ANTHONY

SINGLE DADS OF GAYNOR BEACH

GABBI GREY

Author Website

BLURB

ANTHONY

During my seven years as a social worker in Gaynor Beach, California, delivering orphaned twins to their unsuspecting father is the biggest challenge I've ever faced. These babies lost their mother and they need a loving parent, but is adorable Scott Wexler up to that challenge? Transferring custody is one thing—walking away is something entirely different, especially with the stress of Christmas bearing down on Scott too.

SCOTT

After escaping a miserable childhood, I've made a fresh start in California. I'm in charge at the Gaynor Beach Public Library, I love helping people, and I'm feeling like an actual functional human being. Then social worker Anthony Rodrigues shows up on my doorstep with twins I fathered through a sperm donation, and suddenly I'm responsible for two tiny lives. Accepting help from the gorgeous social worker is a no brainer—admitting I want him to stay is going to take a lot more courage.

———

This 74k word gay romance is a slow burn, mid-angst, instalove with a geeky librarian, a by-the-book social worker, adorable twin-toddler terrors, and a beleaguered cat named Crumpy.

Kaje
ELF
Wendy

CHAPTER 1

ANTHONY

I SHOULD'VE CALLED FIRST.

I eyed the two car seats with sleeping babies at my feet. Everything'd happened so fast. One moment I was sitting in my office writing a report, and the next thing I knew, a pile of paraphernalia was being loaded into my SUV. But I was at my wit's end.

This was probably a bad idea, but every other avenue I tried hadn't panned out. So I'd given up, put the babies into my vehicle, and programmed Scott Wexler's address into my GPS. A stack of papers in my messenger bag was supposed to explain this…whatever this was.

After ensuring the babies were still fast asleep, with the carriers rocking gently on the concrete front step, I rang the doorbell.

Zayden stirred, then quickly resettled.

Alicia didn't move a muscle. Not even a twitch.

The door flew open, and my breath caught.

I'd met Scott several times during the six years I'd been a social worker at Gaynor Beach. Work or pleasure had taken me to the library where he worked/reigned/ran the show.

We'd crossed paths there occasionally—but we'd never spent any significant time getting to know each other.

"Anthony?" Scott's brow furrowed as he adjusted his glasses. His light-auburn hair stuck out in various directions, and an indentation adorned his cheek—like he'd fallen asleep against a pillow with piping. His bright-green eyes lacked focus, and he squinted in the bright morning sunlight.

And he wore tighty whities and a bright, white T-shirt with black lettering that said *Who's Your Daddy?*

I nearly choked.

What am I supposed to say?

Before any words bubbled up, a disembodied, "Who the fuck is that?" came from inside the house.

Well, okay, then.

"Could you, maybe, put on some clothes? And then, may we come in?" I indicated the two car seats. The morning was still relatively cool, but the heat was coming, even this far into December.

He rubbed his forehead. "Let me put on my jeans."

Even as he moved back, a scrawny young man came barreling out, yanking a T-shirt over his head while his jeans remained undone and shoes were unlaced. Once he straightened, the *He's My Daddy* on his T-shirt became clear.

"What the fuck, dude?" He stopped at the sight of me with the babies and ran a hand through his disheveled hair. "This is so not my jam. I'm outta here."

"Jerry, if you'd just—"

"You said you'd be my daddy. Not that there would be *actual* brats. This is way too creepy. I'm gone."

He slung a backpack over his shoulder as he hotfooted down the driveway.

I swivelled back to stare at Scott.

A wince crossed his face. "It's not what you think." He rubbed his forehead again. "So you're saying…" His eyes went comically wide. He glanced from the twins to me and back to the babies. "You have kids?" It might've come out as a squeak.

"Actually—" *Rip off the Band-Aid or gently peel it back?* If I were in this predicament, I'd prefer brutal honesty. I hoped he felt the same way. "—they're your kids."

He squinted. Then he removed his glasses, rubbed his eyes, and put them back on. As if somehow his ability to see impacted his hearing. "Yeah. Uh, no. I hate to tell you this, but I don't have kids. Trust me, I'd remember if I had kids."

Yep, just what I suspected. "Eliza didn't tell you she was pregnant?"

"Eliza Markham?" He scratched his head. "Well…" He coughed. "Oh, shit."

"Yes…shit." I wasn't big on swearing in front of little ears, but today it felt appropriate.

"Yeah, but that was supposed to be anonymous." He glanced down again. "I wasn't ever supposed to know." Again, he rubbed his forehead. "Like, I'm assuming she used my sperm—like from the sperm bank or something? Because she and I…"

He gestured with an inarticulateness that I found sort of endearing.

"We never hooked up or anything. So…yeah."

Which got us precisely nowhere. "She's named you guardian and given me paperwork." I patted my messenger bag. "She also provided irrefutable proof that you're the twins' father. Matched through a blood test and a corresponding entry in the genetic ancestry database. Am I correct you put your name in there?"

"Yeah, but that was, like, for medical emergencies. Family history. Not for… She didn't… This wasn't supposed to happen." More squinting.

This time, I squinted back. Then I sighed. "She told me she changed her phone number, and she refused to say where they were going."

Scott made a strangled sound. "Well, shit."

Again, we weren't moving forward. I tapped my bag. "If you don't want custody, then we can go to a judge, and you can relinquish custody. I know a foster family in Marina Park who can take them quickly. He's a lawyer, and she's a home-maker, with three children of their own. I've placed emergency cases with them before, and I know they'd be thrilled." I winced. "Except the three kids all have chicken pox, so it's going to be a few days. There's no one else local." I'd looked—hard. "I can see if there's a family in Oceanside or San Diego. But cross-county/inter-county paperwork is always slow, and they might end up parked at the local hospital till a transfer goes through—"

He held up his hand. "Give me a goddamn moment. You drop this fucking bombshell on me and then you want to just, I don't know, leave?"

"I understand this is a shock for you. Obviously, I'd prefer that Eliza speak to you herself. Perhaps you can email her? She's likely only halfway to San Diego or LA. Or on her way to Las Vegas. Maybe you can convince her to turn around."

"Was her husband with her?"

"Yes."

A strangled guffaw escaped him. "Then no. I can't think of anything less likely. Eliza's that immovable object you hear about. If she's decided she's leaving with that asshole husband of hers, then she's gone." Yet another squint. "Did he sign the papers as well?"

"Yes. The documents are signed by both of them and nota-rized—there's a power of attorney as well as medical and educational consent forms. This wasn't a last-minute decision. Serious planning went into this." Which was why it made no sense they hadn't contacted Scott to let him know the plan. Maybe they were afraid he'd say no?

Maybe they don't care one way or the other. Eliza hadn't struck me as uncaring—but she hadn't been emotional as she dropped off two babies and a ton of their stuff. Good quality stuff. At one point, the little ones' d been well cared for. Been wanted. *What happened?* Perhaps the contents of the sealed envelope with Scott's name on it might provide answers. No guarantee he'd let me see it, though.

I glanced down at the sleeping infants. "Are we coming in, or am I heading back to my office to see if I can find somewhere else?"

After what felt like an interminable amount of time, he opened the door fully. He stepped forward and grabbed the handle of Alicia's car seat. "Well, discussing it on my front porch is only going to lead to potential speculation by my neighbors."

His Willis Heights neighborhood was friendly and relatively safe, but lower class. Probably all he could afford on his public servant's salary.

I'd managed to snag a house in Conway Heights, but it'd been a stretch. Social workers weren't raking in the dough any more than librarians. The private-counseling clients I took on during my downtime helped pay the mortgage.

I grabbed Zayden's car seat and the diaper bag and entered the house.

The rancher appeared typical of the area—three bedrooms, one bathroom, living space with an open-concept dining room and a narrow galley kitchen. One of my other clients, Patricia Peterson, had a house with almost the same layout.

Former client.

A pang hit me. And my chest tightened. Sometimes I screwed up.

Pushing aside the guilt, I moved into the living room. I placed Zayden's car seat next to the sofa.

A lithe and sleek cream-colored cat leapt from its perch on a dining room chair and headed over to investigate.

Scott placed the other car seat next to Zayden's and stood back. "Twins?"

"Alicia and Zayden."

"A to Z."

"Huh?"

"Eliza said she wanted kids from A to Z. I always thought she'd name them in order. You know—starting with A, then moving on to B..."

"She wanted children?"

He met my gaze. "More than anything in the world. Not so much when I first met her in college, but, I mean, her entire existence for the past five years has been to get pregnant. We sort of lost touch a couple of years ago. She and her husband Mark were up in LA. About two years ago, she stopped responding to my emails. Stopped taking my calls. I mean, I was hurt, but we were never *that* close. I just figured she'd moved on with her life. Before that, she used to share all her infertility woes with me. I guess I thought maybe she wanted a clean break." He eyed the twins. "I don't think it ever occurred to me that she might be pregnant. You'd think that was news she'd share with everyone."

"Especially the father." I tried not to stare at his bare legs with their fuzzy red hair. "Why don't you get dressed?"

He squinted—which he seemed to be doing a lot—then he looked at himself. He rubbed his forehead and sighed. "I can't believe I went outside like this."

I couldn't either, but hauling both carriers inside would've been a challenge, so I hadn't said anything. I'd assumed he didn't care about modesty. Maybe I misjudged him on that score.

He scampered out while I eyed the room. The coffee table was neat as a pin with a folded Gaynor Beach Gazette sitting on it. An e-reader lay atop that. The green pile carpet looked recently vacuumed. A laptop sat on the dining room table. I didn't spot any dust or mess. That relieved my anxiety a fraction.

An infinitesimal fraction.

Scott was a single man. Would be a single father if he took the twins. That kind of responsibility could overwhelm a well-adjusted couple. Some mid-twenties kid? The whole *daddy* thing aside, this was going to be a huge adjustment.

Not a kid.

No, he wasn't. About half-a-dozen years younger than my own thirty-one, by my estimation. He'd been working in the library for three years and had, quite surprisingly, been promoted to head librarian five months ago.

Ms. Ducking suffered an unexpected heart attack while on the job. She'd gone to the hospital and, upon recovery, had moved to Tucson to live with a younger sister. After thirty years as head librarian, the woman'd earned her rest. Still, the town missed her.

Alicia's eyes fluttered open.

My heart sank.

She took a deep breath, scrunched up her face, and let loose an almighty wail.

Scott scurried back into the room, pulling a T-shirt over his head.

Phew, the yellow T-shirt didn't have any risqué logos or writing. I held up the diaper bag. "With babies, it's usually hunger or needing a dry diaper. Or both."

He snagged the bag. "Diapers?"

"Yes, and I can do bottles. Let me get some stuff from my SUV." As I headed back out, a second wail carried. Great. Both babies. They'd slept through the entire ordeal back at the office. Their mother dropping them off, that was. And while she'd handed over the papers she brought and refused all my pleas to do this right, legally, through a court, her husband— Mark Markham—had unloaded a shit ton of baby stuff into the back of my SUV. Then, almost as quickly as they arrived, they departed.

With the babies secured in their car seat by my desk, I searched for an approved foster home while I sorted out this mess. I checked the paperwork. I confirmed the DNA and the power of attorney. But when every option other than the hospital ward struck out, there'd been nothing left except to strap them in the SUV too, and come here. Truthfully, I'd expected Scott to send me on my way. In my mind, I'd been trying to figure out what I was going to say to my boss. How I was going to explain all this. How I was going to try to find a foster home for the babies until things could get sorted.

I snagged the bag with infant formula and bottles. Okay— at least for now—I was going to be here a while.

Scott had a plastic sheet spread out on the floor with fresh diapers, wipes, and cream lined up.

Oh, and two squawking babies close at hand. It appeared Alicia was on the floor while Zayden continued to wail from his car seat.

I hustled into the kitchen and set about making bottles.

Soft cooing noises intermingled with high-pitched wails.

Crying wasn't unusual in my line of work—plenty of infants cried. And toddlers. And kids and teenagers. Very few kids saw me and smiled. But my job was to ensure they were in the safest spot possible—and sometimes that meant not with their parents. I didn't do removals often, but it happened. My goal was to keep families together and get them the support they needed. Sometimes, though, that wasn't possible. I preferred the cries of hungry babies to the sobbing of a child I was taking from their home.

When the bottles were the perfect temperature, I made my way back to the living room.

The babies lay on their backs—in fresh diapers—and Scott bent over them.

He'd blow on one tummy, then quickly move to the other

and repeat the process. Then he made goofy faces and talked nonsense.

The little ones appeared entranced.

So was I.

"I have bottles."

He turned to meet my gaze, and two disgruntled little ones let us know what they thought of that.

"Here."

I handed him a bottle, and he snagged a baby.

I scooped up the other one and settled it on my lap. Him? Her? They both wore identical onesies.

"You've got Alicia." Scott stuck the nipple in Zayden's mouth. "At least they're not identical twins—I've never figured out how parents could tell them apart."

"There's got to be a way."

Eventually, Alicia allowed me to entice her into taking the bottle.

Scott sighed. "Is this really happening?"

"Well, frankly, yes. It is happening."

He slowly nodded. "And it's all legal?"

"I'll say your friend Eliza was as thorough as she could be on her own. This couldn't have been a spur-of-the-moment thing." My nose twitched as I resisted the urge to scratch it. "If you decide to keep the babies—and feeding them now in no way commits you—we'd still have to go before a judge as soon as possible to make this legal. And you'll need a home visit—"

"Eliza's a huge planner—she'd never do something on a whim or the spur of the moment." He lightly skimmed a finger over Zayden's hair. Sparse—but clearly red. Same as Alicia's. And although their eyes were blue now, there was a chance they'd eventually turn green. Even without the DNA test I'd examined, Scott's parentage was clear.

"And you had no idea?"

He winced. "None. I mean, I know they've been

15

trying. And Eliza started asking questions more questions about my sperm donations. I thought she was maybe looking at in-vitro or something." He gave me a wry smile. "My, uh, contributions helped pay my way through college. I donated to several places around the country. Also did blood and plasma whenever I could. I didn't like taking money for that, but college isn't cheap."

"And you have a master's degree?"

"Yes. I'm working on my PhD right now. But that's online." He scratched his nose with his elbow. "All I ever wanted was to be a librarian."

"You're not from around here."

"Gaynor Beach? No, I'm not native."

I considered his response. "I meant California."

He met my gaze. "I've done my best to get rid of the accent."

The mid-western one that snuck through on certain words. "Kansas?"

Crickets.

He finally said, "Oklahoma."

Ah. Sore spot.

"Is Eliza from the Midwest as well?"

He shook his head. "She's SoCal all the way. We met in college. Mark's from Arkansas. I guess maybe that's where they're headed."

And we'd circled around. "How would she have known which sperm was yours?"

His cheeks reddened. "She, uh, helped me write my bio. My *pen portrait*. The sum of me without pictures—what made me unique. Why people might want to choose me to be the biological father of their children. And, of course, she knew where I donated. I suppose it wouldn't have been too difficult." He sighed. "But why do that only to leave them behind? It doesn't make any sense."

"You think it might have something to do with her husband?"

He bit his lip. "Mark was…fanatical. About a lot of things, but most especially about having biological children. I know he and Eliza were planning in-vitro. But I assumed they'd use his sperm." He looked down at his child. "As you saw, Mark is blond, and Eliza has black hair. Mark used to make fun of my red hair—called it a sign of no soul. Probably means he didn't have redheads in his family."

"So if she snuck one past him, it could've been obvious…"

"Yeah, pretty much." He pressed a kiss to Zayden's forehead. "I suppose she figured Mark would either never know, or be too much in love with the kids to care. Jesus Fucking Christ, how can they walk away? Why is she doing this?" He looked up. "Was she under duress? Was he forcing her?"

I considered, but the answer came swiftly. "If so, it wasn't obvious. He didn't dominate the conversation, and he wasn't afraid of leaving her alone with me. If she'd wanted to say something, she had every opportunity. Trust me, if I'd spotted anything amiss, I would've acted on it." All that being said, emotional abuse was insidious and easy to hide. Her lack of affection had concerned me, but it could've been chalked up to stepping back now her mind was made up.

"And leaving two babies in a social worker's office isn't amiss?" No missing the disbelief.

"Did I wonder? Of course. Did I consider calling in reinforcements? Of course. But could I have articulated a single thing wrong? No. She gave me nothing to work with—despite my attempts to engage her. I had no doubt that if I didn't take the babies, they were going to be dropped off somewhere else. At least doing it this way, I had some control over what happened to them."

"She could've brought them here." Defensive. Hurt.

"Would you have opened your home and let her come in? Let her just drop everything off and wave goodbye?"

"Well—"

"You'd have tried to talk her into staying. You would've offered her refuge. You would've tried to find a way to stop her from doing this."

He nodded slowly.

Yeah, I had his number.

But what did that mean?

"We need to seriously discuss what you're planning to do. Are you thinking about custody? Are you willing to work the steps?"

He blinked several times. "I..." He looked frantically around the room.

What's going on? "Do you rent? Are you worried about a landlord?"

"No, nothing like that." He wiped his brow with his forearm.

The room didn't feel hot to me.

"I just...this place isn't designed for kids. Ms. Ducking passed it on to me. She never had kids. I was renting a place in Oakdale, trying to save for a down payment. After her heart attack, she just wanted to get to Arizona. We worked out private financing, and I was able to buy this place. I never could've afforded it otherwise."

"Fair enough." *Where is he going with this?*

"One spare room is a sewing room, and the other is a library—crammed with a couple hundred books."

Ah. "Well, the crib won't take up much space. You have a garage, right? We can move some of the stuff out there. Or you can list it for sale or give it away. This close to Christmas, people'll be looking for bargains."

"Sell Ms. Ducking's things?" His expression of shock morphed into pure horror.

"Is she coming back for them?"

"Well...no."

"Has she asked you to hang on to them?"

"Uh…no."

"Would she want you to take care of the little ones?"

"Of course." He said this firmly.

Is he already thinking of them as his?

"I suppose the garage will work—for now. I, uh, actually like the idea of re-homing some of her things. Surely there are families in need." His expression eased.

"There are, I promise you." Several in my caseload came to mind. Whether they could use sewing gear or old books, though, was another thing.

He eyed me. "Aren't you supposed to be working?"

I nodded toward the bundle in my arms. "This *is* working. If you decide to take custody of the children, you're going to need support. To start with, I need to unload the baby gear from the back of my SUV."

"Oh, my God. This is really happening."

"You don't have to do this—"

He shook his head vigorously. "Yes, I do. I really do. What if Eliza changes her mind? What if she comes back? If I've signed custody over to some stranger, it'll be harder for her, right?"

Slowly, I nodded. "Yes, she'd have to petition the courts. And prove she's a fit parent."

"Well, then, I have to keep them."

"But, Scott, she's not coming back."

"You don't *know* that."

Over the years, I'd had several women relinquish custody of their children—usually when they realized they were incapable of caring for those children. I'd seen that steely determination in Eliza. "No, I don't *know* for sure. But I've seen enough in my line of work to distinguish between a mother who's taking a break to get herself together and a mother who's severing all ties. It's rare, mind you, but it happens. Eliza's not coming back. I might be wrong, but I'm sure I'm not. You need to move forward with that assumption."

"You're such an arrogant ass."

His words struck me like an actual blow. He didn't know me. How could he level such an accusation? And sure, he wasn't the first—and he wouldn't likely be the last—but his words hurt deeper than they normally would have.

Why?

Because a client had accused me of that once upon a time. And she'd died less than twelve hours later of a drug overdose.

Maybe I was an arrogant ass. But I believed in doing what was in the best interest of the children I was responsible for. I trusted my instincts and my experience. If that made me a jerk, I'd have to own it.

"So, am I unloading the SUV or am I driving the twins to the hospital?"

CHAPTER 2

SCOTT

Time.

I need time.

Yet as I gazed at the baby in my arms, time slipped through my fingers like sand in an hourglass. I glanced at the old-fashioned mantel clock. Ten-fifteen. Of course, I had no idea what time Anthony'd arrived. I'd been up late last night —role-playing with Jerry.

Jerry.

I needed to find a way to get in touch with him. To apologize. Because as shitty as him taking off was, he was totally within his rights to do it. Last night was only our second scene. And since neither of us was looking for long-term, the likelihood of much more hadn't been an issue. Plus, since I had today off, I hadn't worried about staying up late. When my *guests* arrived this morning, we'd been fast asleep.

"Scott?"

I met Anthony's gaze. His dark-brown eyes pierced me. Oh, I'd noticed him prior to him showing up here unannounced. With tanned skin, those memorable eyes, and his jet-black hair, he'd always caught my notice. "Hey, when did you grow a beard?" I squinted. "And your hair's longer."

He sat a little straighter, and the nipple slipped from Alicia's mouth. She scrunched up her face, and I was about to speak, but Anthony caught the slip and quickly rectified it. "It's been almost a year since I, uh, decided to change my looks."

"You look older."

He arched an eyebrow.

"More mature." I made the correction quickly. *Thank fuck I didn't tell him how sexy I find him.* I'd pretty much lusted after him since the first time we met—mere days after I arrived in Gaynor Beach. Standing behind him at the grocery store, I'd been…eyeing his gorgeous ass. Okay, I could admit it. The man was the whole package.

He'd turned in line and caught my gaze.

My cheeks heated, and I was certain I'd turned fifty shades of crimson.

He'd cocked his head, given me a nod, and turned back to greet the cashier just as his turn came.

When he was gone, the cashier, perhaps sensing my curiosity about the man who had just departed, had given me a recitation about Anthony—his job, his vital stats, when he'd arrived in town, and so on. Although I appreciated the information, the obvious curiosity of the clerk made me wary. I'd been in town all of three days, and when the woman started her inquisition of me, I was as vague as possible.

I learned that Anthony's jeans and a distressed T-shirt was unusual attire for the man. He wore suits while working and tended to favor more formal wear when he was off the clock. Whenever I saw him, he looked polished and put-together.

I favored casual at work and even more casual outside of it. Sure, I'd wear a polo shirt or button down to the library, but off-hours I was happy to wear shorts and a T-shirt. A hoodie if it ever got cool. In SoCal, though, it rarely did. So different from Oklahoma winters. Twelve days from Christmas, and we were in the middle of a heat wave. Normally in the mid-sixties at this time of year, we'd hit eighty-five yesterday and were likely to see that again today. Thank God my place had air conditioning.

"Aside from me looking more mature—" His eyes darkened. "—I know this is sudden. I can try to find a foster home, but I can't guarantee when you'd get them back in that case, assuming you wanted to."

Damn. My mind had wandered again. I could focus at work—most of the time—but once I stepped out of the library, I struggled to keep thoughts in my head. Amazing I'd managed to obtain not one but two post-secondary degrees. And how was a scatterbrain like me supposed to take care of these infants?

If I said no, I could keep my life intact—stable, organized, and orderly. Or I could at least take time to consider all this— the implications of what such a monumental decision involved. Yet, as I caught sight of a soft, wispy red curl, my heart knew what I had to do.

"Bring it in. If you don't mind watching them, I can move the sewing stuff into the garage. Thank you, that was a good suggestion. We'll see if I can re-home it later."

Zayden pushed at his bottle.

Oh, burping. I moved the baby to my shoulder and started to pat his back.

"You need a—"

The baby burped.

"—receiving blanket."

Anthony's words sank in as I felt warm liquid hit my shoulder and soak into my T-shirt.

Right.

I'd known that. Or I thought I must've. I didn't do babies. As the second youngest of nine, I hadn't had help. Martha'd been eleven months younger than me.

My parents hadn't believed in birth control, so Mom'd popped out kids with terrifying frequency. And there would've been more, but she'd hemorrhaged after my youngest sister.

They'd performed an emergency hysterectomy, and I'm not sure she'd ever forgiven the doctors who saved her life.

She believed her duty as a wife was to produce as many children as possible. She'd started at age nineteen and had popped out nine kids by age thirty-one. I suppose it helped she had two sets of twins, including myself. Still, my mother felt she had another fifteen years of fertility, and to have that abruptly ended hadn't gone over well.

My twin sister, Scotia, planned to give our mother a run for her money. At twenty-seven, she already had five kids—or so I'd heard through the grapevine. All girls, likely much to her consternation.

They needed boys to continue and work the farm once she and her husband were too old.

My family never believed women could do a man's work on the farm, though plenty around the country did.

She'd lose her shit if she knew I had a son.

Oh well, she never would.

Anthony snagged a receiving blanket and draped it over his shoulder. He positioned Alicia and started patting her back.

Her burp wasn't nearly as delicate as Zayden's had been. She belched loudly and produced quite a bit of spit-up.

Is that normal?

Kids should come with instruction manuals.

Wait, maybe they did.

"Did Eliza include any parenting books?"

Anthony met my gaze. "I'm not sure. There's a lot of stuff." He resettled Alicia and tried to coax her into taking the rest of her bottle.

Not interested. She wriggled, she squirmed, and, eventually, she scrunched up her face.

A few moments later, Anthony winced and an odor wafted my way.

I tried not to laugh. As Zayden sucked on his bottle, I took a moment's comfort—but my turn was next.

Anthony, in his slightly rumpled suit, knelt on the floor by the plastic sheet.

"You know how to change diapers?" I asked.

"Yes. Occasionally I have infants in my care for more than a few hours, so I have done this before." He glanced over his shoulder at me. "You seemed to do okay."

I waved my hand in a so-so motion. "I babysat my eldest sister's kids one time when she was desperate. Long story. Anyway, I changed my niece's diaper a couple of times that night. It's pretty straightforward. Oh, boys can sometimes pee when their, uh, comes into contact with air, so be prepared."

"It's called a penis." Anthony removed the very-stinky diaper and wiped Alicia. A bit of cream and he had a fresh one on her. "I'll redress her and put her back in the car seat. Hopefully she'll go back to sleep and I can start hauling things in from my SUV."

"That sounds deceptively easy."

He managed to get her back into her onesie and looked inordinately pleased with himself.

"If you can watch the kids, I can move some of the stuff from the sewing room into the garage. Do you have empty boxes?"

"Yeah. I broke them down and stored them in the garage. There's packing tape in the kitchen."

Zayden pushed at his bottle.

I grabbed another receiving blanket and put it over my shoulder. A little late now, but at least I wouldn't get wetter. I needed to change out of my damp T-shirt, but that thought felt like a distant dream.

Alicia continued to fuss, so Anthony rose with her and

walked around. He tried jiggling and cooing and a bunch of other things, but nothing seemed to work.

She grimaced and let out an almighty wail.

Anthony's brow was furrowed, and his dark eyes were wide.

Not good. I considered him the expert. He was a social worker, for crying out loud. That meant dealing with kids all the time. Right?

Zayden's burp was more delicate than his sister's.

I sniffed.

Nothing.

Nothing yet, I corrected.

Zayden looked at me for a moment, then he scrunched up his face.

I popped off the couch and tried to jiggle and coo and—

No use. His wail soon rivaled his sister's.

Anthony met my gaze.

I pushed my glasses up my nose and tried to focus. "Any ideas?"

He cocked his head. "I think we need help."

I'd be the last person to disagree. Problem was… "I don't know anyone. Well, no, not anyone I could bother. No one who owes me that kind of favor. So, uh, do we look in the help-available ads?" I tried to grab for the Gazette, but Zayden wanted none of that, and started howling afresh.

Anthony managed to scoop up the pages as Alicia'd settled for a sniffle and a snort. He moved the newspaper to my dining-room table where he spread it out. "Does anyone even use newspapers anymore? I thought everything was online."

My cell phone sat on the coffee table. Unlike most of my generation, I rarely used the thing. "Don't you have a bunch of people you can call for baby advice?"

He winced. "Emergency foster parents and, like I said, their kids have chicken pox. Anyway, it'd be inappropriate for me to call when I'm just looking for advice, given they're dealing with sick children." He glanced down at Alicia. "Or whatever rescue we need. I think we're on our own."

That sounds ominous.

I'd been on my own for almost ten years now—so the idea shouldn't have scared me. Anyhow, I wasn't truly alone. For this moment, at least, I had Anthony.

But how long will he stay?

Likely long enough to unload his SUV. Maybe long enough to make sure I'd be a fit parent. At the moment, that didn't feel realistic.

Zayden chose that moment to do his business.

Once I was certain he was finished, I knelt on the carpet and placed him on the plastic. "Did Eliza leave me that contraption that makes diapers disappear?"

Anthony's brow knit. "Disappear? No. Smell less? Yes, I believe there is one of those." He disappeared into the kitchen and soon returned with a plastic grocery bag. "Let's put them in here for now, and I can run them out to the garbage in the garage when I put the boxes in there."

Zayden, apparently pleased with the turn of events, yawned.

I scooped him up and put him in his car seat. I had no idea about the safety of letting a baby sleep in one of these, but airlines let babies sleep in them, and parents took their infants on long car rides all the time. Until we had a crib set up, this seemed a viable option. Perhaps the only option.

Alicia continued to fuss.

I opened my arms.

Anthony placed her in them with a grimace. Whether because he felt he should've been able to calm her, or whether he worried her howls might wake her brother, I wasn't sure. What I was certain of was that the frown didn't look good on him.

He headed toward the garage door and, after about five

minutes, reappeared carrying a pile of broken-down boxes under his arm. He headed down the hall and was back moments later. "That's a lot of pink."

I shrugged. "I'm not big on gender stereotypes." And I definitely didn't care enough to repaint a room that didn't need it.

He held up his hands with a grin. "I'm not saying Zayden can't stay in there...I'm saying that color might frighten them."

Well, he has a point. The bubble-gum color startled me every time I stepped into the room. Reminded me of my upset-stomach medicine. Something I was likely to need in the next few hours.

Anthony returned from the kitchen a moment later, with a roll of packing tape. He'd rifled through the recycling container and found a pile of newspapers for padding.

I should've taken them out to the curb, but I hadn't gotten around to it. Well, I wasn't a hoarder—I just didn't do well with letting things go. Hence hanging onto sewing things and books that I'd never read in a million years.

The rhythmic sound of taping filtered through to me, and Alicia must've found the sound soothing, because eventually her eyes drooped. Moments later, she was down for the count. When I put her in the car seat, she didn't stir.

I closed the drapes as quietly as I could and made my way to the sewing room.

The pink assaulted my senses. So did the dust, and I sneezed. Repeatedly.

Anthony looked up from his task. "You okay?"

I held up my hand, asking for a moment. Then I scurried to the kitchen where I retrieved the extended duster from the broom closet. A moment later I was back, holding the thing away from me. "It won't solve all our problems, but it'll help."

He nodded and stepped to the doorway as I tackled dusting every surface.

This wasn't a great solution, but it was a kindness to the people who'd come to take the stuff. Once I was finished, I stepped into the room I thought of as the library, and Anthony set to work on the sewing notions. I returned a moment later with my camera.

"We should photograph what's going into each box. Then we can post the photo with a number and people can say which boxes they want. Might as well put all the like things together. If someone winds up with too much of anything, they can do what we're doing."

"If they're fanatical sewers, there's likely no such thing as too many."

Point taken. Ms. Ducking appeared to have multiples of everything. Soon, though, we were snapping pictures of boxes.

"Oh, I forgot to ask, how old are the babies?"

Anthony's gaze snapped to mine. "Nine months."

"And you said she had all the possible paperwork?"

He nodded.

"That would've taken time to put together, right?"

"A good lawyer likely could've done it in a day or two. That being said, it's thorough. Like every contingency is laid out. Except..."

"Except?"

"Except you saying *no*. It's not legal until you agree and a court approves it. I tried to ask what I was supposed to do if you turned down this awesome responsibility. She said I didn't need to worry about it—that you'd never say *no*."

I pushed my glasses up my nose. "She might've been wrong."

He stilled.

"I grew up surrounded by kids. Siblings, nieces, nephews,

cousins, schoolmates…everyone had so many kids. I didn't want that. I swore I wasn't going to get tied down like that."

"Never?"

"Well, not until I was at least thirty and in a solid, permanent relationship." I gestured. "Aside from living in a house that's mortgaged to the hilt, I don't have permanence." I sighed. "The latter half of my twenties was supposed to be dedicated to a job I love, and making up for the fun I missed on my journey to get here." I eyed the contents of the room before finally meeting his gaze. "I'm sure you're wondering why I put my DNA in the database, given they may have used my sperm a number of times."

"That thought had crossed my mind."

"I wanted the kids—when they were older—to be able to connect with me. To get a medical history or to just know me. I was expecting curious young adults, not two babies requiring around-the-clock care." Yet another sigh. "I don't regret this, but I'm not sure I'm equipped for this." Was expressing my doubts the right thing to do? Better now than later, right?

He put his hands on his hips. "You have a great job that you love. You're a valued member of the Gaynor Beach community." He held my gaze. "If you put out an SOS, I bet ten people will be on your doorstep by the end of the day, offering to help."

"I…" Words failed me. Was he right?

"But you're afraid to ask." He pointed to the boxes. "You're happy to give things away, but are scared to ask for things in return."

Nailed it in one.

"I, uh, need to check on the babies." Too much intimacy scared me. Sharing my fears overwhelmed me. Sure, Eliza and I'd been close, back when, but that was rare in my life. Most of the time I kept to myself. I'd go out of my way to help others but, as Anthony'd so neatly discerned, never asked for help myself.

Checking the babies was easy—sorting through my feelings was much harder.

Oh, Eliza…why did you do this to me?

I'd likely never get an answer—unless she came back. I didn't know where Eliza might've gone. Mark's family was from Arkansas. I couldn't begin to guess the prevalence of Markhams out there. Surely I could track the couple down via social media. Unless they truly dropped off the grid. Anthony hadn't said the words, but child abandonment was a thing. If Eliza'd prepared all the paperwork, did that mean she hadn't abandoned her children? Or could they still go after her for not making it legal? For everyone's sake, I needed to get this arrangement court-approved as soon as possible. But what if I could find her?

To what end?

I couldn't very well show up on her doorstep and try to hand the babies back. She'd been so determined to be a mother, but… handing the babies to Anthony, the paperwork, the cancelled phone number—those made it pretty clear she wasn't likely to change her mind. Unless she left her asshole husband. I knew, unequivocally, that I'd have walked out on the bastard. To force someone to choose between two helpless babies and himself was the height of selfishness. I'd always thought the guy was a prick. But I'd held my tongue because Eliza was head over heels for the asshole. I thought once she figured out his true nature she'd leave him. Turned out I was wrong.

Painfully wrong.

I dropped to the couch and stared at the babies.

Can I do this?

Do I have a choice?

Not really. Short of turning them over to foster care, I was the only person who could do this. Was I willing to take on a lifetime commitment, just because my ex-friend stalked my DNA and created two helpless little babies I hadn't asked for? I just didn't know.

I snagged the diaper bag and surveyed the contents. Hopefully the boxes contained more diapers as we'd likely go through them quickly.

How expensive was that going to be? Formula, diapers, clothes, and eventually beds and university. Holy crap.

Don't panic.

Yeah, right. Panic was the only way to go. My salary at the library was good, but after my mortgage and car payments, I didn't have much left over at the end of the month. Did the government provide child-support money? Hugh, my Canadian friend, once told me that parents in Canada received money every month to help support their young children and they also got tax credits on their income tax.

How did I not know about these things?

I needed to speak to an accountant. They'd help me out, right? And if Eliza hadn't included books about childcare, I needed to get to the library to sign some out. And what about a lawyer? A will? Odds were, nothing would happen to me, but what if it did? Who would take the babies if I couldn't?

The anxiety welling within me refused to be tamed. I was hurtling toward the abyss with no way to stop the panic attack.

CHAPTER 3

ANTHONY

WHEN I WALKED INTO THE LIVING ROOM, THE SOUND OF SCOTT'S short shallow breaths hit me first. I hustled over to him. Distress washed over me, and my heart sank. His extreme pallor starkly contrasted with the two points of color high on his cheeks.

I approached carefully, ensuring I was in his line of sight.

Could he even see me?

Positioning myself between him and the car seats was a risk, but I didn't see that I had any other choice.

He'd wrapped his arms around his waist. How could he breathe with that tight grip?

The cat, who'd been conspicuously absent since the babies arrived, now sat beside Scott and headbutted his arm.

Scott didn't react.

"Hey." I used my soothing social-worker voice.

Still no change.

"I'm going to touch you."

Nothing.

Touching without express permission was always risky, but sometimes the situation dictated drastic action.

I placed my hand on his knee.

His gaze shot to mine. Unfocused green eyes settled on me.

Progress.

"Hey, can you take a deep breath for me?" I inhaled noisily and deeply, all the while holding his gaze. Then I exhaled in a long stream of breath.

I inhaled again.

He followed suit.

I exhaled.

He did the same.

We continued like that for a long time. If I wasn't able to calm him enough this way, then I might've had to go looking for a paper bag—something few people had these days. Worse-case scenario would be to call an ambulance. I didn't want that. And, from what little I knew about Scott, he wouldn't want that either.

I squeezed his knee. "I think your cat is trying to get your attention." Giving him something concrete to focus on would help.

He glanced over at the cream-colored cat with weird stripes on its face.

"Crumpet." He winced. "Well, Crumpy." He petted the creature who instantly purred. "He's been with me since my days in LA. He was a stray I took in. I think, honestly, that he chose me." He eyed me. "But he's not great with strangers."

"Do you think he'll be okay with the babies?"

Scott's eyebrows shot up. "I, uh, I don't know. He'd better be. I mean, I don't think I could re-home him."

"Well, we're not at that stage yet. Just keep an eye on him, and we'll see how things go." How much reassurance did I need to offer? How much could I offer? I'd once had to threaten to remove two children from a home because the family's beloved pet kept biting them. After the third visit to the emergency room, Doctor Lam called me. I'd felt guilty, for sure, but I'd done what was necessary for the children. In the end, the dog had been re-homed with a guy who was ex-military. He was able to redirect the animal's tendency to bite, but never to the point where she could be trusted around children again. Yes, the family'd been devastated, but the safety of their children should've been their first priority.

Or at least that's how I'd seen it. I hoped like hell Crumpy wouldn't make safety an issue.

Scott's breathing had normalized, and his color was gradually returning.

I eyed the dozing toddlers. Had Eliza slipped them something? Aside from waking up hungry, they'd been unnervingly sleepy.

But what did I know about babies?

Not much.

Or maybe her ex, the jackass, was responsible.

I still didn't understand this—whatever *this* was. And maybe I should've eased into this situation. Given Scott a chance to prepare. I'd honestly thought he might've known this was coming. Eliza'd mentioned several times how close they were, so I'd assumed an ongoing friendship—not the kind of distance that led to her having his babies nine months ago, and him not knowing anything about it.

They're probably just about out of California by now. Although it was a big state.

Something continued to niggle, but I couldn't put my finger on it. Although they hadn't said they were leaving California, I had little doubt they were. It'd be harder to track them down, and getting child support from people across the country wasn't impossible—but it was more difficult.

"I need water." His voice shook.

"I'll get it." I leapt up and headed to the kitchen—grateful to have been given a task. I ran the water cold until I figured it was chilled enough. As I returned, I realized I should've put in ice, but Scott was already reaching for it.

He downed the entire glass in one long series of pulls. His

throat worked as he took in the much-needed liquid. I didn't see any signs, but I wondered if he and his boy toy'd been drinking last night. That the kid was legal helped—and I needed to stop thinking of Jerry as a kid. But I'd had no idea Scott was in to that particular kink. And it didn't reassure me that he was. Not that I worried for the babies. Just...would it be appropriate to have much-younger men around like that in the Daddy/boy context? What if they were into spanking? They'd keep that behind closed doors, I was sure. Or I hoped. Well, the age gap wasn't the thing—but the power dynamic certainly was.

I'd been relieved when Scott put on a normal T-shirt and jeans.

That being said, the image of him when he answered the door was seared into my memory. Those long, slender legs with the fine fuzz of red hair. The bare arms with the freckles that carried across his chest and decorated the bridge of his nose. Or at least I presumed they were across his chest. I wanted to verify that for myself. Talk about wildly inappropriate.

Zayden stirred.

I tried not to panic.

His eyes slowly opened.

Scott tensed.

The baby took one look at the two of us, screwed up his face, and howled.

Before I could even react, Alicia's eyes popped open. She didn't wait to take the measure of the room—she started howling as well.

"I guess..." Scott gestured to the restraints on the car seats.

"Yeah."

Alicia was closest to me, so I unbuckled her and tried to pick her up. Unlike before, when she'd been mildly compliant, she offered resistance. She squawked. She batted her little arms when I tried to lift her shoulders—mindful of her head.

The harder I tried, the more recalcitrant she became.

Zayden, on the other hand, had ceased his yowling. He allowed Scott to scoop him up and gently croon.

"Want to trade?" I asked. Maybe Scott had the magic touch.

He eyed his daughter. "Uh, I'm good. Anyway, this guy needs a new diaper." He knelt on the floor, organizing the plastic sheet.

Crumpet came to inspect the infant.

I managed to get Alicia into my arms—but it was a near thing. She continued to howl out her protests.

Frankly, I didn't blame her for being out of sorts. I'd feel the same way if someone dumped me into two strangers' laps in an unfamiliar house. But I couldn't see how it would've been better to put them in a foster situation only to bring them here tomorrow. That would've been more upsetting to them.

Right?

I just didn't know.

After settling Alicia against my shoulder, I jostled her as I paced the room. Her diaper felt heavy to me, so as soon as Scott had Zayden in a new diaper, I indicated we needed to switch.

He started to rise.

"Uh, no. You're already down. You take Alicia and I'll take Zayden."

Zayden, enjoying a moment of Scott's inattention, rolled onto his stomach.

I thrust Alicia into Scott's arms and snagged her brother before he could go investigating. This house wasn't babyproofed. Like, at all. Significant work needed to be done before they could just be allowed to wander.

Crumpet was clearly displeased with the turn of events—

losing the placid baby for the yowling one. He turned tail and bolted from the room.

Scott didn't even appear to notice.

Alicia squirmed. She kept trying to turn over and wasn't appreciative of Scott's attempts to keep her still.

"Maybe she's hungry?"

Scott glared. "Diaper first. And clearly, I don't keep baby food around."

Obviously he'd forgotten they'd come with some—but I wasn't going to point that out right now.

And I hadn't unloaded everything from my SUV. I still couldn't believe we'd crammed all the stuff for two babies, as well as the two babies themselves, into my vehicle. I had serious respect for the engineers who designed the car, and I gave props to the people who figured out how to compress baby stuff into small-enough pieces to fit. But we still had to reassemble everything.

"I'm going to put Zayden back in his car seat. I can feed him in there, right?"

"You think I know? I mean, he should be sitting up, right? Or something?"

"We...need an expert. Surely you know a woman with kids—"

Scott shot me a death glare. "I can figure it out."

"There's nothing wrong with asking for help."

"I can manage. I mean, if you have to leave—"

"Oh, I'm not going anywhere. I'm certainly not leaving you alone with two babies to care for."

"Yet you showed up on my doorstep intending to do just that."

Guilty.

Maybe I hadn't thought this through. "Don't you have someone you can call?"

"Like a random mom?"

"Well, sure."

"Uh, no. In fact, I don't keep a list of women who can drop everything and run over here to help. Don't have a list of men either."

I flashed to his boy toy. No, definitely not.

"Then I guess you're stuck with me." Without waiting for another word, I snagged the diaper bag, dropped it on the table, and started rifling through it. I was sure I'd seen—

Yep, baby food.

Peas. Khaki green. Gross, for sure, but…whatever.

I scanned the instructions. The stuff didn't need to be heated. Fortunately, I located two little baby spoons. I moved back into the living room as Scott scooped Alicia into his arms. Awkwardly he rose, managing to balance the baby.

Impressive.

As always, I admired him. He was serious for someone so cute. In fact, before today, I'd have seen *him* as more the boy-toy type. Sure, he was tall. But he was also slender. Lanky. And he didn't look his twenty-seven years.

He jostled Alicia, trying to soothe her. His coos did nothing to slow the girl down.

I knelt to put Zayden in his seat.

Talk about a look of pure displeasure.

I had that jar of peas open and was coaxing the spoon into his mouth in no time.

He didn't appear pleased, but he didn't start wailing either—so I'd take that as a win.

As I glanced up, I met Alicia's gaze. She'd stopped screaming and was watching me feed her brother.

"Quick." I held up the other spoon.

Lightning fast, Scott had the little one secured in her seat. He snagged a tissue to wipe her nose, and although she didn't look happy, she didn't start the siren wailing again.

Scott managed to give her a mouthful of food without too much difficulty.

"This feels way too easy." I fed Zayden another mouthful.

"Yeah, it does." Scott offered another mouthful to Alicia—and she opened willingly.

"They're going to need protein as well, right?"

"Another bottle?" Scott eyed the half-empty ones sitting on his once-pristine table.

"Yeah, I think so. Do you want to keep feeding them while I make them?"

"Sure." He eyed me. "Then I think we need to get the playpen in here. I don't think they'll want to stay in their car seats and, if I don't miss my mark, playpens are easier to assemble than cribs."

Half-an-hour later, he was eating those words.

I'd made bottles, and we'd fed the babies.

Perhaps because they were overwrought from all the morning's activities, they both went to sleep after having been fed and changed. Zayden fussed a bit, but eventually settled.

Scott and I went to work on the playpen.

Honestly, one of us should've been able to put it together. Somehow, though, we couldn't.

"Do you think this is easier for mothers?" Scott tried again to raise the side, only to have it fall in on itself.

"I have no idea." That made no sense. "I wish it came with instructions."

Scott snapped his finger. "Internet."

Fortunately the noise didn't wake the babies, who appeared dead to the world.

"While you do that, I'm going to bring in the pieces of the crib."

He nodded. As I left, he was plugging in headphones to his tablet.

After four trips, I had all the pieces as well as the baggie with the hardware and the appropriate screwdriver, which they'd given me.

Considerate. Didn't make up for fucking abandoning their

babies—but I could at least acknowledge this'd go faster with the right equipment.

I'd tucked two suitcases into the footwells in the backseat. One turned out to be stuffed with baby clothes and the other was filled with blankets, stuffed animals, and toys. Again, such loving care in making sure the twins had everything they needed—everything except two loving parents.

Scott would do his best to make up for that lack, but he was just one guy. Wouldn't he be overwhelmed? Always short of hands? He'd never get a break. I'd seen new parents overwhelmed with one kid, let alone two.

No changing table, and nothing that could be used as a dresser. No high chairs either. So either they hadn't brought everything, or they'd been making do.

Likely hadn't brought everything. They'd skimped on little else—as far as I could see. With just one crib, though, I assumed the twins slept in it together. I'd say they were too big. Or at least almost too big. So, somehow, we'd need another crib.

We? Shouldn't you be leaving soon?

I had a shit-ton of paperwork waiting for me back at the office. And Mr. Winters, my boss, would likely wonder where I was. I'd told Lottie our receptionist, but I couldn't be certain she'd remember the details. Of course, she'd observed me receiving the twins—that was memorable enough, right?

With her, I was never certain.

As I was reaching for my phone, I heard a muffled curse. Or, at least it sounded like *shit* to me.

I sprinted back to the living room to find Scott holding Zayden against his chest. "He started choking. Or I think he was choking. And she—"

Alicia having awakened by the noise, now started wailing again.

Despite my head starting to hurt—and knowing the pain

was about to intensify—I moved to her and scooped her into my arms.

Again, she squirmed and fought.

"Did you get the playpen set up?"

He nodded, still patting Zayden's back. "I think this might be because we tried to feed him while he wasn't completely vertical."

That didn't seem probable to me, but I couldn't offer another explanation. "They sleep on their backs."

"I don't think he's going back to sleep anytime soon."

"Right." Still, I bounced Alicia. "I opened a suitcase of toys. Maybe we can try putting them in the playpen with a few toys. After we get them settled, we need to talk."

Scott's mouth drooped.

He likely knew this wasn't going to be a straightforward conversation. "It's just about things you're going to need if you decide to do this."

"What do you mean, *if* I decide to do this? Of course I'm going to do this." He held Zayden protectively against his chest. "That isn't open for debate."

Right.

Alicia'd begun to calm.

I walked her to the bedroom and, ignoring the crib parts, I showed her the toys in the suitcase.

She pointed to the pink dinosaur. Then she pointed to the yellow bear.

Deciding these'd be a good start, I snagged them both and headed back to the living room.

Scott stood, looking out the window.

Across the street, a father held a bicycle while his daughter tried to figure out how to ride it.

No training wheels.

That was what this situation felt like—no training wheels. Or like we were walking across a tightrope with no net below us. Kind of crazy, and yet completely necessary.

I moved to the playpen and dropped the stuffed animals in there. Then I gently placed Alicia in with them.

She grabbed the pink dinosaur and hugged it fiercely.

I understood the desire to grab something familiar and hold on for all I was worth.

Scott lowered Zayden to the playpen. When he tried to reach for Alicia's toy, Scott distracted him with the yellow bear. "They're going to need more than this. I might not know much about babies, but I know they have a very short attention span."

"I thought you said you hadn't spent any appreciable time around children."

"True, but we welcome kids into the library and, well, they can be very loud if someone doesn't keep them distracted."

"Why don't you go grab a couple of things that might work?"

He nodded and left the room.

Alicia looked around.

Was she looking for her mother? Would she ever realize her mother wasn't coming back? How long before she accepted this new reality? And, most importantly, how much would Eliza's abrupt departure affect her? I didn't—not for a single moment—doubt the children would be profoundly damaged by this.

Scott would do everything he could to mitigate the damage, of course, but he wasn't a psychologist. And the twins wouldn't be able to verbalize their pain. So I suspected we were in for many more tantrums, upsets, and just general chaos.

We?

I glanced at my phone.

Then I sighed and texted Mr. Winters to let him know I wouldn't be in for the rest of the day.

CHAPTER 4

SCOTT

I wanted to stay ensconced in the spare room forever.

The twins' room.

Jesus.

Reality hadn't truly sunk in.

Eliza was gone—possibly forever.

I had twins I was responsible for—possibly forever.

My dreams and hopes were gone—possibly forever.

Because whatever happened from this day forward was entirely dependent on the two babies in the next room.

Being watched over by Anthony Rodrigues.

I kept expecting him to leave, but he didn't seem in a hurry to go anywhere. I sorted through some blocks and a toy that made barnyard noises when the babies depressed certain buttons. Oh, and a dog that spoke when you squeezed his stomach. That'd entertain them, right? Except they wouldn't be strong enough to squeeze, which meant one of the adults had to do it.

After we get them settled, we need to talk.

Well, that didn't sound ominous at all.

Was he going to tell me that I couldn't handle the twins? That he was concerned about their safety with me? That donating sperm was possibly the biggest mistake of my life—except if I hadn't then I wouldn't have a university degree.

If I hadn't, I wouldn't be a father.

I'd never—not in my wildest dreams—imagined I could be a father. I liked twinky boy toys. Few of them were ready to settle down and be parents. And sure, I might find a life partner later whose desires matched my own, but I had plenty of time to figure that out. My late teens and early twenties had been dedicated to education. The latter half of my twenties was meant have fun. To build up the speculative fiction section of the library. To play around with men who liked to pretend to be *boys.* All the sexy good times I missed while in college and first securing this job.

Kids.

"Hey."

I spun to find Anthony in the doorway.

He gestured to the toys, yet cocked his head in question when I pressed them to my chest.

"Just…" I gestured around the room.

"We'll tackle the crib, I promise."

The crib wasn't the real problem, but I wasn't going to bare my soul to the man. "Yeah, that'd be great."

He glanced behind him. "Look, I didn't mean to freak you out. All I wanted to say is you need a couple of high chairs and some kind of dresser or changing table. Somewhere to stow their clothes."

I eyed the suitcase. Putting the clothes into some type of furniture meant they were staying. "I have no idea how to get those things."

"Yeah, I thought that might be the case. I know an inexpensive place in San Diego. If I call right now, I might be able to get the stuff delivered before dinner. Or at least before bedtime." He cleared his throat. "Your call, of course. We might be able to find used things here in Gaynor Beach. We'd need to—"

"Just call. I'll give you my credit card." Gruffer than I liked. "And, uh, thank you. I'm sure you must be needed back at work or something."

He muttered, "or something" under his breath.

I tilted my head.

"I've texted my boss to let him know what's going on and to say I wouldn't be in for the rest of the day. I haven't heard back yet, but I'm assuming it won't be an issue. I didn't have anything pressing today anyway." He glanced behind him again. "And I became a social worker to work in the child-welfare system to ensure children were cared for. Helping you means I'm doing what I want to be doing."

Asking him probing questions was set to the side when one of the twins let out a howl of what I'd term indignation.

Anthony and I moved swiftly to the living room.

Alicia gripped both stuffed animals and clearly had no intention of sharing.

Zayden's lower lip trembled.

"Hey, buddy."

At the sound of my voice, he turned.

"I've got these toys." I placed the barnyard thing before him and started pushing various buttons.

Alicia abandoned the stuffies and crawled over to check out the new thing.

Zayden, unimpressed by the noises, snagged the yellow bear back and clutched it to his chest.

Was this his security blanket? Did he have an actual security blanket?

"You said she left me some papers?"

Anthony nodded and his eyes widened. "Yeah…we got kind of distracted."

"Well, we seem to have won a small reprieve. Perhaps you can get me the papers, and while I read them, you can place the order." I looked around. "A dresser, changing table, and two high chairs. Is there anything else we need?" I probably should've said that *I* needed but, in that moment, I liked the idea of having someone on my side.

Don't get used to it.

Right.

Pretty soon I'd be all alone.

Anthony retrieved an envelope from his messenger bag. He handed it over, then headed into the kitchen, phone in his hand.

Gingerly, I sat on the couch. Keeping an eye on the twins —my children—I opened the envelope.

The top few papers were the legal documents Anthony'd referenced. As he'd said, everything was laid out clearly and notarized. Would this stand up in court? If someone thought I was unfit, would I be able to defend myself with this? And Anthony'd said something about a judicial order. What would that require? I needed to consult a lawyer.

After the legalese came several pages on child care. The schedule—which we'd completely blown—as well as the likes and dislikes of each child. Eliza'd dropped a couple of hints about the emerging personalities of my charges. Basically, Alicia was a hellion, and Zayden was along for the ride.

Good to know.

But no explanation. Why she gave them up after she'd told me for years that all she wanted was to be a mother? Why she chose her asshat husband over these two beautiful babies? Why she used my sperm instead of someone's who looked like her husband? Deceiving him by not using his sperm was bad enough...but to pick someone who looked nothing like either of them? Maybe she thought her genetics would trump mine. Ah well, the redheaded children left no doubt they weren't Mark's. That being said, their blue eyes were all Eliza. With the tufts of red hair, both had the poten-tial to be stunning.

Looks don't matter.

No, they certainly didn't. And being a redhead usually

meant being the butt of plenty of jokes. But I'd be here to support them—let them know it got better and, if they met the right person, their hair might be an advantage.

Oh, my God. I was getting so far ahead of myself.

I leafed through the rest of the documents, but found nothing satisfying. Nothing to explain Eliza's state of mind. At least she could've written me a personal note.

Maybe he didn't let her.

That had distinct possibilities. I'd tried to warn Eliza that I felt Mark was too possessive and too jealous and that those weren't admirable traits in a partner—but she hadn't listened. Even before I moved to Gaynor Beach, we'd drifted apart. I blamed Mark. In truth, I could've made a bigger effort.

Anthony reappeared. "This is several hundred dollars worth of furniture. Don't you want to check what I picked before I finalize it?"

Did I? I should, right? Yet even that thought over-whelmed. I shook my head.

He went back to the kitchen.

Why did I trust him to do all these things? Why was making a decision for myself so difficult? How was I supposed to cope on my own?

"Okay, they've got a delivery truck that can make the trip this afternoon. Barring major traffic on the Five, they should be here around five-thirty." Anthony tapped his phone against his hip.

I checked the schedule, feeling as if this was something I could do. "The babies usually eat at six."

He scrunched his nose. "You think we can keep them to their schedule?"

"Uh…" I glanced over. Alicia was reaching for Zayden's bear. "Hey, sweetheart, how about this dog?" I showed her the one I'd placed on the floor. I squeezed its tummy, and it spoke.

Her interest was immediately riveted back. She held open her arms.

I handed her the dog.

She clutched it.

A reprieve.

Exhaustion was setting in, and we hadn't hit one o'clock yet. I checked the schedule. Well, we'd messed up lunch by feeding them the peas in the late morning. And bottles should've been... I rubbed my forehead. Even if we were able to keep to this schedule, what was to say chaos wouldn't follow? Their entire lives had just been disrupted, so something told me that whether I fed them at a precise time was going to be the least of our problems.

"Do you have to work today?"

At Anthony's words, I had a moment of pure panic and my stomach lurched.

Phew, it was Friday. "No, I have most Fridays off."

"But you work tomorrow."

Shit.

"I'm working Saturday and Sunday this week. Then I have Monday and Tuesday off next week." Panic set in. "I'm going to have to find someone to watch them. And, like, I can't afford a nanny. So that means day care, right? Do they take babies in day care?" I waved my hand. "Of course they do. We don't offer maternity leave in the lovely U S of A, so lots of women have to go back to work right away."

Anthony's mouth opened.

"I was talking to a Canadian the other day about their system. Women get a year. And in some Scandinavian countries, it's even more than that."

"A Canadian?" Anthony's brow knit, and he looked vaguely disconcerted.

What was that about?

"Yeah, some tourist. Wanted to borrow the library's internet for a few minutes—trying to save on the horrendous data charges, I think. Anyway, I don't remember how it came up…" I snapped my fingers. "We were discussing healthcare —universal versus insurance-driven. And after that we started comparing other things they have that we don't. I tried to find things we do well. Like, Canadians don't have free speech enshrined in their constitution."

"Is that so?"

Anthony seemed to have recovered himself. Weird, that the thought of a Canadian set him off.

"Yeah. But they have statutes against hate speech. Like people can't just say whatever they want and claim free speech. Apparently, he doesn't feel that it stifles people from saying whatever they want anyway." I scratched my nose. "And then his husband came in with their two daughters, and they started in about how Canada had gay marriage almost ten years before we did and…yeah, I kind of felt like we were behind on a bunch of issues." I winced. "And regressing on others."

Anthony met my gaze and nodded.

At least we lived in California. At least Gaynor Beach was a liberal and inclusive town. At least I felt safe here. Thank God, I wasn't back in Oklahoma these days. I'd have felt compelled to protest the current injustices, and that would've driven a further wedge between me and my family.

Ugh.

"You okay?"

I nodded. "Just thinking how lucky I am."

"Except no paternity leave."

"Well, I can ask Ms. Wallace. She handles human resources and payroll for the library. I mean, I'm the boss, so I should know. But these aren't, uh, normal circumstances. And, to be brutally honest, I haven't read all the rules and regulations. All my staff are healthy and work hard. I haven't had a single issue since I started. I was just hoping to coast through for the next forty years or so."

"That's optimistic of you."

I tilted my head.

"If there's one thing I've learned from my work, it's that things rarely go as planned. And sometimes even making arrangements for every contingency doesn't work."

"You mean like having a woman drop off two babies and then drive away?"

"Well, frankly, yes. Definitely one of my more interesting moments." He scratched his beard. "Look, I can help you find someone for childcare. I have a few ideas. And I'm sure if you check the classified ads, you'll find listings. I know a service that will do background checks. Why don't you call Maggie at Tiny Tots Day care? Or Corey Stokes at Charmers? Surely one of them will have a spot. And isn't the library closed over Christmas?"

I shook my head. "We only close for Christmas Day and New Year's Day. I'm the one who works the most over the holidays—no family and all that. Many of our lower-income residents rely on services the library provides. And some of the older people in the community drop by to socialize. And we get frazzled parents bringing in kids over the holidays when they need a break."

"In other words, these two couldn't have come at a worse time."

Just because he spoke the truth, didn't make the words any less painful. "I'll manage." Only I had no idea how.

A howl of protest drew my attention.

Alicia'd snagged Zayden's yellow bear again.

Damn.

I grabbed the dog and squeezed his stomach. I hoped one of them would be interested—honestly, I didn't give a shit which one.

Both ignored me as the tug-of-war over the yellow bear continued.

Alicia won, but then Zayden smacked her on the head.

Anthony and I were there in an instant.

I grabbed a screaming Alicia while he snagged Zayden.

I tried to get a look at her head. Surely her brother couldn't have caused that much damage, right? Carefully, I brushed her hair in different directions, trying to see if I could spot a contusion. The fine strands were easy to manipulate, and I didn't spot anything amiss. "Did he startle you, little one? I'm sure he's very sorry. But you shouldn't have taken his toy. You need to learn to share." Or we needed to get a second playpen. Apparently imprisoning them together didn't bring out their better angels.

"You can't hit your sister," Anthony crooned. "Brothers take care of their siblings. They do everything in their power to keep them safe. They…" His breath caught on the word.

I turned toward him, but he ducked his head against Zayden's neck.

"Just don't do it again."

The likelihood of a nine-month-old baby understanding and never hitting a sibling again was, like, less than zero. I could guarantee it'd happen again. Likely repeatedly. My older siblings beat me something fierce as I was growing up— my twin sister Scotia most especially.

Somehow, whenever I fought back, I was the one who got in trouble—even if I wasn't the instigator. I learned my lesson quickly and resolutely—take whatever was dished out and just deal with the consequences. Of course, it didn't help that my dad beat on me the most. To this day, I didn't know whether he'd sensed I was different, or if he just saw me as an easy target.

Maybe a bit of both?

"Do you think they might be hungry?" Alicia's wailing had decreased, and I wanted to find a way to make it cease entirely. I needed a painkiller. I felt like I'd tied one on last night—even though I hadn't.

"If we each hold one on our laps, we should be able to feed them, right?"

"I'm quite sure other parents manage." Even as I said the words, I wanted to pull them back. We weren't parents. Okay, I was. Stunningly. But Anthony wasn't. This wasn't his mess to try to clean up.

"So let me find some food." He rooted around in the diaper bag, coming up with another jar. "Chicken."

"Protein." Somehow, this felt like an enormous accomplishment. "And we should get them drinks, right? Milk or something? Are they old enough for...what're those things called...?" I gestured, hoping he'd understand.

"Sippy cups. I haven't spotted any yet, but there's at least one box left for me to bring in." He gazed down at Zayden. "Food. Then maybe a bottle and we can put them down for a nap?"

"We can try." Since both toddlers looked fully awake to me, I wasn't holding out much hope on that one. Still, perhaps with full bellies they'd mellow out.

An hour later, we had two sleeping toddlers tucked in their car seats.

The house was in utter chaos.

I had grown-up things to do, even if I just wanted to crawl into bed and sleep for a month.

Or until these two turned twenty-one.

CHAPTER 5

ANTHONY

As Scott called two of the day-care centers in town, I attempted to wipe the spilled formula from my formerly once-pristine cotton shirt. Certainly, I had days when things went sideways. I chose functional clothes that could be tossed in the washing machine. It only made sense—I worked with kids on occasion.

Had not seen hurricanes Alicia and Zayden coming.

Neither, apparently, had Scott.

I'd known when Eliza turned up at my office instead of going directly to him that something was off. But she made it seem like she was just going through official channels so no one would question Scott's custody later. Like, for instance, wondering why a single man suddenly had nine-month-old babies.

Give up, already.

Yeah, this was a lost cause.

Scott appeared at the bathroom door and caught my gaze in the mirror. His green eyes were dull—not the sparkle I normally spotted.

"Corey at Charmers said she can take the twins."

"That's great." I tossed the washcloth in what I assumed was the laundry hamper.

"In January."

"Shit." Succinct and heartfelt.

"Yeah. Maggie was a no-go for two nine-month-olds at the moment. She gave me two people to try—both of whom didn't have space. Seems a whole pile of babies have been born in Gaynor Beach the last year."

To my relief, only one case had passed through my door. A neighbor had reported hearing violence in a house with an infant. Mr. Winters had investigated and found the allegations couldn't be substantiated. In fact, the couple were remorseful their arguments were heard outside of their home. The husband had recently lost his job. Mr. Winters put him in touch with someone who could give him a job. I'd checked recently to see how things were going, and the family looked good. Looks could be deceiving, of course, but I had high hopes.

I shook my head. "So, Corey…"

"New Year. And I've got a call in to Ms. Wallace, but she only works mornings on Fridays, and she's gone."

My phone rang.

Mr. Winters.

I held up my finger and indicated I had to take the call.

"Hello, Mr. Winters."

"Where are you?" For a smaller man, my boss had a booming voice.

"Helping out a new father."

"Scott Wexler?"

"Uh…yes."

"Lottie showed me the copy of the paperwork. You delivered the babies immediately? Without consulting with the county's legal team? Verifying with the judge? Putting the babies into foster care, thereby giving Mr. Wexler twenty-four hours to prepare?"

"Uh…" Some of that was overkill…but some was logical —steps I would've followed if my head had been in the right place. Somehow, though, I hadn't questioned whether Scott would take the babies. Or, rather, I figured if he reacted badly then I could take them away and that'd be an end to it.

Stupid.

I hated calling myself stupid, but I couldn't argue with the sentiment. "I apologize, sir. Those are things I should've considered more diligently. But I'm here now, and—"

"You're to come back to the office. Immediately."

"That's not going to be possible. Mr. Wexler still needs assistance."

"Well, he's not getting it from you right now. I want you back—right now."

Sounded like I was due for another reprimand. "Sir, isn't the mandate for Child Protective Services to, you know, protect?" God, I sounded like an idiot. "Mr. Wexler just needs a little more time, and I'm here now—"

"If you want a job come Monday morning, you'll be here in thirty minutes."

He hung up.

I glanced up to face Scott's stricken expression. "I'm so sorry. I'll come back as soon as I can—"

He held up his finger. "We'll manage. I don't want you to lose your job. The kids around here count on you. Mr. Winters too, of course. But you've become part of the community, and we can't lose you. Go. We'll make do."

"Okay, I'll go."

His expression didn't lighten.

"Firing me is an entire process, and I can appeal it and, honestly, I've mostly gotten good performance reports, and no child has been injured or died on my watch—that carries a lot of weight."

"*Mostly* good performance reports?"

Trust the librarian to catch the slipup. Or maybe just me needing him to know I wasn't perfect.

"I made a mistake on a case a while back. Well, I'm not sure it was a mistake, but perhaps a rush to judgement. The result was a negative outcome—although things are much better in that situation now." *Please don't ask me details.*

"That sounds kind of ominous, but you didn't lose your job."

No, just an off-the-record dressing down and informal reprimand.

"My record's still clean."

"Okay, well, go. We can manage."

I didn't want to leave. The crib wasn't made, the last of the boxes hadn't been removed from the room, and I hadn't finished unpacking my vehicle. "Shit, we have to get the last of the stuff out of my SUV."

We did—removing the double stroller, several boxes, a few bags, and a few other things I couldn't even figure out. Weird, they sent all this but not high chairs.

I waved to Scott as I drove away. As I checked the time on the dashboard, I realized my shirt was a disaster. No way did I have time to go home and change. I didn't keep a spare shirt in my SUV, but I did in my office.

My hopes of sneaking in and putting it on were dashed when Mr. Winters stepped out of his office just as I entered the building.

Lottie glanced up from her magazine. She snapped her gum, smacked her fire-engine-red lipstick-covered lips, and resumed reading her magazine.

She'd started before me—and I'd been here six years. I could get a read neither on her age nor her sentiment toward me.

She treated me with the same disdain she treated everyone who worked here.

Great with the clients—crappy with the staff. Almost two-faced. Almost. She was kind and deferential to Mr. Winters.

We all were.

Guessed we all valued our jobs.

Mr. Winters indicated I follow him into his office.

I pointed to the stain and then at the door of my office.

He crossed his arms.

That's a hard no.

I ignored my shirt, my feelings of disquiet, the swell of fear for Scott, and the rising panic as I made my way into my boss's office.

His was more than double the size of mine.

This is what I covet.

Or rather, the power to help kids that went with it. But, today, I was as far away from it as I could get.

He pointed to the chair. He was doing a lot of that today.

I sat.

He didn't. "We have rules and protocols, Anthony. I'm sure you're aware of them." He ran his hand through his graying, thinning hair. "Sometimes you do exceptional work, and then sometimes you miss the mark entirely."

"You're talking about Patricia Petersen." Might as well lay it on the line.

For a moment, he hesitated. "We discussed that case. I believe your overzealousness contributed to the young woman's death, yes."

"I did what I thought was best." And I had. I'd been concerned about the child—about Marilee. I'd been blind to how my actions might've affected the mother.

"And I reprimanded you for that. You didn't follow protocol—you exceeded the required visits by a huge amount without any evidence the child was endangered. You caused distress to Patricia. She turned back to drugs and overdosed."

I fought the lump in my throat. I'd been protecting the baby. But I hadn't meant to push the mother back into using.

And I wasn't convinced I was entirely to blame. That being said, the woman's friend and her father blamed me. They'd convinced Mr. Winters I was responsible.

That almost cost me my job. A job I loved. A job I was made for. Losing this employment would cost me far more than just a salary—it'd destroy whatever sense of self-worth I had left. I didn't consider myself arrogant, but I believed I was important to Gaynor Beach. And Mr. Winters wasn't getting any younger. There'd come a time when he'd need to retire, and I thought I wanted the supervisor's job.

Still, contrition was important—even if it hurt. "I apologized to Mr. Bracken, Patricia's father, and to Mr. Collins, Patricia's friend. Those two are now married and have made a wonderful home for Marilee. I acknowledge all that. That was one instance."

Please let him not bring up—

"Then there's the Unger family."

Fuck.

"I did all my due diligence. I followed up, I checked in with everyone who knew the family." They lived on the outskirts of town. Their home was dilapidated, but everything had appeared tidy and organized. The kids went to school every day in clean clothes. All were doing well in school. Except one day the youngest of the three, a young girl aged six, had turned up with bruises on her thigh. Her teacher noticed and pressed for an explanation. Lana said she fell. A classic excuse, and one the teacher didn't buy.

The school authorities called me in.

I investigated. I questioned everyone. I searched for any signs she—or any of the other children—were being abused. No evidence turned up. At every turn, the kids insisted nothing was wrong. And after botching the Patricia Petersen situation, I was wary of being overzealous again. So I backed off.

Less than a month later, Ralph Unger came home one

ordinary day after his work on the local military base. He slaughtered his entire family—his wife Irma and their three children, including Lana. Then he turned the gun on himself.

Naturally, I was under harsh scrutiny—I'd been there less than a month previous, how had I not seen this coming? The fact no one else in the family's lives had seen it either hadn't mattered because I was the professional. The one who should've known better.

An autopsy proved Lana'd been abused. We assumed it'd been Ralph until police discovered Irma's diary, hidden away. Their thirteen-year-old son had been the one. He'd admitted as much. Instead of seeking counseling, the family'd attempted to carry on. The working theory now, months later, was that the abuse hadn't stopped, and rather than put his family through the shame and possibly a trial, Ralph had decided to put an end to all of it.

I'd never know, of course. He hadn't left a note. Hadn't confided in a single person. Just taken four lives of people he purported to love. Then killed himself. Knowledge of the abuse was hidden under judicial seal. Letting that fact be known would likely be damaging to me. I'd been tasked with discovering if Lana was being abused. And I'd asked pointed questions about her father—but hadn't considered the brother as a potential perpetrator. That was stupid on my part.

There's that word again.

I hadn't predicted Ralph Unger would turn into a family annihilator.

That was a failure I had to live with.

But there'd been no professional misconduct on my part— no one could point to a single instance where I'd missed something obvious.

I'd moved on.

Or so I told myself.

And Mr. Winters hadn't brought it up, so I believed it in the past.

More fool you.

I eyed my boss. The silence dragged on, and still he stood there—stoic—waiting for me to break.

Well, fuck him.

Two could play this game.

Finally, at length, he cleared his throat. "The Markham twins."

"Alicia and Zayden."

He nodded. "Am I correct the parents dropped them off this morning?"

"Yes."

"Intending the babies to go to Mr. Wexler."

"Yes."

"And this didn't strike you as odd?"

Jesus.

"Of course I thought it was odd. Naturally I questioned every aspect of the entire thing. I double-checked their paperwork. I asked repeatedly if they were certain. At one point I was able to get Mrs. Markham alone, and I asked if she or the twins were being abused. Or if her husband was coercing her. I offered her protection and sanctuary. In short, I did everything I could to ensure they were both certain this was the course of action they wanted to take." I met my boss's steely gaze head-on. "They were immovable. If I hadn't taken the infants, they would've left them elsewhere. I figured better here where we could ensure they were cared for."

"And your solution was to drop them off to an unsanctioned household."

Inwardly, I winced. Outwardly, I held my stance. "Mrs. Markham named Mr. Wexler as the biological father, and all the documents gave him custody."

"So you figured you'd just show up and say *hey, here are your kids, good luck*?"

When put like that, my actions didn't sound logical. "I thought placing them into emergency foster care only to

61

move them a short time later would be doubly traumatic. Mrs. Markham also left me with the distinct impression Mr. Wexler was aware of the paternity of the babies. She might've also intimated she'd let him know she was doing this."

"And you didn't question her on why she didn't deliver them directly?"

"She made it clear she wanted everything to be done through official channels—so Mr. Wexler wouldn't later have to deal with the authorities about how he was suddenly in possession of two babies." This sounded so rational and logical to me. Yet, seen through my boss's eyes, the entire situation was preposterous. I took a deep breath. "At this point, removing the children from Mr. Wexler's custody doesn't make sense. He's already organized a room for them, and they're settled. Unsettling them just for a night or two, only to move them back, would be too disruptive."

Don't let him see you sweat.

Mr. Winters's eyebrow arched. "And I suppose if I went by for an inspection that everything would be in order?"

Oh, Jesus, no.

Did I have time to call Scott? To warn him? And to what end? Surely he'd already done everything he could. He needed help—not scrutiny.

Brazen it out.

"You'd find everything in order."

"Well, I have a dinner meeting with an old friend in Oceanside tonight, so an inspection will have to wait."

"Household inspections are below your pay grade. That's what you pay workers like me for."

He crossed his arms. "The children were brought here—putting them under our jurisdiction. It'd only be prudent of me to ensure their welfare."

"I can do that."

"Frankly, Anthony, I question your objectivity."

Ouch. "I'm being objective. Mr. Wexler is prepared to

care for the infants—I'm merely ensuring he has everything he needs to succeed in this. In other words—I'm doing my job."

With far more confidence than I felt, I rose. "I'm going to return tonight to ensure everything is going well. If I have any concerns, I *will* remove the children. Is there anything else?"

He held my gaze for a long time. The lines on his face were more pronounced than I remembered from when I first started. But six years was a long time.

I'd changed profoundly in that time. Whether for the better or worse was up for debate—especially on a day like today. At this point, I didn't know if today was a win, a loss, or a draw.

"You may leave."

Not giving him a chance to change his mind, I exited as quickly as I could. I unlocked my door, dropped my messenger bag to the floor, and yanked open my filing cabinet where I kept my spare shirt. Despite the creases from where it'd been folded it was a sight better than the one I had on. I yanked off the stained one and tossed it into a plastic bag. I'd take it to the dry cleaner's—better than trying to get the stains out myself.

I double-checked my planner to ensure I didn't have any other appointments on the calendar. And I didn't do virtual counseling on Friday nights, so that was clear. God, had it only been this morning that I'd thought about going down to San Diego and visiting one of the gay bars?

Clearly off the table for tonight.

For the foreseeable future.

I dropped into my chair.

What's the plan?

How long would Scott need me? Hell, did he even want my help? If I returned there, I was making a series of assumptions.

Perhaps I should text him to determine if he needed assistance.

I discarded the notion—of course he needed help.

Write up the Markham file now, or do it later? I wasn't likely to forget a single detail of today, so that wasn't the concern. But Mr. Winters might decide to look for the report. He said he was heading to Oceanside, and tonight was Friday. But he was on call this weekend, which meant he might be called into the office at any point. Or he might just drop by anyway.

Sighing, I opened my laptop and created a case file. I texted Scott.

—I will be there but not for a bit—

I'd been writing for about ten minutes before I realized he hadn't replied. And given his predicament, that wasn't surprising. Still, worry niggled at me, but I needed to focus so I could get back to him sooner.

Offering a prayer that everything was okay, I dug back into the report.

CHAPTER 6

SCOTT

From the moment Anthony left to the moment I managed to get the two babies strapped into the stroller and the group of us headed down the driveway was pure insane chaos.

When the social worker closed the door, Zayden woke. Within a heartbeat, his whimpers woke Alicia. Only, she went from zero to ten in a nanosecond. Out of self-preservation, I picked her up first. After I changed her diaper, I put her in the playpen and turned to Zayden.

She howled her displeasure.

I got him clean and put him in the playpen.

He grabbed the yellow bear, but fortunately this time Alicia wanted the pink dinosaur.

After preparing bottles, I tried to feed them.

I had this image of me sitting on the couch, a baby placidly resting in each arm, and us having a quiet moment while they ate.

Holy fuck, was that an absolute impossibility.

Eventually both consumed enough liquid that I didn't have to worry about them starving.

Amongst their stuff was a diaper thingy. Which was a good thing, because both pooped within about twenty minutes of each other. I barely had one clean when it was time to do the next.

Still, they were restless.

I remembered my sister saying she took her kids out for car rides to calm them down. Shit, I didn't have the bases for the car seats. In all the chaos, Anthony'd driven off with them. And no way was I going to jury-rig something. Inspiration hit when I remembered the stroller. Took me fifteen minutes to unfold the fucking thing, but I succeeded.

By then, the babies were at each other's throats. Literally.

Alicia was trying to grab Zayden's collar and choke him. Of course, she had no concept of what she was doing.

I figured separating them in the stroller would be a good idea. Maybe if I walked them long enough, I could calm them down.

Even as I loaded them, I realized I hadn't eaten anything today.

And we were pushing four o'clock.

I strapped the twins into the stroller in the garage and ran back to the kitchen, where I chopped off a huge chunk of cheese, then darted back, belatedly realizing leaving them alone might not have been the brightest idea.

Alicia pounded the little tray before her.

She's going to be a handful.

Not to be too judgemental after, like, seven hours. Perhaps, once she settled, she'd be a perfect child.

Yeah, right.

She reminded me so much of Scotia. My twin sister was hell on wheels when we were growing up. I secretly hoped her own children were as much hellions to her as she'd been to me.

But I'd never know.

I managed to get the stroller out of the garage and the garage door closed while remembering my keys. Even that little thing felt like an accomplishment. I'd thought about sunscreen, but sunset was in about forty minutes. And I debated not going at all, but I needed to get these two out and into some fresh air. Plus, the stroller kept them a bit apart. They sat next to each other, but it was harder to strangle someone next to them.

Or so I theorized.

At the end of the driveway, I turned right.

I loved my neighborhood, but didn't walk nearly as much as I should. In fact, I didn't exercise as much as I should. Being naturally lean, and without a big appetite, I was unsurprisingly on the slender side.

Now, Anthony was another story. He was my height, but he had a few muscles under those button-down shirts. Oh, he wasn't bulky, but he had some nice definition. I'd spotted him running on the beach one day when I'd ventured down. I'd forgotten to wear sunscreen and had decided that was my effort at outdoor excursions for the next ten years. The sun in Oklahoma felt very different from here.

Now, if I ventured down to check out the ocean, I did it on cloudy days. Stormy days were the best—watching a squall whip in off the Pacific was magnificent.

"Hey, Mr. Wexler."

I blinked, then spotted the young man on the other side of the road. Kevin was on the verge of being a teen—still motivated to come to the library just to learn. In a few years, he might not think it was so cool.

Except this was Kevin—who loved to learn about nature. Hopefully he'd carry that love into adulthood.

As I waved, he nudged the man walking next to him. One of his fathers…

What was the guy's name? Another newer Gaynor Beach resident. And an attractive one at that.

Kevin, the guy, and their dog crossed the road. This far into the suburb, we didn't see much traffic—only local cars.

Pretty dog. Big, but attractive with its multi-colors.

I didn't know breeds.

But Kevin had her on a head collar, and she wasn't pulling. In fact, she hung back behind his legs.

Must be shy.

"Nice to see you, Kevin."

The dark-haired, snub-nosed boy offered a wide grin. "I was just telling Alec how I want to go to the library tomorrow."

Alec. Right.

"Well, we'd love to have you. For anything in particular?"

The lanky young man was level with his father's shoulder. He'd shot up during the almost year I'd known him.

"*Octopus and Squid: The Soft Intelligence* by Jacques-Yves Cousteau." He vibrated with excitement. "It has one hundred and twenty-four color photos, and you can't find a copy on the Internet. If I really like it, I'm going to ask for a copy for Christmas."

Alec smiled, caught my eye, and gave a subtle nod. His blue-gray eyes sparkled.

He was a damn handsome man, and I noticed he smiled a lot more since the first time I'd seen him.

"Zelda!"

The dog, who'd previously been cowering behind Kevin, had moved and now had her snout stuck right in the stroller.

Pure panic shot through me and I was about to yank the stroller back when Alec dropped to his haunches and calmly took hold of the head collar right under the dog's chin. "Are you making new friends, Zelda?"

She turned to meet his gaze, then looked back at the twins.

Alicia, apparently completely unconcerned, reached out to grab the dog's snout.

Zelda licked her little fingers.

Those big teeth were an inch from the baby's hand.

Alec's calm demeanor, though, and the dog's soft expression, eased my fears. I didn't want to make any sudden moves, lest I startle the large animal.

"Are these your twins? I didn't know you had children." Alec's tone was light, and he stroked the dog, easing her back a foot or two, while she continued to observe the twins who now were gesturing toward her.

"It's, uh, a very long story." *Might as well come clean.* "I didn't know about them, but they're with me now. We just…" I drew a breath. "Needed some fresh air."

"I remember that age—they get into everything. Are they crawling yet? Trying to stand?"

Lordy, I had no idea. I hadn't let them beyond the playpen. That felt vaguely like child abuse.

"Well," I hedged. "I don't know them all that well."

Alec gently pulled Zelda to heel as he rose. He cocked his head. "Long story?"

"Yeah."

"I think twins are cool. Like, you always have someone to play with." Kevin's enthusiasm was adorable.

I flashed to the memory of Alicia trying to strangle her brother. Not so much fun.

"They do entertain each other." Like bopping each other on the head when the other steals their toy…

"We need to be headed home." Alec gave the twins one more look.

I'd have said almost…wistful.

Kevin petted Zelda's head. "Time to go."

The dog looked longingly at the twins, then warily up at me. As they walked away, she gave me a wide berth.

My heart rate finally returned to normal. I'd held my cool, but all I kept thinking was the dog could bite one or both of the kids, and that I'd be the worst father ever. In the end, I was lucky, and Zelda's gentleness had won me over.

She's a special dog.

And kids should have a dog in their lives, right? I eyed the twins, leaning against their seatbelts to watch Zelda go.

Oh my God, take a breath. You've had them for about seven hours. They don't need a dog. And Crumpy would lose his shit anyway.

The one time a friend had come over with their dog, Crumpy'd jumped onto the dining-room table and had hissed continuously. We'd taken the dog to the backyard to hang out, but my friend had never come back with the lovely pooch.

Speaking of Crumpy, he'd be expecting his evening meal shortly.

As I spun the stroller to head home, I watched with horror as Alicia stuck her hand in her mouth. The hand Zelda'd licked.

Worst father ever.

The first thing I did, once we were home, was to wash hands. I wanted to rinse her mouth out, but didn't figure that was a thing. I put the babies into the playpen while I put a bit of wet cat food on a plate.

Crumpy appeared at the clink of a spoon like Pavlov's dog and inhaled the food in just a couple of mouthfuls. Then he wound around my legs, begging for more. He never got any, but it didn't slow his attempts.

Several times I'd nearly tripped over him.

He didn't care.

Food.

The doorbell rang.

In concert, the two little ones started howling.

My neighbors were bound to wonder what the hell was going on in here.

A young woman stood before me when I opened the front door.

"Yes?"

She thrust a clipboard in my face. "Two high chairs, one changing table, and one dresser."

"Oh, yes, of course." Holy God, I'd taken the twins for a walk having completely forgotten about the delivery—I might've missed them entirely.

"I'm Nikki, and this is Fred."

A much older gentleman appeared, carrying a box.

I stepped aside to let them in.

Nikki let Fred pass first.

"Kitchen?" Rough-voiced. Like a smoker.

I pointed.

He grunted.

Nikki stepped inside. "Show me where the dresser's going."

I led her to the bedroom.

She eyed the frame of the crib and gazed up at me.

"Next on my list."

And still the twins howled.

After a moment, Nikki headed back out. But instead of going outside, she veered to the living room. She walked right over to the playpen and peered in.

"You realize they're playing with, uh…"

I stepped closer, and the smell hit me.

How…?

Zayden's little pants were down, and apparently he'd figured out how to get the diaper down as well.

Or Alicia'd done it.

Crapshoot as to which of the two hellions was responsible.

Nikki stepped back. "Look, you paid extra for us to put the high chairs and changing table together."

This I hadn't known, but gratitude rushed through me at Anthony's obvious thoughtfulness.

"And we're not allowed to take cash for anything."

Where was she going with this?

"But if you make a donation to a local shelter for domestic-abuse survivors, I'll put the crib together too."

"Uh…" Nope. No words. Tears pricked my eyes, and I blinked.

She looked up at me. Those piercing eyes saw right through me. "You clean the kids—we'll fix the stuff. I trust you to make the donation." Without another word, she stalked off.

Two stinking messes.

My eyes swam.

Both kids needed to be cleaned. Right now.

Bathtub seemed the most logical option.

Both kids needed to be moved. Right now.

At the same time or…

Fuck it.

I scooped Alicia into my arms, then bent and managed to balance Zayden against my hip. I hustled us to the bathroom while Alicia clung to my shirt.

Shit.

Quite literally.

I sat them on the bathroom floor and shut the door.

Fred and Nikki might rob me blind, but at least neither of the twins was venturing beyond this room.

I moved to the bathtub, shoved in the plug, and ran the water.

Warm, right?

Next, I gingerly removed their clothing. All of it was covered. I'd left them alone only long enough to feed the cat and answer the door. That was what, two minutes? Tops? Yet, in that short amount of time, they'd created chaos.

I tossed everything into the sink, then I snagged a washcloth. I needed to get as much off as possible before I put them in the tub, right?

God, I didn't know.

Diligently, I cleaned as much as I could while trying not to gag. Mouth breathing was a thing and this was truly the grossest thing I'd ever done. No dogs or younger siblings at home. No pledging fraternities. Just a plain suburban life. Hell, even the cat litter was automatic, and I only had to empty the container. My entire life was orderly.

Now I was up to my elbows in piss and shit and I hadn't forgotten the vomit from earlier.

When I determined each child was as good as they were going to get, I put them in the bathtub. The water only rose to mid-chest, but panic seized me that they'd drown.

I didn't have any baby stuff, so I used my gentle body wash in the nooks and crevices. No baby shampoo either, so I used the body wash for that as well. I didn't want to use my harsh dandruff shampoo on these tender scalps.

Somehow, after an interminable amount of time, the kids appeared to be clean. I'd even managed to wash their hair without getting soap into their eyes. Truthfully, I felt pretty damn proud of myself.

A gentle knock sounded at the bathroom door.

"Yes?"

"Uh, Mr. Wexler, it's Nikki. Everything's set up. I need you to come and sign off on the work being done."

"Can't you just, you know, forge my signature?" Jesus, did I just ask a woman to commit a crime? "Never mind. Uh, give me a second." While holding both children, I snagged two towels. I managed to get a squirming Alicia onto one just as Zayden was about to pitch forward into the water. God, the child had no sense of self-preservation. I caught him and managed to get him onto the towel. I wrapped each of them like burritos, tucked one under each arm, and opened the bathroom door.

Nikki stood outside. She looked me over and, for the first time, a small smile crept onto her face.

I looked down.

Soaked. Pretty much from head-to-toe. With the bulk of the water having soaked into the crotch of my jeans. And smears of dried shit on my arms.

"You've had quite a day."

Meeting her gaze, I blinked. "It gets better, right?"

"I have no idea. I deliver furniture. Kids are my brother's jam. He's got five of them. I avoid them all." She pivoted and walked into the spare bedroom.

Obediently, I followed.

Not only was the crib set up, but the dresser and changing table were as well and…

"Is that a mobile?"

She nodded. "Found it in one of the boxes. I assumed you wanted it set up."

Mutely, I nodded.

"As agreed upon, we secured the dresser to the wall so it can't get pulled over. We moved the last of the boxes to the garage—I assumed you'd be okay with that."

"Yes…of course."

"Fred opened the box labeled linen and found the baby stuff. So he put that away in the dresser after doing the high chairs."

"And I'm not allowed to pay you." This didn't feel right.

"Donation," she reiterated. "And sign here."

I held both bundles in my arm. Maybe if I…

She stuck the pen in my mouth.

I signed holding it between my teeth.

She held up her hand to indicate I could keep it when I tried to hand it back. She snagged the end I hadn't drooled on and put it on the window sill. "Where no little hands can grab it."

"Yeah."

"Your house is not childproofed. I'm going to assume it's because you didn't know you were having babies move in, although…" She eyed them. "The pee stick would've been, what, sixteen months ago?"

I didn't even try to replicate her math. "The mother didn't tell me."

"Ah." She tucked the clipboard under her arm. "Fred's chomping at the bit to get back to San Diego. I wish you all the best, Mr. Wexler."

Then, in a moment of what I assumed was an uncharacteristic show of emotion, she quickly kissed both toddlers on their heads.

Just as quickly she was gone.

I stood in the middle of the room and gaped.

The room actually looked like a child's room. Okay, the horrid pink might scar them for life, but the rest actually looked nice. The crib was set up in one corner with the mobile above it. Against the short wall was the changing table and, next to it, the dresser. One of the delivery drivers had set up a little blanket in one corner with many of the kids' toys laid out on it.

This time, the tears didn't just prickle, they fell.

CHAPTER 7

ANTHONY

I parked on the street in front of Scott's house, because his driveway held a delivery van. As I alighted from my SUV, a burly older man hopped into the cab of the truck.

By the time I made it to the front door, a young woman was coming through. She halted when she saw me.

"Friend," I offered.

Her gaze narrowed.

Was she…judging me?

"You're from Tufts. In San Diego." I named the furniture store I'd hired to deliver the stuff. "Did you manage to put together the high chairs?"

Her mouth pursed.

Okay, well, the truck's logo was on the side, so that didn't help my credibility. But surely knowing about the delivery contents would gain me admittance.

"He's in a tough place. Take care of him." She swept past me, clipboard tapping her hip. Within moments she was in the passenger seat of the truck, and the two were on their way —presumedly back to San Diego.

What the hell happened?

I stepped into the house and the smell hit me.

Okay, yeah, and all that.

Gingerly, I made my way over to the playpen.

Pretty obvious what happened there.

Aside from an empty plate on the floor and a couple of half-consumed bottles in the sink, the kitchen was empty.

I headed to the bathroom.

Absolute chaos. Shit-covered baby clothes were tossed haphazardly in the sink. A used diaper lay to one side. The bathwater remained in the tub.

After rolling up my sleeve, I pulled the plug. Then I washed my hands. I made a note to later clean the tub.

I considered making a start on the bathroom, but I still hadn't set eyes on anyone.

The door to the babies' room was ajar.

Scott stood in the middle of the room. Unmoving. He had two wriggling bodies against his hips, held football style, and wrapped in matching towels.

Okay, well, no blood. No one appeared injured. A hell of a mess to clean up—but nothing that couldn't be dealt with.

Thank God Mr. Winters didn't come.

I winced on that one. No, my boss wouldn't have made a favorable decision based on what I was seeing. Parents had bad days, for sure, but this place was chaos. "You need help?"

Scott spun, clearly startled by my words.

His tear-streaked cheeks were nearly my undoing. I snagged one bundle. Upon close examination, I guessed Alicia. "Hello, sweetheart."

She eyed me suspiciously.

"Time for a diaper."

That hard look didn't ease.

I moved to the changing table, relieved to see everything organized. Somehow, I didn't get the feeling Scott'd done this. The delivery woman, then? The crib was put together, and hey, brackets held the dresser to the wall. Plastic plugs capped every outlet. Everything was perfect. Likely the high chairs would be perfect as well.

Changing Alicia proved relatively easy, and I snagged a onesie from the dresser while holding her tight. She wriggled, squawked and whined, but I managed to get her dressed.

I held her up to Scott. "Trade?"

Glassy eyes met mine. "I can't…"

He handed me Zayden and fled the room.

Not an auspicious beginning.

Struggling to hang on to both babies, I put Alicia in the crib and worked diligently to get Zayden into a fresh diaper and bedclothes as well. Then I snagged both kids again—with difficulty—and we made our way to the kitchen. Someone had emptied the box of food, and all the jars sat on the dining room table. After securing each baby in a high chair, I snagged two plastic baby spoons, a jar of something purple, and plopped down on my own chair.

I was already exhausted, and I'd only been here twenty minutes.

Feeding the two was a challenge, but I managed. I spotted a box of Cheerios. A small handful wouldn't hurt.

While they were occupied, I set about making bottles.

And still, Scott didn't reappear.

Was he finished? Like, he'd had enough and I could just take the babies and go? Awkward as fuck, but I could call my contact in Oceanside and see if they had a spot. Hell, the car seat attachments were still in my car. It'd take little effort to haul them up the highway.

Except I didn't want to do that.

Instinct insisted that Scott didn't mean that he literally couldn't do this ever. Just that he needed some time for himself. It'd clearly been a brutal day, and maybe he just needed a few moments to breathe.

Given the microwave clock read almost seven, I figured I

could do diaper changes, pretend to read a bedtime story or something, and then I could put these two to bed.

When was their bedtime? Eliza'd said something about a schedule when she pointed to the package for Scott. I hadn't looked it over. Aside from the fact I hadn't been invited, I figured there might be something personal from Eliza to Scott —something explaining this seemingly impetuous, yet clearly well-thought-out, insane plan.

Carry two at once? One at a time? I still hadn't cleaned the playpen which, thank God, had a plastic bottom. I'd thought that'd be cold to sit on—now I was incredibly grateful to the ingenuity of whoever knew what kind of trouble babies could get into.

Coaxing the babies to drink some formula proved challenging. Alicia especially showed zero interest.

I offered her my warmest smile. "You need this. Dehydration is a thing."

She didn't look convinced.

Zayden grabbed his bottle and drank a bit. It'd be easier to sit on the couch with them in my lap. Better to have Scott do one and I do the other.

Another ten minutes passed before I decided we'd done our best. I wet a washcloth. Once I had Alicia in decent shape, I removed her from the high chair and hightailed it to the bedroom. I deposited her in the crib, handed her a stuffie, and hustled back to the kitchen.

Zayden appeared on the verge of...something...but he seemed to calm when he spotted me.

Another smile from me in what I hoped was comfort. I knew enough about child psychology to understand that kids were incredibly intuitive and could pick up on the stress of the surrounding adults. They had to see me happy and unstressed.

Which meant I had to *be* happy and unstressed.

After verifying Alicia was okay, I set about changing

Zayden's diaper and getting him ready for bed. Next came Alicia. Somehow, we managed without descending into chaos.

Neither baby appeared sleepy.

I closed the door and flipped off the overhead light, opting instead for a lamp with a low-wattage bulb. Then I moved them to the blanket on the floor. Both immediately started to crawl away, but I hauled them back. I snagged a book that looked interesting and started to read.

Zayden was immediately captivated, but Alicia showed zero interest. Still, the room'd been babyproofed, so I let her wander while I read three books to Zayden. By the end, his eyes drooped and Alicia'd stopped moving as well.

I laid Zayden in the crib first, carefully removing the stuffies. No pillows or blankets either. I put him on his back, offered another smile, and watched as his eyes drifted shut.

Next, I scooped up Alicia.

She struggled.

I held her close and jiggled her. I stroked her hair and tried to offer soft soothing words.

After several minutes, some of the tension eased from her body.

Gently, I laid her in the crib next to her brother.

How long before they'd each need one of their own?

More research to do. For now, they were safe.

Alicia pointed to the mobile.

I examined it until I found a timer. I turned it on and stepped back.

Her attention was completely on the mobile.

A cursory search turned up the baby monitor.

Light on or off?

On for tonight. Not good for sleep hygiene, but I…oh. I spotted a nightlight in an outlet. I flipped it on, and a soft glow illuminated the space. After turning off the lamp, I took a moment to really look around. Hard to believe that this morning the room had been a sewing room. Eventually the walls needed to be painted, but that was low on the list. A nice bright yellow or sage green would work.

Tiptoeing out of the room, with the monitor in my hand, I glanced around one more time. After closing the door, I let out a long sigh of relief. God only knew how long the peace would last—so I needed to hurry, even though I really just wanted to crawl into bed. Any bed would do at this point.

Still, I sought out cleaning supplies—conveniently located under the sink. They'd have to be moved, or we'd need to install child locks immediately. I could absolutely see Alicia figuring out how to open this cabinet.

I checked to make sure the product was safe to use around children. It was. Not to consume, of course, but not noxious.

As I set about cleaning the playpen, Crumpy paid me a visit. He sat on the couch and stared at me with unblinking pale-blue eyes. His stripes were more pronounced with the overhead light on.

For a moment, I just looked.

With that squished face, he reminded me of the grumpy cat I saw in memes sometimes. He could star in his own meme with that look he gave me. Completely unimpressed. Whether by me, the little intruders, or the smell—I just wasn't sure. I didn't speak cat.

No pets during my childhood. Pets cost money. We barely had enough to feed our family.

In the past.

When the playpen was pristine, I moved back to the kitchen to try to achieve some kind of order. Cleaning high chairs was easy—deciding where to put the jars of baby food was a whole other thing. Right now, they covered most of the dining room table. I'd say this much for Eliza—she wanted her babies fed. I didn't have the same neatness gene Scott clearly possessed, but I didn't like looking at all the food taking up room on the table either.

One more day. Whatever Scott's decision was in the morning—that'd determine where we went from here.

Exhaustion hit in a crashing wave—hard, but ebbing. Barely eight o'clock, and I was ready for bed. I eyed the couch. Nice and long. I eyed my clothes. They'd be rumpled as fuck in the morning if I didn't strip down to my underwear. And what was the propriety of that? I supposed I could just leave, but Scott still hadn't emerged. I assumed he was behind the closed master-bedroom door, but I couldn't be certain. In all the chaos, he could've walked right out the front door and just kept going.

I wasn't sure I'd blame him—he didn't sign up for this.

Still, he needed to step up or step away. I almost said *man up*, but that was not only misogynistic, but something my father said to me all the time. I'd been as *manly* as I could because, even at an early age, I'd realized being prissy would earn me a dressing down. I wasn't physically abused, but the psychological torment was nearly as bad. Being gay wasn't going to be accepted in my family—and I'd do better to remember that. Now, my mother, my brother, and sister were dead, and my father was in prison.

I no longer felt the need to hide who I was.

Making my way to the bathroom, I consider all that'd happened today. In all of twelve hours—just how many lives had been irrevocably changed?

Mine included.

I scrubbed the bathtub to a polished shine, loaded the stinking baby clothes into the washing machine and turned it on. Then I pissed, washed my hands, splashed cold water on my face, and searched to see if Mr. Orderly had a spare toothbrush.

He did. Four, in fact. All in original packaging.

And since I kind of felt he owed me, I snagged one.

His toothpaste happened to be the brand I preferred, and within a couple of minutes, my teeth were clean.

Except…I hadn't eaten.

Since breakfast.

Shit.

I put the toothbrush off to the side of the counter, flipped off the light, and headed to the kitchen. I would've been happy to skip food, especially after having breathed in the smell of poop for the last hour, but that never ended well—invariably, I'd wake up with a headache and a mile of regrets.

Deli meat, brown bread, cheese, and a slice of tomato later, I had a sandwich. I added mayo and then stood in the kitchen to eat. Took me less than five minutes to polish it off. I started to put everything away, but decided I'd make another two. Hopefully I'd be able to coax one into Scott—if he ever appeared—and having a spare wouldn't hurt if I needed to eat on the run.

When he appeared. The guy was responsible. Above all else, he was responsible. Plus, he had a shift at the library tomorrow and no way was he going to miss that. I might not be certain of his willingness to take on the babies, but I knew he'd rather die than miss a shift at the library.

Funny, the little things I knew about him. Neat, meticulous, helpful, and gentle. This morning's *Who's Your Daddy* incident aside, I felt I had a good grasp on him.

Or so you believe.

The truth was, I knew very little about him.

Just like he knew very little about me.

I wrapped the sandwiches and put everything back in the fridge. I cleaned my teeth again and headed to the linen closet. If I was sleeping on a couch that didn't look all that comfortable, I was at least using a bottom sheet, a light blanket, and pillow.

Ever grateful Scott had a/c, but also he didn't jack up the temperature, I organized a makeshift bed. I removed my shirt and pants. The only debate was socks, but my feet often got chilled, and that made it tough to sleep. So they stayed on.

Opting to leave a low lamp on, I crawled into bed. Aside from the flu episode two years ago, I couldn't remember the last time I turned in so early. I was a night owl—which made hitting my desk at eight-thirty every morning a challenge.

Setting aside the flu episode that kept me home for a week, I hadn't missed a single day of work in six years.

I expected sleep to be slow in coming after the day I'd had, but I was gone within a few breaths and didn't awaken until I heard cries coming from the monitor. I didn't hesitate —I sprinted as fast as I could. Maybe if I made it in time, whoever was crying could be soothed and—

Nope.

By the time I was in the room, both twins wailed. They stood, gripping the edge of the crib, and both their faces were screwed up in obvious displeasure.

Instinctively, I placed my hand on both foreheads. Warm, but not hot. Why I felt *that* was the most important thing to check, I wasn't sure.

I flipped on the light and quickly assessed whether diapers needed to be changed. And not that I wanted to show preferential treatment, but picking Alicia first felt like self-preservation. Sometimes Zayden was able to self-soothe when his sister stopped wailing. Thus far, I hadn't found the reverse to be true.

Alicia's wails did diminish as I changed her.

I was trying to decide whether they needed bottles when Scott burst into the room. He still wore the same jeans and T-shirt, but they were rumpled.

He scooped up a whimpering Zayden and pressed a kiss to his forehead. "Hey, buddy. You need a new diaper?"

Alicia kicked and her foot connected with my gut. I oofed.

Scott looked over and, finally, he took me in. All virtually naked me. He raised an eyebrow.

I nearly pointed out he'd been MIA for hours, but now wasn't the time. "Alicia and I are going to do bottles."

He nodded.

My precious bundle and I headed to the kitchen. Doing this would be easier with her in the high chair, but we'd reached a place of understanding. As she tucked her head against my shoulder, my heart melted just that little bit. I managed to get the bottles done just as Scott arrived. His green eyes were a little more focused. His frown line was a little less visible. His red hair was a little less mussed. Likely, he'd taken a detour somewhere to make himself more presentable.

For me?

He needn't have bothered. I found him cute, but didn't see him in *that* way. Adorable? Sure. Fuckable? Yeah, not really. Not that I was particularly choosy…more that now he felt like a client. Any attraction I might've felt in the past had been shoved into the closet this morning. I was a social worker—his children were my clients.

We headed into the living room.

"Aren't you cold?"

"Kind of." I snagged the blanket and tried to wrap it around me. My effort was haphazard at best until he helped.

Success.

I huddled under it as I sat at one end of the couch. I tucked Alicia into my arm and, within seconds, she was latched on.

Scott replicated everything except the blanket, and soon Zayden settled.

"How do working parents do this? I have to be at work in less than five hours. Not that I'm going…but still…"

"You're not going?"

He looked at me, the babies, then back at me. Our gazes met.

"It's not like I can just leave them here. And I haven't secured childcare for them."

"I'm off for the weekend. I was planning to stay while you worked."

He shook his head. "I can't ask you to do that."

"You didn't ask—I offered."

Silence descended, punctuated by sucking noises.

When Alicia'd consumed half her bottle, I righted her.

"Crap, receiving blanket." I did not want to wind up covered in spit-up. I flung off the blanket and darted to the diaper bag, coming up with two. We were nearing the end of the supplies, so I needed to restock. Having everything close was handy, and if we needed to take off for any reason, having something we could easily grab would be good.

Burping Alicia was easy, and she soon settled against my chest.

Zayden was fussing more, though, and I worried Scott might get frustrated.

He didn't, though. He got the baby burped and after soothing and quiet words, he got him back into the crook of his arm so he could feed him more of his bottle.

"What time do they wake up?"

Scott gazed at me blearily. "I have no idea."

"Didn't Eliza give you a schedule?"

He nodded, scrunching his nose. "I'm honestly too tired to check right now—and I doubt they'll stick to it anyway. Their entire lives have been disrupted. I mean, would you want to follow a routine if everything was upended?

I flashed to the night the police came to the house. In the days that followed, I continued my routine religiously. With a neighbor's help, I did all the things necessary to bury my sister, my brother, and mother, but I also continued to go to school. The authorities weren't impressed, but I fought hard to keep going. I wasn't going to let the deaths of three people in my life disrupt my path. High school graduation, then getting the fuck out of town.

"We'll put them back to bed after fresh diapers. You and I

need to talk, but you need sleep more. We can regroup in the morning before you head to work."

Instead of providing him with another opportunity to argue, I headed to the babies' room.

By the time he arrived with Zayden, Alicia was already in the crib. I cranked the mobile for her, but she was out within a few seconds.

In no time, Scott had Zayden down as well.

We snuck from the room, closing the door.

"You must be cold, let me get you some clothes."

I shook my head at Scott's suggestion. "I'm crawling under the blanket and going right back to sleep, and I have my clothes for tomorrow—it's all good."

He looked ready to argue, but obviously decided there was no point. "Well, thank you." Then he headed into the bathroom.

I stood, waiting my turn.

We passed in the hall, and he said, "thanks for cleaning that up," but he didn't meet my eyes.

Nor did I meet my own in the mirror's reflection. Instead, once I'd done everything that needed to be done, I headed to bed.

This time, though, sleep was slower in coming.

CHAPTER 8

SCOTT

My phone alarm blaring at seven a.m. pulled me into full consciousness.

The twins were the first coherent thought in my mind.

I held my breath, but no sound came. I let out that breath and slumped back into bed. All the things I needed to do before I could leave the house flashed in my mind like an old-fashioned movie flickering in my brain.

Which made me think of the times we gathered in our gym as kids for Friday-movie nights. Why they thought *Old Yeller* was appropriate to show children, I'd never know. Twenty years later, and the trauma hadn't eased. My kids were never watching that movie. Even when they were fifty.

When I'd be seventy-seven.

Yep, I had children.

Babies.

Little ones I'd completely neglected last night.

Anthony'd come home, and as soon as he had a grasp of the situation—or even possibly before, who knew—I abandoned him and the kids. I bolted to my room and gave in to the full-on panic attack. Had sunk down into it and let it drag me under. I'd pulled out the tranquilizers I never used, downed two, and crawled under the covers.

Only cries hours later had pulled me out of the haze.

Sitting up, I opened the drawer of my nightstand. I picked up the pill bottle and held it in my hands. Part of me wanted to chuck them in the garbage, and part of me acknowledged if I hadn't had them yesterday, I'd have likely wound up in the hospital—which would've been ten times worse.

Anthony doesn't know.

No, he didn't.

I shoved the bottle to the back of the drawer and slammed it shut.

For now.

Then I shoved off the blankets. I'd stripped last night after dealing with the babies, so I was down to my underwear. I yanked them off and grabbed my robe—the robe Eliza'd bought me for a graduation present. Pink satin—always smooth against my skin. She'd meant it as a gag, I was pretty sure, but I loved it. Used it all the time.

I poked my head into the spare room to check on the twins.

They lay next to each other on their backs with their hands clasped. As if, even in sleep, they were seeking comfort from each other. When would they realize their mother wasn't coming back? Would it be gradual or had it already happened? Would there be a big meltdown or just these continuous little ones? Would they even find equilibrium?

Oh, Eliza, what have you done?

I hopped into the shower and, for just a moment, thought of my erstwhile companion. Last night? Even with the panic of dealing with crying infants—even knowing I'd completely flaked out earlier in the evening—I'd noticed him. Hard not to, seeing as he wore only gray boxer briefs and socks. The man was fucking beautiful. All tanned skin, light dusting of hair, and beautiful muscles. I shouldn't have seen him that way—certainly shouldn't be thinking of him that way now—but I'd have to be blind not to see the beauty.

And before, while I'd known he was competent at his job and a good person, I hadn't known how profoundly caring he could be. He hadn't needed to come back. He certainly hadn't needed to care for the kids, clean the entire mess, and stick around to help. I owed him more than I could ever hope to repay—and we weren't even twenty-four hours into this clusterfuck.

I needed to get into the office. To sit down and look carefully at the schedule for the next three weeks. Find any places where I could schedule other people to cover for me.

Lydia, a library student from L.A. was due back in three days. She planned to volunteer a few shifts.

What if I offered her paid employment for that time? On the one hand, she'd get great experience that'd serve her in good stead when she graduated. On the other hand, she'd just finished a grueling semester and deserved a break. As a scholarship student, though, a few extra bucks would come in handy. I'd call her and feel her out.

Where are you going to find the money?

Ah, the eternal problem of librarians. The Gaynor Beach city council gave me a workable budget every year—but it didn't cover everything I wanted. Some days I wanted to throw the papers in the air and give up. But I wouldn't. I'd work through the numbers again, and then I'd look forward to another fundraiser and try to figure out how to make it a success. What I really needed was a rich patron.

Fanciful.

Sure.

But I was allowed to dream.

Then come crashing back to the earth upon realizing two babies were likely to wake soon.

Scrubbed clean, I exited the shower.

Hey, the laundry hamper was empty. When had Anthony

taken care of that?

More guilt.

I dried myself off using the last towel. Must put a few fresh ones on the rack. Ms. Ducking had been a huge fan of towels—or many people had gifted them to her over the years. Either way, she had an entire shelf in the linen closet full of them. That was clearly going to come in handy. I added gel to my hair that made it a little spiky, but I didn't have time to dry it. I slipped back into my robe and opened the bathroom door.

Anthony stood on the other side, equally surprised to see me.

Our gazes met and held.

His dark-brown eyes were extra-deep in the crappy light of the hallway. He held his finger to his lips.

I nodded.

He pointed to my bedroom.

I nodded.

Then, realizing he was waiting for me, I headed in that direction.

He followed and closed the door. He held the baby monitor.

"You did the laundry."

Great, just blurt it out.

No *good morning*, no *how are you*, no *thank you for saving my ass last night*.

"I didn't figure you'd mind. Eliza included a bottle of baby laundry soap, so I tackled the dirty clothes. Then I planned to do a load of towels and the, uh, adult clothes."

Oh, God. I wracked my brain, trying to remember what else was in my hamper. Well, he'd seen the daddy T-shirt— that was about as bad as it got.

I hope.

"Of course I don't *mind*. That's great. Uh, you said you could stay here today? While I sort things out?" I grabbed my wallet from my nightstand and yanked out my credit card. "Whatever you need."

"Won't you need it?"

"I have my debit card and some money in the bank. I…" I faltered. "I don't know what I'm doing."

His gaze softened. "It's okay to feel that way. Some parents have nine months and still aren't ready for the rigors of parenthood." He tapped the card against the opposite palm. "You don't *have* to do this, you know."

"I know." I stood a little taller. "And I know some people will think I'm crazy…but I have to try. Although genetics play a role—they're clearly my children—I'd do it for Eliza anyway. Just in case—"

"She's not coming back, Scott. I think you need to accept that reality."

Knowing he was right and actually admitting it were two different things. I kept hoping this was all just a big misunderstanding, and she'd come back and…something…and everything would be okay.

But the world didn't work that way, and surely, after twenty-seven years, I'd have figured that out by now.

In the next moment, though, I'd go into a rage at Eliza and Mark for what they'd done. Dropping this mess into my lap. Leaving me to cope. To pick up the pieces. To provide a good life for the babies that obviously meant nothing to them. I shook my head to rid myself of the anger. "I'm going to pick up some parenting books while I'm out today."

"That sounds like a good idea. I might read some of them as well."

Did that mean he was planning to stick around, or was he just doing it for professional development?

I was too scared to ask.

Likely because I was scared of the answer.

"Oh, you need my cell phone number." I reached for the

phone, attached to the charger and sitting on my nightstand, when my robe fell open.

I scrambled to put the flaps back together and studiously did *not* look at Anthony.

He cleared his throat.

I peeked up.

"It's okay. I mean, I'm a guy and you're a guy and, you know, locker rooms."

Tightening my belt, I winced. "I got made fun of a lot in locker rooms—not my fondest memories."

"I apologize."

"Well, I was scrawny. And the only redhead in my class. They razzed my sister Scotia as well. Kids…they can be so cruel." I blinked several times.

Oh. Things were out of focus because I hadn't put on my glasses. I did that and then snagged my phone. I unlocked it, selected the phone app, and handed it to Anthony.

A moment later, his phone—in his back pocket—beeped.

"Text. That way we have each other's numbers and an open text dialogue. I doubt you can take calls at the library."

"No, you're right, I can't. If it's urgent, call the main phone number. That's always answered."

"Okay." Anthony's gaze narrowed. "Are you okay? Yesterday was pretty intense—"

"I'm fine." Instantly, I regretted the snap in my voice. "Sorry."

He held up his hands in the universal *I mean no harm* gesture. "I was, uh, reprimanded for just showing up here with the twins. I should've given you more warning."

"But would they have gone into foster care?"

"Probably. Somewhere. But they would've been okay for a night or two."

I shook my head. "Eliza wanted them here."

Anthony blew out a quick breath. "Have you heard from her?"

He'd handed my phone back, and I checked.

Nothing.

I hadn't expected anything, but it would've been nice. "They must be halfway across the country by now."

"Depending on if they drove all night or if they're making any stops along the way. But yeah, you can get pretty far in just over twenty-four hours."

That felt too neat. Too tidy. Like she was starting her life over right now while I faced a lifetime of being a father. "I need to get dressed." I needed a minute to compose myself as well. At least I'd hidden the pills.

"Of course. I'm going to make some oatmeal. Oh, you said Eliza included a schedule. Do you mind if I look through the papers?"

I wracked my brain to remember if they contained anything incriminating, but I didn't think so. "It's fine. Hopefully the key to the universe is in there as well."

"Isn't that forty-two?"

He left before I could answer.

Huh. Wouldn't have taken him for a Douglas Adams fan.

You don't know him at all.

No, I didn't. Being a social worker'd gained him admittance, but shouldn't I do some due diligence or something? Make sure he was safe to be around the kids?

Well, he might just do it back.

In fact, he might've already done a search on me. He wouldn't have found anything.

Or at least I hoped not.

Medical records were sealed, right? Especially the ones from when I was a teenager in Oklahoma. I had to believe it, anyway.

God, help me.

I slipped into my baby-blue button-down shirt and a pair of khakis. I selected matching socks and then a pair of loafers. Ms. Ducking used to insist on ties, but that'd been the first rule I'd gotten rid of. She'd also been a proponent of skirts and low heels for the women. I was happy with jeans and family-friendly T-shirts.

The women in the library appreciated it.

As I reappeared, I heard Anthony humming softly. I glanced into the spare room and he was changing Zayden.

Alicia still slept.

Were we supposed to wake her or let her sleep? Would that affect her napping schedule later?

Ah, yes, the schedule. I made my way to the living room to find the envelope. Despite yesterday's chaos, I spotted it easily. I opened it and located the schedule. Scanning it, I realized we hadn't done a single thing yesterday at the appointed time. Was that good in that we adapted or bad because getting the babies back on track would be tough?

I didn't have a ready answer for that.

After entering the kitchen, I attached the paper to the fridge with a magnet.

Then I pinned the food list, pleased to find there weren't any allergies or sensitivities—that could've been disastrous.

Again, just to be certain I hadn't missed it the first time, I thumbed through the papers. Medical records of the kids, a few miscellaneous articles about various things…but nothing personal. Nothing from Eliza to explain any of this.

Oatmeal.

Damn.

I located a container in the piles of baby food on the dining room table. Not that I had the right to expect it, but why hadn't Anthony put the food away?

Because you flaked and he wasn't sure you were keeping the kids.

Ah.

Fair enough.

So as the oatmeal heated in the microwave, I shifted things around in the tiny pantry to create an entire shelf of little jars and boxes. I did my best to organize it, but I'd need to make a more concerted effort later.

And when precisely would *later* be?

Good point.

Anthony breezed in with Zayden on his hip. He spotted the schedule and approached it with what I could only term trepidation. "Ah."

"We'll do better today."

He arched an eyebrow. "You mean I will."

"Yeah. Look, I should arrange some help."

"I'll be fine." He tucked the baby into the high chair. "Don't get oatmeal on yourself, but would you mind watching him? I want to wake Alicia. She'll likely be cranky, but I want to try to keep them on the same schedule."

"Those parenting books I'm planning to bring home— better make sure at least one is about parenting twins."

"With so many multiples these days, I'm sure there must be something."

"If all else fails, I'll go down to Boardwalk Books and Bites. Nash should have something."

"Great."

Just before Anthony moved away, he pressed a hand to my arm.

Our eyes met.

"You okay?"

His gaze penetrated down to my soul. How easy would it be to blurt out the truth? That I had no goddamn clue what I was doing. That I wanted to honor Eliza's wishes—and to take care of my babies—but that terror overtook me every time I thought more than two minutes ahead.

But I wouldn't say those things. He'd seize on the weakness. He'd take the babies away. Hell, he might do that anyway. For now, I had to show strength. "Yeah, thanks, I'm okay."

Whether he believed me or not was a whole other story. Still, he let me go.

I missed the comfort of the contact.

Feeding Zayden proved easier than I expected, and I even managed to get down a bit for myself—and none on me—by the time Anthony brought a groggy Alicia in and got her settled on the high chair.

"You head out, I've got this."

My hesitancy must've been obvious. He put the bowl down on the counter and clasped my upper arms.

Again, our gazes met.

"We will get through today. You're going to work. I'm going to take care of the kids. Everything else will sort out, okay?"

He seemed to be asking me that question a lot.

"Yeah, okay."

Then, with an impulse I couldn't explain, I hugged him.

He went rigid, of course—because who wouldn't when accosted by a virtual stranger—but as I started to pull back, he tugged me toward him. He held on tight, letting some of his strength seep into me.

I'd take everything I could get.

After one last squeeze, I pulled back. I had the absurd urge to kiss him. Not a peck on the cheek with a *have a good day*, but a full-on mouth-with-tongue kiss that said *I'm going to miss you and I hope you miss me*.

Ridiculous.

I held up my phone.

He nodded.

I kissed each baby on the head.

Zayden leaned into the touch.

Alicia batted me away.

After one last glance at the very domestic tableau I was leaving, I walked away.

And my heart broke just that little bit.

CHAPTER 9

ANTHONY

That hug.

I wasn't sure who needed it more—Scott, myself, or us both equally.

Two hours later, the embrace should've been a distant memory.

Except it wasn't.

He'd felt so good in my arms. A solid weight and presence. Not some ethereal being like he'd seemed last night when he'd first dropped the twins into my arms and took off. This morning he felt more grounded. And he looked great in his outfit.

Smart.

I, on the other hand, looked pretty rough. I had circles under my eyes, I wore yesterday's clothes, and I was just...rumpled.

Not a good look.

But this was what parents endured, and if anything was to come out of this disaster, it'd be an increase in my empathy toward parents—especially single ones.

Despite the fact Alicia somehow got oatmeal in her hair, breakfast was a relative success. Okay, I didn't get much oatmeal. But I eyed the sandwiches in the fridge and planned a mid-morning snack.

Then I tried to put the kids in the playpen so I could get some work done.

To say it didn't go over well was pretty much the understatement of the millennium.

Zayden would play for a few moments with a toy, but Alicia had no interest. She thought the playpen was a prison, and she wanted out on parole.

Now, I didn't have actual proof of this—but the fact she howled the entire time was some indication.

Giving up, I moved the three of us to the spare room. I spread out more blankets on the ground, closed the door, and left the kids to their own devices. I figured with that stack of toys, we were golden. While they played, I tried to create lists on my phone. Top priority was getting all the things necessary to childproof the rest of the house.

Alicia kept trying to grab my phone by crawling all over me while Zayden clutched his yellow bear to his chest and kept rocking back and forth.

At one point, I tried to pull him into my arms.

He squirmed and fought back.

I relented.

He resumed his rocking.

Alicia, trying to stand by using his head, nearly knocked him over.

He protested vociferously.

And on it went.

I was surprised, at ten-fifteen, when the doorbell rang. I pocketed my phone, swept the babies into my arms, and headed to the front door. Opening it, my heart seized.

Mr. Winters stood on the other side of the door. He held his briefcase in one hand and a business card in the other. Clearly, judging by the expression on his face, he was as surprised to see me as I was to see him.

For a fraction of a second, I considered barring him. But the thought passed, and I held open the door.

He stepped inside.

I said a little prayer of thanks that I'd managed to tidy the place. Everything was put away—including the bedding from last night.

Alicia stared at the newcomer.

Zayden cuddled into my neck and hid his face.

Mr. Winters cleared his throat. "You appear rumpled."

For a moment, I worried he'd realize I was wearing yesterday's clothes. But he wouldn't, because he hadn't seen me after I'd gotten changed. I owned several pairs of khaki pants, so he couldn't be positive these were the same from yesterday. "I've been playing with the babies." At least I wasn't wearing oatmeal.

He stepped toward Alicia and leaned forward.

She attempted to grab his glasses.

He stepped back. "Well, perhaps you can give me a tour."

And so I did. Every room, including the master bedroom where—thank goodness—Scott had made the bed, and the room with all the books. He did a thorough inspection of the babies' room and we moved into the main living area. He'd withdrawn a notepad and was busy scribbling notes.

I shouldn't have been nervous, but I was.

Finally, once we finished in the kitchen, he cleared his throat. "This house isn't babyproofed."

"I'm aware. For now, the twins are restricted to the playpen, high chairs, and the floor of their bedroom. We have a plan to get everything organized tonight." Or at least I assumed we did.

"And where is Mr. Wexler? I assumed he'd be here."

"He, uh, had to work. I'm helping out today and tomorrow."

"It is difficult for me to approve him through a home visit if he isn't even here."

And if you'd called ahead of time, we might've arranged something.

But I knew why he'd done it. I would've done the same thing. "Mr. Wexler will be home this evening, if you would like to come back. Or he'll be up first thing in the morning before he has to work tomorrow. I believe he has Monday and Tuesday off—so you could visit then."

"How does he intend to care for the children while he works?"

"I believe he's secured spots for them in Charmer's Day Care with Corey in the New Year."

"And until then?"

"He's working on arrangements." I didn't add that I'd be here whenever I could for as long as he needed me. We hadn't talked about long-term. I figured that conversation would come once things settled. And if he gave me the kiss-off, I'd be on my way. But I hoped he didn't, because I liked the idea of being able to stay and watch over the twins.

Mr. Winters harumphed—which was more emotion than I'd ever seen him display. He was known for holding his cards close to his chest. "Well, I don't see anything that would disqualify Mr. Wexler, but I'm concerned he isn't here. Please let him know I intend to return." He made a sweep of the living area. "And that I'll expect the house to be babyproofed by the time I return." He tucked his notebook back into his briefcase, left his card on the front hall table, and saw himself out.

I'd managed to put the twins in their playpen and they'd actually behaved the entire time. Relief flooded me as I envisioned all the scenarios that could've happened but hadn't.

Alicia squawked.

Ah, snack time.

The doorbell ringing again caught me off guard as I wasn't expecting anyone. I was about to step away when Alicia screwed up her face. Panicked, I scooped her up.

I knew that face.

After ensuring Zayden was okay, I was making my way to the front door as the bell rang again.

"All right, enough. Be patient." I moved to the hallway where I managed to flip the bolt and open the door.

Oh, holy hell.

The young woman on the other side of the door gaped. She narrowed her eyes. "You."

"Uh, me." How was I supposed to answer? I knew why I was here—I had no clue why she was. Twenty some odd thousand people lived in Gaynor Beach. That was thousands of houses.

So how'd she end up at this one?

Lacy Collins put her hands on her hips just as Alicia grabbed a lock of my hair—making me wish I'd kept the crew cut.

Despite myself, I winced.

The teenager before me grinned. "Scott said you could use help. That there're things you might want to do and I could watch the twins." Her dark-brown eyes lit. "Twins are cool. I mean, I love Marilee…but two? Double the fun."

"You mean double the chaos." I tried, but found myself lacking her enthusiasm. "You're qualified?"

She rolled her eyes. Something I'd witnessed before. "Duh. I took a babysitting course when I was younger and had done some sitting for kids in the neighborhood before Oscar had Marilee."

Oscar hadn't *had* Marilee, but I wasn't going to argue semantics with my potential savior.

She continued. "And I've been watching Marilee whenever Oscar and Hugh need a break. I mean Miss Agnes is Marilee's nanny, but she isn't on duty all the time. So I get plenty of time with my niece."

And since Marilee'd been ten months when Lacy'd moved down from Los Angeles to stay with her older brother and his...found family...I couldn't argue with her bona fides.

"They're a challenge."

"I can handle it."

"You have to watch them all the time."

She offered me a *duh* look.

"Well, you'll have to go to the bathroom. So, like, call me."

The girl was uncommonly tall, and well on her way to being her brother's height—a major growth spurt since the last time I'd seen her.

Alicia reached for Lacy, who caught her easily. "Hello, little one."

"This is Alicia. Her brother Zayden is in the playpen. I was thinking maybe you can take them to their bedroom? I need to run out and get baby-proofing supplies and a few other things."

The baby appeared fascinated with Lacy. She kept stroking the young woman's dark skin and was grabbing for the black curls when I intervened.

"No." I tried for gentle. "We don't pull on hair."

Alicia squawked with indignation.

I sighed.

Lacy laughed. "She can pull my hair—one time. Then I'll set her straight." She indicated I should let her in the house. Which I did. With just a moment's hesitation.

"How much is this going to cost me?"

She eyed me. "First visit's free—so Scott can make sure I'm a good fit."

I didn't miss how she'd invoked Scott—implying he was her boss. And she likely wouldn't take any shit from me.

In that moment, I again admired her moxie. I didn't intend to tread on her—but I was also glad she wasn't going to let me.

She made a quick survey of the room and located Zayden. "Hey, little man."

He turned at the unfamiliar voice. The rapidity with which he did it had me questioning whether Eliza'd called him that. He held up his arms, and I scooped him up. Lacy was powerful, but I doubted she could safely handle carrying two at once.

I moved to the spare room with her hard on my heels. I stepped inside.

She whistled. "Isn't this the color of that medicine stuff?"

I hadn't actually thought of that, but she had a point. "Ms. Ducking owned the house before Scott. I guess she, uh, liked pink." The other spare room was floral. Scott's bedroom was a soothing sage green.

"Well, it's bright." She eased Alicia to the floor, and I replicated the action with Zayden.

Alicia started crawling.

Backwards.

Zayden sat placidly and snagged a stuffie.

Meanwhile, his sister'd turned herself around and was heading for the door—ass first.

Lacy stepped in her way and gently guided her back to the blanket.

"The big man was just on his way out." She threw a look over her shoulder. "When did they last eat?"

I glanced at my phone. "An hour? Or more? I think…"

"And do they have a schedule?"

"It's on the fridge, but frankly, we haven't followed a single thing. We, uh, didn't plan for this."

She drew in a sharp breath. "Something Anthony Rodrigues didn't plan for? How shocking."

Even I recognized mocking sarcasm. "I'm doing my best." A tad defensive, but I was.

Finally, at length, her expression softened, and she offered a small smile. "I get it. I really do. When Oscar was alone with Marilee for the first time—after Patti died—he panicked. At least you and Scott are in this together."

The mention of Patti, my former client, hit hard. Lacy's brother still blamed me for her death—and I wasn't sure where Lacy's allegiances lay.

"You go." She offered me a smile. "We got this."

Part of me felt this was all kinds of wrong. I was responsible for the babies. On the one hand, I'd given my word to Scott that I'd stay and care for them. On the other hand, Scott called Lacy and asked her to rescue me. And childproofing this house had to be a priority—the twins couldn't live in their playpen or bedroom for the next ten years and Mr. Winters could return at any time.

Truthfully, I couldn't contemplate ten minutes, let alone ten years. After snagging the shopping list, I headed for my car. I popped off a quick text to Scott—letting him know that Lacy'd arrived, and that I was off shopping.

He didn't respond, but then I hadn't expected him to. He seemed like a diligent guy, and if they had a rule of no phones on the library floor, then he'd abide by it.

My first stop was the hardware store. Fortunately the young woman working had me weighted down with everything I could possibly need within a few minutes. Since, unbeknownst to Scott, I was paying for this myself, I studiously ignored the price and moved to the grocery store. The twins had plenty of food in jars as well as formula, but Eliza hadn't included fresh food. I'd searched the internet for healthy baby foods and come up with a list that worked. I also nabbed a few ready-to-serve meals for adults. Scott and I were going to need all the help we could get.

So you're staying?
Obviously.
For how long?
No clue.

I honestly had no idea what I was doing. I had work on Monday. Scott was working today and tomorrow and had Monday and Tuesday off. Where did Lacy fit? The high school was in session for another week before winter break. And how often did Scott plan to make use of the teenager's services?

Shoving away the calculations of complications, I went through the check-out line and was soon stowing the food in my car. I was missing something, but getting home was important. Not that I didn't trust Lacy. Well, maybe like, ninety percent. But that this was all so new—for me, for the twins… They needed constancy in their lives and between my schedule and Scott's, they weren't likely to get it any time soon. Which could have disastrous consequences for their attachment and stability. They were old enough to feel the acute loss of their mother. Our goal had to be minimizing the damage, the pain the twins couldn't express verbally.

I arrived home and was met at the front door.

Lacy snagged the grocery bags.

"The twins?"

"Fed and asleep. They were starving."

Hadn't I just fed them? Or was time slipping away? "And they went down?"

"Alicia cried a bit, but I got her calmed. Zayden was down fast." She carried the groceries to the kitchen. "But you've got a bigger problem."

Oh, God, I didn't think I could handle anything else. "And that is?"

"Crumpet's straining and peeing little drops of blood."

Even the word *blood* sent my blood pressure skyrocketing. "The cat?" I should probably have asked how she knew the cat's name, but that seemed like the least-important unknown information at the moment.

She nodded. "I've put him in his carrier. You should run him to the Gaynor Beach Veterinary Clinic right now."

"Right now?" I couldn't conceive why this couldn't wait until Scott got home.

"There might be a blockage. He could die."

"But there might not be a blockage. He might be fine. It might be..." *Seriously? You know nothing about cats and you're arguing with a teenager.* "How do you know so much?"

"I've been volunteering at the clinic for over a year now. More importantly—" She pointed at my chest. "—I called and spoke to Dr. Louisa myself. She said time was of the essence. So get moving."

"What if I paid you to take a cab?"

She shook her head. "I'm not old enough to authorize medical procedures."

"Well, wouldn't Scott need to do that?"

"I tried calling his cell phone. He didn't answer."

"Did you try calling the library phone?"

"I did." She gave me her patented *duh* look. "No one answered."

"Okay, well I'll just go down there."

She sighed. "What part of *he might die* are you not understanding?"

"Where's the carrier?" No point in prolonging the argument. "Will you keep trying to reach Scott for me?"

"Yeah, I can do that." She indicated a hard-shell case where a very pissed-off Crumpet glared.

Good to know where I stand. "And you'll manage the kids?"

"I've got your number."

I wasn't even going to ask how she had it. Instead, I dropped the bags with the hardware stuff and groceries, picked up the case, and headed for the door.

"Drive safe," were her words that carried me out and to my car.

Did she think I normally drove recklessly, or was this a standard warning she gave everyone? Given she used to live in LA, I could see that. I was a skilful driver, but not a fan of their freeways. Even the side streets drove me a little crazy.

As such, Gaynor Beach was the perfect size, and soon I

found myself in front of the vet clinic. I parked, snagged the case, and headed inside.

To my relief, the waiting room was empty. Surprising, since this was the only vet in town. The two exam rooms had closed doors. Maybe that was where all the action was. I approached the desk with trepidation.

An older woman rose to greet me. She peered into the cage. "Hello, Crumpet."

He hissed.

"I know, you don't enjoy your visits here." She met my gaze and shrugged. "Some animals love their visits and some have bad associations. He had a nasty urinary tract flare-up last year. Guess he remembers us."

"Or he doesn't like any strangers." I wasn't sure where to go with this. "I'm Anthony Rodrigues. You know Crumpet. Uh…"

"Lacy called and said you were on your way in. Doctor Blair is just finishing up with a patient. Oscar will get you settled, and she'll see Crumpet right away."

My stomach dropped to the floor. Of course Oscar was working today. Because what were the odds I could sneak through this endeavor without drawing attention to myself? I wanted to be under the radar, but apparently the screen was flashing my name loud and clear.

One of the exam-room doors opened. A tall, slender woman with a sleek chignon of blonde hair and bright-brown eyes exited with a little dog on a leash.

The poor dog had a cone around his neck.

Another striking woman followed. She wore a lab coat, had dark-brown hair, and her eyes were also bright— although they were a stunning shade of blue.

"Peaches will be just fine, Melinda."

The woman smiled. "I'm supposed to be at a wedding this afternoon. You know me, always in my scrubs."

The vet indicated her own clothes. "Part of our jobs.

Although your work as a nurse is pretty intense." She crouched down to scratch Peaches's ears. "You be good."

Surprisingly, the dog licked her hand.

I wasn't sure I'd be so generous if someone had just stuck a cone around my head.

"Christa will settle you up." The vet gave me a quick look. "Oscar will get you settled, and I'll be right in."

I managed a nod before she disappeared into the back.

Sounds of what I assumed was cleaning carried through from the exam room and, within moments, Oscar appeared.

The Black man was as strikingly handsome as ever. I saw little bits of his sister in him—the nose, in particular. Also the stubborn set of his jaw. From the moment we'd met, we'd been antagonistic. That was on me. Well, he might've also had a chip on his shoulder.

He didn't appear surprised to see me, which provided a modicum of relief. He indicated I should enter.

I did. After surveying the room, I placed the carrier on the metal exam table.

Oscar peered into the case. "Hello, Crumpet."

"He's not very—"

Heedless of my warning, Oscar opened the case.

Crumpet stepped out. He eyed me before turning his attention to Oscar. He approached the vet tech's outstretched hand, headbutted it, and started purring.

"See, now how can he be dying if he's..." I gesticulated.

"Seriously ill cats can still be affectionate and purr." He petted the cat and scratched behind his ears. "I want to weigh him, and then Dr. Blair will come in and give him a thorough examination. She'll likely order tests to determine the cause of the blood. Did you see how much?"

I shook my head. "Your sister presented me with the cat in the crate and ordered me to come here." In retrospect, I really should've asked more questions.

"My sister was right to send you in. This might be very serious." He held the cat. "Could you remove the crate?"

Naturally, I did as bade. He placed the cat on a little scale and noted the weight. He stroked a few more times. "Good boy. Just the same weight as the last time. You're a good boy."

I thought the praise of maintaining weight might've been excessive, but Oscar had a clear calming effect on the cat that I couldn't argue with.

At that moment, Dr. Blair entered. She met my gaze. "Mr. Rodrigues."

"Please, call me Anthony."

She nodded. "I'm Dr. Louisa Blair. I understand Crumpet was straining over the litter box and you spotted some blood."

"I didn't." I pointed to Oscar. "Lacy Collins was babysitting for me and she noticed Crumpet... Anyway, she told me to get right over here."

"You have kids?" Oscar's disbelief was clear.

Not that it was any of his business, but he was bound to hear eventually anyway. "Scott Wexler has two babies—Alicia and Zayden. I was watching them while he worked, but I needed to run some errands, and Scott asked Lacy to help." I pressed a hand to my forehead in an attempt to stem the rising headache. "Lacy saw Crumpet, and when I arrived home from shopping, she insisted I come here."

"It's a good thing you did." Dr. Blair held the cat and appeared to be feeling the cat's abdomen.

From my angle that's what it looked like. I was truly clueless.

"He has a blockage. This requires immediate sedation, and we need to clear the blockage."

I scratched my scalp.

"He can't urinate. We need to unblock the urethra and get his bladder emptying immediately. Otherwise, the toxins in his system will build up or his bladder could rupture and he could die."

Not that I'd ever question her, but the steeliness in her blue gaze held me captive. No mincing words.

"Do you need my authorization? Do you need to speak to Scott? I mean, of course, do whatever you have to do—"

Before I finished the words, the door to the exam room opened, and Scott barreled in.

The room suddenly felt quite small with so many adults and a poor cat.

"Glad you're here, Scott." Dr. Blair pivoted to him. "As I was explaining to Anthony, it appears Crumpet is blocked. I need to sedate him immediately and clear the obstruction. This is urgent."

Scott's green eyes went wide with panic. "Lacy said...is this, like, life or death?"

Dr. Blair nodded. "Yes, he'll die if we don't get him unplugged in the next few hours."

He sagged, and I moved quickly, pulling him against me. Still, he didn't respond.

"Scott?" I tipped his face toward me. "Dr. Blair needs an answer."

He met my gaze, but I still read pure panic. "Is this about the cost?" I glanced at the vet. "Because I can figure it out—"

"Scott has insurance on Crumpet." Oscar's voice was sure and strong. "This'll be covered. He'll likely only have to pay the deductible."

"Then you need to agree to it." I caught Scott's gaze again, willing him to fight through the panic. "Just tell Dr. Blair to do whatever it takes to save Crumpet's life. You have to do this." I didn't repeat *or the cat would die*. That might just be a step too far. That might push him into full panic mode— although we appeared to pretty much be there anyway.

At length, Scott turned his gaze from me and met the

doctor's concerned one. He cleared his throat. "Yes. Whatever."

She nodded, pulling Crumpet into her arms. "Oscar's going to bring out the paperwork for you to sign. Then you and Anthony can wait in the waiting room. I'll have news in a half hour or so." She was gone before either of us could adequately respond—just making it even clearer how dire the situation was.

Oscar left behind followed her out.

"Anthony?"

"Yes, Scott?" I continued to hold him against me.

"What's going to happen?" His voice was small.

"Dr. Blair is going to do everything in her power to take care of Crumpet. And if everything goes as planned, he'll be fine."

"And the twins?"

Sheesh, he wasn't asking for much. "Lacy's with them. We need to call to make sure she's okay. I take it she spoke to you?"

"She called me at the library. She said you were bringing him here." He stared into my eyes. "I can't lose him."

"I think Dr. Blair feels we got him here in time." Perhaps the vet was holding back greater concern, but she seemed like a straight shooter to me.

Oscar reappeared with some paperwork and a clipboard.

He took Scott through a list of things, but I mostly tuned out.

Instead, I focused on sending all my positive energy to both Scott and the darned cat. It had to all work out, because I wasn't sure Scott could withstand any more shocks.

CHAPTER 10

SCOTT

How I'd managed to drive from the library to the vet clinic was beyond me.

Anthony expressed concern about me driving home after the visit, but with Crumpet safely catheterized, in his cage and fast asleep, I was calm enough that I felt safe to make the quick trip.

Mikayla, my assistant at the library, had watched the floor until closing. She'd locked up and run the keys over to the vet clinic—for which I was incredibly grateful. Her concern for Crumpet was touching.

By then, I'd been able to give the good news that the blockage had been removed and he was expected to make a full recovery. I might've been near-tears while delivering that news.

She headed home after promising to see me the next day. She was great for emergencies, but not capable of handling the library on her own. I was doing my best to train her, but she didn't have a degree. I had been speaking to Ms. Wallace about funding an education for the young woman. Keeping her on staff while offering her opportunities was my top priority.

Anthony and I drove up to the house at the same time. I parked in the single-car driveway while he pulled up in front of my little home. With bone wearying-fatigue, I exited my car and made my way to the front door.

It opened to reveal a very calm-looking Lacy. "Perfect timing. The twins are eating." She led the way into the house while Anthony and I followed.

The house felt strangely empty without Crumpet, despite the surfeit of bodies, and I was grateful he'd be home in a day or two.

A heavenly aroma tickled my nose. Tomato sauce with the scent of spices. I gazed at the stove.

A pot of pasta was heating.

"Spaghetti." Lacy looked mighty pleased with herself—as she deserved to be.

The twins sat in their high chairs, eating peas and carrots. Well, perhaps playing with was a better description—although it appeared, perhaps, they'd consumed some of the food. A bowl with a couple of spoons and a light-brown substance sat on the table. Beef? I needed to learn how to identify jarred foods accurately.

"How were they?"

Lacy offered a wide grin. "They're scamps—much as Marilee was at that age. Watch out for Alicia. I'm sure I don't need to tell you that she crawls backwards. At one point she got stuck and, let me tell you, she was indignant."

"You installed the child locks." Anthony tugged at the door of the cupboard under the sink.

"Well…" Lacy bit her lower lip. "Hugh brought Marilee over. She played with the twins while he installed the locks. I watched the kids and cooked. I have to say, for a toddler of two years, Marilee's an effective babysitter. The twins were fascinated by her and kept trying to replicate the things she did—like walking. I think your little ones will be walking soon." She pointed to an outlet near the floor which now had plugs. "We did as much as we could, but you'll want to do another sweep before you let them loose. But you *will* need to let them loose—they're incredibly curious, and you can't restrict them to their bedroom."

"Don't see why not." Anthony muttered the words under his breath.

Lacy rolled her eyes. "You can't show fear."

He cleared his throat. "No, of course not."

"You both need to eat before I leave." Lacy pointed to the pot. "So have at it. These two also need baths. Will you be able to manage that, or do you want me to do it?"

"Have you eaten?" All this work and I wasn't sure if she'd had a moment to herself.

"I grazed on some cheese and crackers while they napped. Miss Agnes cooked her signature grilled fish for dinner, so I'll head home as soon as I know you guys are settled." She pointed to the food. "In fact, why don't I do baths while you guys eat?"

I should argue. She'd done more than enough for one day. But my stomach rumbled. The vending-machine chocolate bar was a distant memory. Normally, I packed a lunch. Today I hadn't had time. I'd nearly taken one of the sandwiches I spotted in the fridge, but I hadn't been sure if Anthony had plans for those—so I hadn't touched them.

"We'd be so appreciative." I eyed the twins. Zayden was still in relatively good shape, but Alicia had smooshed peas in her hair.

To my relief, Lacy snagged her first.

"Would you like a bath?" She asked the question in a sing-songy manner.

Alicia eyed her dubiously.

That was my girl—never quite trusting. Not that she had a reason to trust these strangers after a mere thirty hours. We'd yet to prove to her that we could be trusted. I was certain, in her mind, she believed that stability would come back. That surely her mother would return. Even if I said the words that her mother wouldn't return, she wouldn't understand them.

Zayden watched his sister and their babysitter disappear.

While Anthony refilled the sippy cup, I dished out the pasta.

"That smells amazing."

Anthony'd stepped right into my space and was so near me I could feel his presence resonate within me. "Uh, yeah, she did a great job. She, uh, said something about today being free…"

I handed Anthony the plates, then snagged the parmesan from the fridge. "Water? Or I have wine. I'm not a beer drinker—"

"Water's perfect."

"Yeah, she said something to me about that as well." Even though Lacy'd only been gone a few moments, I checked to make sure she couldn't hear me. "I'll pay her, of course. And secure her for whenever I can. But she's got school and, as amazing as she seems to be with the twins, I want to see her excelling in her studies." I sat at the table, heartened to see Anthony digging in. "She wants to be an astrophysicist. Or a Supreme Court Justice. Or…" I flailed my hand. "She's come up with any number of noteworthy professions—all of which require stellar grades."

Anthony scratched his trimmed beard. "I didn't know that. I'll admit I know little about her."

"Why would you? She's not one of your kids." The truth slammed into me. "But Marilee was?"

His gaze shifted away. "It's a long story that I can't comment on."

"Right. Privacy." I knew the toddler's mother had died, and that Oscar and Hugh had adopted her. I remembered Lacy moving down to Gaynor Beach not long after all that took place. I'd thought it was sweet she wanted to help. She'd trundled into the library soon after arriving in town.

Although she had access to everything she might need at home, she loved the feel of books and often visited us. A bright young woman, she'd been the first one I'd thought of to help. "So we don't want to take her away from her studies. And obviously I'm paying her for today. But damn, those costs are going to add up quickly."

"You'll be entitled to some benefits and tax credits. I have some paperwork about all that. But won't be enough." Anthony shook his head. "It's never enough—kids are so expensive. How low-income parents do it, I'm never sure."

"I'll cut back where I can. I mean, I don't have a lot of frivolous spending, but I can scale some stuff back."

"Like?"

I shot him a glance. "My membership in the online dating apps."

"Well…that's quite a step. You don't think you could meet someone who might help you? Someone who'd want to be a parent?"

Laughing was a distinct possibility. So was weeping. "Most of the guys I met…they wouldn't be into that kind of thing. Or, if they were, screening them would be a nightmare. I think…" I gazed at Zayden who was studiously mushing carrots between his fingers. "I think dating is off the table for the next eighteen years."

Anthony startled me when he placed his hand over mine.

"You say that now. You're just getting started. You'll meet people along this journey—single fathers, single mothers…"

"I'm pretty much as gay as they come."

"Ah."

Was that his subtle way of being sure? Although I loved women, I wasn't attracted to them. I'd bonded to Eliza, and losing her friendship had hurt, but nothing more. "But I agree I should be looking to find other people in a similar situation to myself. I'm sure Oscar will have advice—he was alone with Marilee before Hugh arrived, right?"

Anthony held my gaze. Something flickered in his eyes, but I wasn't sure what it was. He always seemed on edge when we spoke of the vet tech. I didn't think Anthony was racist, but he definitely had some kind of firm opinion when it came to the other man.

"What is it about Oscar?"

He winced. "I...might've misjudged him when we first met. That's on me."

"You mean you were an asshole."

Lacy breezed in with a placid looking Alicia in her arms. She plunked the baby on my lap.

Good thing I'd managed to eat most of my meal.

Alicia reached for the plate.

I pushed it out of reach.

She went for the fork.

I moved that away as well.

She gazed up at me.

Offering a smile, I touched her nose.

Which she promptly scrunched.

"Asshole?" I wasn't sure of the propriety of foul language around the babies, but if anyone knew, it'd be these two.

"Very soon, that language won't be appropriate." Anthony's rebuke was mild.

Lacy glared.

"I admit I was wrong about Oscar. And I've apologized."

"Not like you meant it." Lacy scooped Zayden into her arms. "Bath time, little man?"

He clapped his hands, showing far more enthusiasm than his sister.

Lacy left the kitchen.

Anthony resumed eating.

I waited.

After a couple of minutes, he sighed. "I had formed a judgement about the type of person I believed Oscar to be. I didn't give him the benefit of the doubt. Like I said, I was wrong. He's—" He cleared his throat. "He's proven to be a good dad to Marilee."

I'd witnessed that myself. Both Hugh and Oscar regularly brought Marilee to the library to check out books. Apparently they read to her every night. And she was such a happy baby. Or at least she was when I saw her. And she'd lost her mother at the age the twins were now…so did that mean these two might wind up having happy childhoods as well?

I just didn't know.

"So…" This time I cleared my throat. "You'll be heading home tonight, right?" I fought the panic rising within me.

Anthony held my gaze. "I stopped by my place to pick up some extra clothes and some nightwear. It's your call, of course, but I'm okay at staying right now. I don't want you to feel overwhelmed—especially if they both start crying at the same time."

"I think I need to get a pair of rocking chairs."

He pursed his lips, as if not quite sure what to make of my non sequitur. "Sure. There's room against the far wall. They'd have to be smaller, but I can see it. Maybe we can find some online?"

"And a tree. Kids need a Christmas tree."

"Scott, they're too young to understand Christmas. Just like—before you get started—they don't need presents. You being here for them is all they could ever ask for. You'll have plenty of Christmases in the future when you can buy them things."

This time, I pursed my lips. He was so right—I had been panicking. About all of it. "You can watch them tomorrow while I'm at work?"

"Of course."

"Then I'm home on Monday and Tuesday."

"Okay."

"But we both work on Wednesday."

"Hopefully, by then, you'll have found someone."

"I can do it." I said the words with more bravado than I felt.

Lacy again breezed into the room. Man, the teenager was silent. She plopped Zayden in Anthony's lap. "They'll need a bottle before bed, but otherwise they're good."

To my surprise, she pressed a hand to my cheek. The gesture was both unexpected and incredibly sweet.

"You're going to do right by them. I'm sure of it. I'm off school on the 20th, so if you can make do until then, I can help over the holidays."

"But your schoolwork."

She rolled her eyes. "You think I've not done with everything up until the end of semester? Oscar's signed me up for a computer class through an online college, but that doesn't start until January."

"You're interested in computers?" I was having a tough time keeping track.

A casual shrug. "I'll need computers if I study astrophysics. And since I want to do a minor in criminal justice, it'll be good if I get some classes out of the way before I go."

Anthony whistled. "That's impressive."

"You think I can't do it?" She shot daggers from her eyes at him.

He held up his hands. "I believe, honestly, that you can do whatever you set your mind to."

That appeared to mollify her. "Well, do you need me back tomorrow?"

I glanced at Anthony.

He appeared to consider. "If you want to come for a few hours, there are some things I can do."

Part of me was curious what those things might be, and the rest of me realized it was none of my business. "Do I have your email?"

Lacy scrunched her nose.

"So I can pay you."

"Oh, right, for tomorrow. Today was a freebie. And yeah, I'll make sure you've got it." She snagged her knapsack from the couch. "See you tomorrow."

With that, Hurricane Lacy was gone.

Anthony let out a breath as he pushed his plate out of Zayden's reach. "I'm not sure who's more exhausting—her or the twins."

"She's a ball of energy. At first, I wondered if she had attention deficit or something. But no, she just appears chaotic. She's got her, uh, stuff figured out."

"That she does." He pressed his fingers to his temple. "And I underestimated her as well. At my own peril. So that'll never happen again either."

I was dying of curiosity, but Alicia pounded her little fist on the table. "Do you think they want to play? I just want to go to bed."

"Why don't you play with them for a bit while I clean up? We'll do bottles, bedtime stories, and hopefully that will have worn them out."

"Yeah, okay. But I feel like I get the better end of the deal."

Anthony eyed Alicia. "No, I think we're about even."

Two hours later—after bottles, multiple stories, and almost an hour of crying jags—I was done in. I managed to peel out of my shirt and pants, but that was as far as I made it. I crawled into bed, pulled up the covers, and was out within seconds.

CHAPTER 11

ANTHONY

When Scott called the next day from work to let me know Ms. Wallace had granted him an emergency family leave of six days, relief washed through me. And I heard it in his voice as well.

Lacy, who was with me, dragged out a calendar and helped me figure out a schedule that'd take us into the new year when she'd return to school and the twins could start day care.

Between the three of us, we had every day covered.

I eyed Lacy as she put the calendar back on the fridge. "I'm not sure we're paying you enough." I knew Scott would pay a fair wage, but I felt I should be contributing.

"Probably not." She glanced at the twins in their high chairs. "But you're going to write me a stellar letter of recommendation when I'm applying to the university."

"Whatever you want—you need only ask."

She gave me a sly glance. "I knew you'd figure it out eventually." She didn't give me a chance to respond. Instead, she snagged Zayden and let him down to the floor.

Alicia was about to start her vocal protest when Lacy let her down as well. The baby sat on her butt for about ten seconds before bending over, rotating, and crawling backward toward the living room.

Lacy caught my eye and grinned. "Once she figures out how to move forward, you're in trouble."

We were. Everything had been babyproofed—including moving some nice items of art up and away from where curious fingers could find them. Zayden'd already figured out how to pull all the books off the bottom bookshelf—even though some of them were quite heavy.

Alicia liked to tug at the pages to try to rip them out.

So we'd tethered the bookcase, moved up what we could, and boxed the rest. By the time Lacy left and Scott got home, things looked different again. I worried this might be disorienting for him, but he merely scooped up Zayden and gave him a big kiss on the cheek. Then he put him down and did the same for Alicia.

I had some weird wish he'd kiss me on the cheek as well. Which was positively fanciful.

He did come over and put a hand against my arm. "Thank you. I only made it through the day because I knew you were here."

I pointed to the calendar. "Everything's settled until you can start taking them to Charmers."

After gripping me for just a moment longer, he pivoted to the calendar. "Wow, you guys did it."

"Lacy did." Not only had she taken the initiative, but she'd also volunteered for several days when she'd be alone —when Scott and I had to work.

"I wish I could give them grandparents, aunts, uncles, and cousins. Good ones." Scott looked wistfully out at the two rapscallions who were banging wooden blocks against the laminate kitchen floor.

"You're doing the very best you can. Why don't you play with them for a bit? I'll heat up some leftover pasta for us and organize some food for them."

He offered me a grateful smile. "Yeah, that'd be wonderful." He was about to drop his messenger bag when I shook my head.

"Bedroom. With the door closed. Trust me."

"Yeah, okay." The smile was weary.

We'd been up with the twins in the middle of the night again. I was someone who didn't require a lot of sleep, but I was under the impression Scott did. And when he'd shown up to deal with the event, he'd only been wearing his briefs. I was pretty sure he'd been sheepish, but we'd both been so desperate to calm the kids down that I hadn't asked any questions. Admired him? Yes. Asked questions? No.

"Hey, you found rocking chairs." Scott appeared at the kitchen entrance with a wide grin on his face.

"Lacy found them. I mentioned you having said something, and twenty minutes later I was driving to two different places to pick them up."

"But they match."

"I know." I injected as much admiration as I could. "She's incredibly capable. I hadn't even told her what we were looking for, and yet she showed me the picture, and I knew she'd found what you wanted. Then she found a second one. I had to drive up to Oceanside, but I think it was worth it."

"Totally worth it."

Scott stepped into my personal space, then threw his arms around my neck and wrapped his arms around me.

I was so stunned, that—for a moment—I didn't react.

He started to pull away.

I pulled him closer. He was a solid presence in my arms. Usually he seemed slight—insubstantial. Slender. Now, though, holding him close? I felt his full weight.

He rubbed his unshaven jaw against my neck. "Thank you."

My first, flippant response was that I was just doing my job. Because that's how all this had started—me wanting to ensure the babies were cared for. That they wouldn't wind up back in my caseload within days or weeks because of neglect or abuse. But the words wouldn't come because they were only partly true. In my heart, I'd known Scott would find a way to care for the babies. My sticking around was as much to support him as it was for any concern for the little ones.

A cry wrenched us apart.

Scott met my gaze for just a moment before hustling out to the living room.

What had I seen in his eyes in that brief second? What else might've been said if not for...whichever child was crying. When I heard Scott's dulcet, soothing tone—and the crying ceased—I opened the fridge to begin work on dinner.

A full three hours later, the twins were in bed. Asleep.

For now.

I held no illusions we'd get a full night's rest. And I had work in the morning.

"Do you need to go home?"

Scott tried for neutral, but I spotted the panic.

"I have a suit hanging in your front hall closet. I can help with breakfast, but then I'll need to shower and be on my way to work."

"Right."

"I'll check in with you around lunch. And I'll have my cell phone with me—just call or text if you need help."

"We'll be fine."

Ah, bravado. I understood. He needed to know he could stand on his own. Hell, he had to. I'd help where I could, but my job was a demanding one. Not a huge number of cases requiring child protective services interventions—but enough to keep me on my toes. I had two follow-up cases in the morning. Both would keep me out of the office, but at some point, I'd have to go in to write the reports—and deal with Mr. Winters.

I'd also warned Scott that my boss would be dropping by for a visit—likely in the next day or two.

"Are you up for talking?" Scott met my gaze.

I read trepidation in his eyes. "Sure. Living room?"

He nodded.

"Okay, you want a glass of water?"

He nodded again.

I set about pouring two glasses, and as I arrived in the living room, he was trying to organize the toys into some semblance of order.

"I feel like we don't have enough."

"They have plenty, Scott." I handed him the glass and gestured to the lovely, large couch. "What's up?"

"Maybe I can check out the secondhand store in town. Or surely there must be people giving away or selling toys for cheap. I just want to make sure they're always stimulated. That I can always keep them busy."

"Kids are just as happy with cardboard boxes." I reached across the space to grasp his hand. "What's really going on?"

"What if I can't do this? What if I've bitten off more than I can chew? Or whatever that weird metaphor is…"

"I'm not sure it's a metaphor and I'm not sure it's appropriate. You were presented with a situation, and you decided to act. You still don't have to say yes."

He met my gaze. "You really think I had a choice?"

"I think I could've found someone—and I still can. I'm not holding this over your head—simply letting you know that you always have options."

"These are my children."

And that was the crux of the argument.

"Yes, biologically, they're your children. And yes, Eliza has handed them over with intent. But you're a human being. You have free will, and if you choose to find a loving home that isn't yours for these babies, that's okay."

"But it's not *okay*. You know I'll never be able to live with myself if I do that."

I wanted to say that Eliza'd clearly found a way, but that was too crass. Didn't stop me from being tempted. I squeezed his hand. "What assurances can I offer?"

"I'm scared to ask."

Ideas flitted through my mind of what he might be reticent to ask. I wanted to make this as easy for him as possible, but I couldn't quite put my finger on what he wasn't saying.

Oh.

"You want to know how long I can stay."

Relief flooded his features, and his brow unknit. "Yeah. I mean, you have a life. And a job, and—"

Again, I squeezed. "Being here and helping you is what matters. I'll be back tonight. I have a couple of video-counseling appointments, but I'll do what I can."

"You can't keep sleeping on the couch."

With my spare hand, I patted it. "Actually, it's damn comfortable. Far more than I would've thought."

"I want you to take my bed. If you're staying here, it's the least I can do."

Wasn't this the plot of tons of movies? *There's only one bed…*

"I've managed before, and I can handle it again. When you're ready to send me on my way, I'll go. Until then, I'm good. I'll need to run back to my house for stuff and to water my plants, but there's nothing tethering me there."

"This place is small and going to cramp your style."

Ah. "I don't know what you imagine my sex life to be like, but it's not all that impressive these days. I've had a few short-term relationships, but nothing's stuck. Now, I know you like to have guests—"

He wrenched his hand from mine and held up both. "Uh, no. That's done. Jerry was…" He winced. "He wasn't forever material. And now…" He gestured in the direction of the babies' bedroom.

I understood. But one didn't simply walk away from preferences and proclivities because one became a parent. "There are other ways to, uh, get your needs met."

"No." His mouth set in a grim line. "I can give that up. We had fun…me and all the other guys. But I need to focus on my children."

Fair enough. I wouldn't point out he had a perfectly good babysitter and Gaynor Beach had two respectable hotels. He'd figure that out. And if he needed to get his rocks off, undoubtedly, he'd find a way.

Why are you hoping it's with you?

The thought shocked me. It'd come out of left field, so to speak. I wasn't attracted to Scott. He wasn't really my type—if I had a type. I generally went for guys who were my size or bigger. Definitely muscles and heft. Because sometimes I liked to hold the guy down and fuck him hard. Very occasionally, I liked to be fucked.

A memory stirred. I'd been with a guy in college—a guy much like Scott—and he'd been so talented with his cock that I hadn't cared that he was smaller.

Focus.

"Okay, so you having sex isn't a priority right now—I totally get it."

"But it might be for you."

Again, my mind flitted to him. Which was nuts. "I can always go back to my place…if I have an itch to scratch. I'll be honest, I'm good with my hand right now. I don't need complications." Especially not with this redhead and his two babies down the hall.

"Well…" He scratched his cheek. "Why don't we share the bed? We're both grown adults. I have one of those special orthopedic mattresses. Certainly better for your back than this thing." He tapped the couch.

"It'll take away your autonomy. You need somewhere to escape to." Flashes of the first night came to mind. If he hadn't been able to retreat to his room, he might've taken off entirely. And where would we have wound up?

"I don't need you to tell me what I need." He angled himself toward me for the first time. "What I need is you. I know the day will come when I need to stand on my own two feet, but I'm not there yet. I know the day will come when I need to parent these two on my own, but I don't have the confidence to do it yet. At least for now…will you please stay?"

An easy promise. "I'll stay. At least until you get on your feet."

"I think that'll be when they're teenagers."

His delivery was so deadpan that I wasn't sure he was kidding.

Better not to ask.

"I'm not sure you'll need me that long, but we'll see how it goes. You might find a rhythm that works for you and you'll find me superfluous."

"Never." He snagged my hand and gripped it painfully. "I'll never be able to do this without you."

Never felt like an exceptionally long time.

"I think you need some sleep."

He faltered. "I'm one of those people who need a solid eight hours to be able to function."

I didn't hide the wince. "You realize that's not likely to happen any time soon."

"I guess I'll learn to adapt."

"And if you need to take naps when the kids are down, then do that."

"But won't I have, you know, cooking and cleaning to do?"

I flashed to how much Lacy could accomplish. I needed to be careful that Scott not compare himself to the little dynamo who had energy to spare. "Cooking and cleaning are important, but your health is more so."

He yawned.

My cue. I rose and tugged him with me.

He came willingly.

"You take your turn in the bathroom first. Then get into bed and try to let the stress of the day go."

"Easy for you to say."

I arched an eyebrow.

"They're not your kids."

"Maybe not, but they're my responsibility—and I take that seriously."

"So you'll come to bed with me?"

I knew what he meant. "I'll join you in a bit. But don't wait up, okay? Just go to sleep."

He pulled me in for another hug. "Thank you."

Before I could hug him back, he was gone.

Emotions swirled through me as I prepared for another night here. I organized my messenger bag to ensure it was ready to go in the morning. I made a pile of sandwiches so I could grab one and there'd be a couple for Scott during the day. Finally, I placed all the bowls and plates that we might need on the table—anything that would help Scott and alleviate some of his stress.

I wasn't convinced my actions were enough, but an hour had passed, and I was flagging. I grabbed my sleep pants and T-shirt and headed to the bathroom. I brushed my teeth, flossed, and then changed for bed. I returned to the front-hall closet where I hung my clothes from today. Amazingly, they weren't in too terrible shape. Not a spill on them—that had to be a record or something.

Finally, after I could procrastinate no longer, I headed to Scott's bedroom.

He'd left the bedside lamp on. The one on what was, I assumed, to be my side. He was huddled on the far side of the bed. I wondered if he was asleep, but I heard gentle snores.

Good enough.

I checked to make sure we had the baby monitor. Once I was satisfied with everything, I gently slid into bed.

I'd barely turned off the light before Scott rolled over and tucked himself against me.

Still, I was certain he slept.

So much for boundaries.

I'd set my alarm, and would ensure I was up before him. He never needed to know what he'd done in his sleep.

Although I would.

Having a warm body curled into my side felt good. Felt perfect. Despite my sometimes-prickly nature, I was actually someone who thrived on affection. I didn't give it or receive it often, but when I did, I cherished it. My mother'd been free with her affection and love.

What would she make of this predicament? Likely she'd be here cooking casseroles and quesadillas and doing whatever else she could to help. She'd view the twins as honorary grandchildren. Grandchildren she'd always wanted. Grandchildren she'd never lived to see.

And on that depressing note, I tugged Scott a little tighter and fell into a dreamless sleep.

CHAPTER 12

SCOTT

WHEN I AWOKE, I HAD THE IMPRESSION OF WARMTH. I REACHED out my hand and found the place next to me warm. Vague memories of Anthony in bed with me flittered back and my mind warred with whether or not I'd...tried to spoon him?

No, that couldn't be right. I'd sworn to stay on my side of the bed. No matter how much I craved the physical contact—the physical reassurance—crossing the middle of the bed was a line I wasn't going to traverse.

Groggily, I checked my phone for the time.

Seven twenty-three.

Well, how the hell had that happened? I'd slept a solid ten hours. Had the twins woken up, and I hadn't heard them? That didn't seem possible, but on occasion I could go deep. One morning I woke up to find my favorite decorative plate shattered on the floor. I'd thought there might've been a clumsy burglar. Of course, nothing was missing and when I turned the television to the news, I discovered I'd missed a three-point-eight earthquake. Had apparently slept right through it.

The baby monitor was switched off, and my heart did a

little dance of appreciation. Anthony really was an amazing man.

But how long is he staying?

I couldn't ask more of him than he'd already given—more than I had the right to ask for. Yet the thought of his departure sent me into paroxysms of panic.

A knock sounded softly at the door. Before I could respond, Anthony opened it.

"You have just enough time for a shower and to run to the vet to pick up Crumpet. Then I need to head into the office. The twins are fed, their diapers are changed, and they are— for the moment—playing in the playpen."

Rubbing my face, I tried to kick my mind into gear. "Wow. Thank you. I'll be quick."

As he left, I made a particular note of how good he looked in a suit.

Then I scrambled out of bed and headed for a quick shower. I waved a quick goodbye as I headed out to my car. A quick shot over to the vet clinic, and I had my boy secure with me and we were making our way home in under twenty minutes. By the time we arrived at the house, I was refreshed, and I felt almost human.

I eased Crumpet from his carrier and placed him on the sofa. He gazed at me unblinkingly for several moments before closing his eyes. Dr. Blair said he'd be completely back to himself in the next day or so.

Anthony handed me an insulated mug of steeping tea when I entered the kitchen. "I hope you like it strong."

"I do." Hopefully he could see the gratitude that shone through me.

"There's a covered plate in the fridge with scrambled eggs and toast. I've also left you a couple of sandwiches—make certain you eat them—as well as cut up vegetables for you. You can give the kids avocado pieces, nice and small, for snacks. There's jarred food for lunch, and if you want to smush a banana for them, that'll work. It'll be messy, but it'll work."

"How do I thank you?" I blinked back tears.

"You hang on and do the best you can. You text me if you need me, and you keep everyone safe until I get back tonight. We'll have dinner, and then I have one appointment but the rest of the time is for me to help you. Okay?"

I let his words of reassurance wash over me. "Yeah, I can do that."

"Great."

He hesitated for a moment, then swept me up for a tight embrace. "I have faith in you."

More, apparently, than I had in myself. Still, I'd take the proffered comfort. "Thank you."

He gave me a quick nod, then was gone.

I snuck a glance at my babies. Finding them occupied, I tossed breakfast into the microwave, added a spoonful of sugar to my tea, and tried to center myself.

Three hours later, that centering was long gone.

When Anthony burst through the door, I nearly wept in relief. Then promptly panicked because he wasn't due home for a few hours yet.

He dropped his messenger bag and came right for me. He held me at arm's length and did a thorough examination. Then he pulled me in for a hug. "I came as soon as I could."

I blinked several times. "How did you know?"

"Well, you messaged me."

"No, I didn't." I'd typed out an SOS on my computer, but hadn't actually sent the message. I kept telling myself I was an adult and should be able to handle two screaming babies. Except I couldn't even figure out what was wrong. They hadn't needed diaper changes, neither would take a bottle. I'd triple checked the list of foods they could eat, and I hadn't fed them anything not on the list. I'd checked for injuries—I'd done everything I could…all to no avail.

Anthony pulled out his phone. He unlocked it, handed it to me, then made a beeline for the living room where the two babies sat—still wailing.

I triple checked. I was sure I hadn't sent the message. I'd wanted to—more than anything in the world—but I'd resisted. Still confused, I moved out to the dining room.

Crumpet sat next to the laptop, indolently licking his paw.

I moved to the machine and discovered that not only had he sent the message, but he'd started another one which was just a bunch of gibberish. "Did you do this?"

He blinked up at me.

Of course he hadn't. He was a lovely cat, but there was no way he'd intentionally sent the message.

Except he'd done something similar with my final term paper last semester. I hadn't been gone two minutes before he'd walked across the keyboard and nearly deleted a month's worth of work. "We need to talk," I spat.

He blinked again.

"Why don't you prepare bottles? I think, at this point, they're overwrought and hungry." Anthony stood, one baby in each arm. Both clung to him and drooled. Oh, and wiped their snotty noses against him.

I was trying to not see this as utterly catastrophic, but I was failing.

Still, I shut the laptop. I'd thought to do a couple minutes of work while the twins played happily in their playpen. By the time I composed the message of desperation, everything'd gone to hell.

Anthony leaned over to place a chaste kiss on my cheek. "It'll be okay."

I wanted to believe him—I really did.

He headed toward the bedroom, and I prepared the bottles. My heart stuttered at an image of the two of us rocking the babies in the new chairs. That image was shattered at the mere thought of him returning to work.

Suck it up. New parents do this all the time.

They did. And some had virtually no maternity leave before having to return to their jobs. Being granted emergency family leave was a stroke of luck—but it didn't fix the problem that I was in charge and responsible for the safety and well-being of these two hellions.

Bottles prepared, I headed into their bedroom.

Anthony had one balanced in each arm. Zayden was curled into his side, while Alicia was more alert, pulling on his hair. He winced, but didn't try to pull away.

"Which one should I take?" I whispered the words, afraid to break the tranquility of the moment.

"Zayden, I think. Very gently."

I handed him the bottle and gingerly removed Zayden from those strong protective arms. Mine weren't nearly as reassuring, I was certain, but Zayden settled and took a bottle.

Slowly, Anthony eased Alicia into the crook of his arm and coaxed her into taking the bottle.

"Can you tell me what happened?"

"I don't know." I wanted to wail. "One moment they were playing happily...the next they were screaming their heads off. I thought maybe I fed them something bad or, I don't know, they'd hurt each other. I even wondered about Crumpet, but he was resting on the top of the couch—fast asleep. Or at least he was when I checked."

"And the message?"

"They'd been crying for over an hour. I mean...I figured they'd tire themselves out, but they didn't. And I knew I needed help, and I typed out the message. But I didn't send it. I swear to God, I didn't."

He cut me a curious gaze.

"Crumpet."

His jaw twitched. "It's okay to admit you needed help."

"I admit it. I needed help. But I wasn't going to interfere

with your workday. I was going to suck it up. I should've deleted the message—and I'd completely forgotten about it until I saw your phone. Honest to God, I didn't send it."

"Crumpet, eh?"

"Yeah."

He didn't appear convinced.

Hell, if I hadn't seen both the computer and the phone, I wouldn't have believed it.

Zayden pushed his bottle away. I snagged a handy receiving blanket, gave one to Anthony as well, and began the process of burping the baby.

After a few moments, Anthony replicated my actions. "I think they'll go down for a few hours."

"You need to get back to work." My heart sank, even as I said the words.

"I could call in sick—"

"Don't. I promise I won't panic again."

"Yeah, that's the thing. The more upset you get, the more they feel that panic and react to it. Not that staying calm in all circumstances is possible—but losing your cool affects them. They're sensitive to your moods. They're still feeling their way around this place…trying to figure out who they can rely on and who'll vanish like their mother did."

Funny, neither of us ever mentioned Mark or whether his departure had any impact on the twins. I think both of us inherently understood his impact and interactions would've been minimal.

"I emailed her."

"Oh."

"I don't know if she got it or not. And I'm not sure what I was thinking…that she might have advice? That she might see the error of her ways?"

"If she came back, Scott, would you ever be able to trust her again?"

"I honestly don't know." And I didn't. These babies were

as much Eliza's as they were mine. If she came back and wanted to be part of their lives, who was I to deprive her of that? I wasn't sure whether I ever wanted to be put in the position of having to make that decision. So, I guessed, I didn't want her to come back. Anger still roiled in my gut every time I thought of what she'd done. Of the choice she'd made. Of the ramifications on these two precious little lives.

Anthony rose and placed a sleeping Alicia in the crib.

I did the same with Zayden.

He flipped on the baby monitor and we slipped out of the room.

"Why don't you grab a sandwich while I do a bit of clean-up?"

I glanced around. The kitchen was a mess—with dirty dishes and the trays on the high chairs needing to be cleaned. The living room wasn't much better—with toys, books, and a few other things strewn about. My neat and orderly house was absolute chaos.

In three hours.

Part of me wanted to refuse his offer, but another part of me appreciated that if things were back in order, I'd be less likely to panic. I was proud of myself from not having descended into a panic attack—but it'd been a near thing.

"That'd be great. Thank you." I snagged the sandwich and sank onto a dining-room chair while he set about putting everything to rights. I eyed my laptop. What had made me think I could sneak in a bit of studying? Except they'd been amusing themselves and happy. I'd thought…just a couple of minutes…who would it hurt?

Admitting defeat, I made a note to email my professor. Maybe if I could hire Lacy for a couple of full days over the holiday, then I could get my project finished. I wanted this PhD so badly…but the kids had to come first. My entire world was turned upside down, and the sooner I got with the program, the better off I'd be.

Anthony completed setting the house to rights just as I polished off the sandwich.

"Are you going to get in trouble for being here?"

He shook his head. "I let Lottie know I was on lunch—I am entitled to those." He dropped to his knees before me, placing his hands on my thighs. "Are you going to be okay? I can call in sick—"

I shook my head vehemently. "I'll be fine. I was thinking of maybe asking Lacy to come over after school—if she doesn't have homework."

"She said something about being done with everything until the end of semester. So yeah, send her a text and invite her over. The twins'll be thrilled."

He wasn't wrong. For some reason, they really seemed to like Lacy. Probably because she didn't panic at every little thing, worrying she might scar them for life if she fucked things up.

Anthony squeezed my thighs. "Text her now. She's probably in class, but she might get the message later." He held my gaze.

His dark-brown eyes mesmerized me. He made it seem like everything was going to work out. That I just had to be patient.

I nodded and picked up my phone. My fingers were clumsy as I was all too aware he was still touching me. I finished sending the text and had barely put the phone on the table when it buzzed. Automatically, I picked it back up. "She can be here at three."

"And I'll be home around five. So, you're going to be fine. But I do have to go."

He used his grasp on my thighs to push up. Then he eased me into his embrace for another hug. "You're going to be fine."

His whispered words brushed my ear, and man, I wanted to believe him so badly. I just wasn't sure how to express my gratitude at his surety.

When he pulled back, I fought the urge to hold on as tight as I could. I had to survive just three hours. The babies were settled, and the house was quiet. I'd eaten, and they'd been fed. Three hours wouldn't be so bad.

Right?

He pressed a kiss to my cheek. "You'll be great." Then, without another word, he went to the front door. He scooped up his messenger bag and left quietly.

In the moment after he left, I fought a wave of panic.

Only to realize not only did I have nothing to panic about, but that I had nothing to do.

Dinner.

Right. I could put on a pot of chili to simmer all afternoon. That'd fragrance the air and provide us with sustenance. And it'd prove I could handle things.

An hour later, the doorbell rang.

No, no, no.

I bolted for the door and flung it open, holding my finger to my lips. Like that could somehow undo the damage of the bell.

The man at the door startled at my appearance. His eyebrow arched, and he gave me a once-over.

I scanned him as well. A few inches shorter than me, rail thin, tanned skin, graying black hair, and dark-brown eyes. Longish hair and a mustache. He looked awfully familiar, but I couldn't figure out why. Maybe he'd been a patron at the library?

I cleared my throat, searching for my manners. "May I help you?"

He straightened. "I'm looking for Anthony Rodrigues."

My senses went on high alert. No one except Lacy knew Anthony'd been coming around. Well...maybe his boss? I hadn't asked how that discussion had gone—or if he'd even had one. Did his boss know about what was happening?

I shook my head to clear my thoughts. "I'm sorry, I don't know you." I wasn't prepared to lie about Anthony having been here. Nor was I going to offer what I considered intensely personal information.

He stared at me. Uncomfortably. Like he was trying to take my measure. Like he was trying to figure out who I was.

Good luck with that.

Hell, I barely knew who I was. I'd gone from a pretend daddy to a real daddy in a heartbeat and now I wondered if I'd ever really known myself. What I was capable of. Who I wanted to be. Everything was wrapped up in the two angels who apparently hadn't woken at the sound of the bell.

Finally, at length, he held out his hand. "My name is Carlos Rodrigues."

Well, that actually explained why he felt so familiar. "Anthony's father?" I shook the man's hand.

He nodded. "Yes. I'm here to see my son."

"I'm sorry you've come all this way." Actually, I'd no idea how far he'd come. "He's not here. Perhaps you can try him at the office?"

"I tried there. The nice young woman told me to come here."

Huh. I couldn't figure out if that was a good thing or not. Probably not—having his coworkers knowing he was here wasn't likely to lead to anything good. Especially if they were nosy—as I suspected they might be.

"Well, he's not here now. Why don't you give him a call?"

Carlos waved me off. "Will he be here later? Or will he go home?"

"I'm not sure." I was sure, of course, but something in the man's demeanor made me hedge. Why not just call Anthony and ask?

The older man gave me a long level look. "Are you his boyfriend?"

I sputtered. "Uh, that's an incredibly private question to

ask." And maybe my non-answer would give him the wrong idea, but I wasn't going to be so blunt. Plus, I didn't feel like classifying my relationship with Anthony. We weren't lovers…but we felt like a bit more than friendly. Certainly we were closer than we'd been when he showed up four days ago.

Had it really only been four days? Time had a weird quality where it seemed to be running at top speed one moment, then crawling along the next.

"Hey, Scott."

I glanced over Mr. Rodrigues's shoulder to find Lacy loping up the drive.

"Aren't you supposed to be in school?"

"Spanish class is so boring. I got Hugh to spring me so I could come hang out with you and the twins."

Anthony's father, who likely spoke Spanish, huffed. He glanced back and forth between Lacy and myself, not stepping aside to let her pass. "You're very young."

She pulled herself up to her full height. Which, admittedly, was impressive for a young woman. "That's none of your business." She cocked her head. "I hear the twins. Scott, we'd better go in."

How had she taken the measure of the situation so precisely? I didn't want to hang out on the porch talking to this man. Something about him felt off. Instead of introducing him to Lacy, I held the door wider so she could scoot past the two of us and into the house. I didn't hear the twins, but this guy didn't need to know that.

"I'm sorry I can't help you. I have to go."

As I turned, I'd have sworn he blasphemed—in Spanish and under his breath—but I couldn't be sure.

I closed the door and, for the first time in a while, locked it.

Lacy's eyebrow arched. "He's an asshole."

"You heard?"

"Him swear? Yeah. But…he gives me the creeps."

Far be it for me to question a young woman. "Well, you don't have to open the door for him, okay? If he wants Anthony, he can track him down himself."

The first wail came from down the hall.

Lacy dropped her backpack in the front foyer. "Let's go."

And so we did.

CHAPTER 13

ANTHONY

Fatigue hit me in a wave as I parked in front of Scott's house. When I'd returned to the office from lunch, Lottie informed me someone had been looking for me—but she couldn't remember who. I wasn't sure I believed her. She'd never warmed up to me. I couldn't figure out if the animosity came from my ethnicity, my gender, or just a clash of personalities.

Mr. Winters accosted me, demanding to know why I hadn't visited the Riviera family yet. I'd always planned to see them in the afternoon—and I explained as much.

The man was unmoved.

I'd quickly written up my morning interview—that'd ended mere moments before Scott's frantic message—and headed out to see the middle-class family who lived in a nice house on a nice street. All had appeared well except Mrs. Riviera had suffered crippling post-partum depression while her husband was away with the military overseas. Her family doctor had stepped in, referring her to counseling and, eventually, calling in child protective services. I worked with a psychiatrist to confirm Mrs. Riviera had post-partum depression—not psychosis—and to formulate an appropriate treatment plan. The concern by the family doctor was warranted as the mother hadn't been caring for herself or the infant. Early intervention—and a good course of anti-depressants—seemed to have warded off the worst of it. My visits were now perfunctory. She assured me she was taking her medicine. In return, I looked around the place, checked on her baby girl, and made sure everything was okay. I figured another two visits and I could close the file.

A success story.

I'd returned to the office to write up the report and to see if anything else had come through. It hadn't. I was due to spend tomorrow morning at the high school and had another couple of home visits in the afternoon. Gaynor Beach might be a small town, but I had steady work.

I twisted the door handle. It turned, but the deadbolt had been thrown. I'd meant to talk to Scott about his penchant for not locking the door, but, at this moment, I was irritated at the fact he'd chosen this afternoon to be smarter.

The door opened and Lacy grinned. "Just in time."

For what?

Do I want to know?

Her smiling face warmed me. We'd come a long way in just two days.

Then the noise hit me.

"Holy hell." *What the actual fuck?*

Lacy held the door aside, and I walked in. I dropped my messenger bag and pivoted to head straight into the living room.

The twins sat on the floor. Each had metal cutlery in their hands and each was pounding on various overturned pots.

"Like a drum set." Lacy looked inordinately pleased with herself.

I hadn't arrived home with a headache, but I was likely to develop one.

Home.

When had I started to consider this home? I lived in a nice house the next neighborhood over. A house I'd barely seen in the past four days. But Scott's house wasn't my home. Soon he'd have everything under control, and he wouldn't need my help.

Alicia spotted me and grinned. She held her spoons above her head for a moment, then slammed them down against the pots with what appeared to be her entire strength.

Lacy chuckled, cheered, and clapped along with the clamor.

I wanted to plug my ears, crawl into bed, and sleep for a month. The twins had awakened in the middle of the night, and Scott'd slept right through it. Which was good because he needed the rest, but tough for me. Still, I'd managed.

"Where's Scott?"

Lacy cocked her head, appeared to consider, then nodded. She pointed back in the direction of the bedrooms.

I headed that way.

He sat on his bed with a laptop open and several papers scattered about. He glanced up when he saw me and pushed his glasses up his nose. "Uh, Lacy said she had things in hand. I emailed my prof to say the paper was going to be late, but I figured I might be able to get a bit of work done on it while she supervised the chaos. I managed to prepare dinner, so we can eat as soon as you're ready."

He shoved all the words out in a rush.

I sat on the side of the bed. "It's okay to take time out to study. And you're right, Lacy's got everything handled. Now, what did your professor say?"

"She said to take all the time I needed, and if I want to defer my winter courses, I can do that. Except I really want to get this degree finished…"

He looked so dejected. "What degree? I thought you already had one."

"Two." He rubbed his forehead. "I got my BA and my MLS. I want a PhD in library sciences, though."

I hesitated. "Won't that make you overqualified to work at the Gaynor Beach Public Library?"

He shrugged. "I'm not doing it for that...I just, you know, wanted to do it. To prove to myself that I could." He glanced out the door toward the cacophony just down the hall. "Now I'm thinking I can't do anything."

"Look, I managed to get my master's in counseling from Humboldt State University. With an emphasis in Indigenous studies." I waved off his curious tilt of the head. "I did that part-time while working at CPS by day and counseling virtual patients at night."

"Twin nine-month-olds." He enunciated each word.

"Help." I pointed to myself.

"For how long?" Disbelief was writ large across his face.

"For as long as you need me."

Uh...what? Did I just...?

Yes. Yes, I did. And I'll stand by it.

"You don't know what you're signing up for."

"Well, I think I know more about kids than you do."

"I was the second youngest of nine. I have some idea of what I'm getting into."

Yet even as he said the words, I caught the wince. Hadn't he said he had little experience with infants?

"Okay. I..." My breath caught. I'd almost blurted out that I'd had two younger siblings. That Mickey'd been more than ten years younger than me and that I'd helped raise him when he was younger? Or how close I'd been with Laura—since we'd only been two years apart?

He cocked his head, clearly noting my trailing off.

"I know that me agreeing to stay and help you isn't a big deal."

He snapped his laptop shut. "It's a very big deal and you

know it. I need to learn to stand on my own two feet and cope."

Which was true, but why did the words hurt so much? If he learned how to handle the twins without my help, then he wouldn't need me anymore. There'd be no more bottles, diapers, and rocking babies to sleep. No more worries and stress.

Except I'd likely worry, even if I wasn't around. I'd wonder how he was doing. If he was coping. Whether he was asking for—and getting—the help he needed.

He snapped his fingers. "I almost forgot...your father stopped by, looking for you."

I cocked my head and stared at him. Were my ears plugged, or had the racket from the living room scrambled my brains? "Uh, I could swear you just said my father came here looking for me."

"I did." Scott rubbed his forehead. "I wasn't comfortable with him being here—what with you not being here. And you'd just left. I mean, I suppose I could've invited him in."

"You must be wrong."

His brow knit. "He said his name was Carlos Rodrigues. He even looks a bit like you—although shorter, older, balding, and not nearly as handsome."

I bypassed the entire handsome comment.

Another time.

"You're certain he said he was my father?"

Scott slowly nodded. "Lacy met him too. Frankly, he was kind of rude to her. And I didn't know if he was that way because she was a teenager, a young woman, Black or—"

"All the above." My blood pressure shot through the roof. "He's not supposed to be here."

"Yeah, you're starting to freak me out a little bit."

How was I supposed to explain? I certainly didn't want to...but did I owe Scott an explanation? "He's supposed to be in Northern California. I mean, I don't even think he's allowed down in SoCal."

"Allowed?" Scott's confusion mirrored my own.

"It's a long story."

He opened his mouth, but Lacy poked her head in the door. "Miss Agnes made her famous lasagna for dinner. You guys are good, right?"

"Of course." I moved toward her. "Thank you so much for coming over."

"No problem." She went through the hall and to the front entryway where she snagged her backpack. "I don't think Hugh will let me skip school tomorrow. But if it's urgent, I can get Oscar to spring me." She winked. Then she opened the door and bounded down the steps. I didn't even have the chance to ask her if she needed a ride before she was down the street and out of sight.

I noted the silence and quickly pivoted. I slammed the door and headed into the living room.

Alicia'd managed to put one of the smaller pots on her head and it balanced precariously.

Zayden was interested in his yellow stuffed bear, but held a spoon in his hand.

"Are you guys hungry?"

Both looked at me with expressions I couldn't begin to read.

"Okay, well, I'm going to go organize food. Carry on." I motioned to the pots.

Alicia grinned, picked up her spoon, and started banging on a pot on the floor.

I made my way to the kitchen and scrounged carrots and peas I could nuke and smush as well as jarred beef. While I did all this, I kept an ear out to make sure I still heard two babies banging. Well, so much for Zayden's interest in his bear. I wasn't certain whether to be grateful for Lacy's ingenuity, or to curse her for the ridiculousness of the dissonance I was enduring.

"Hey." Scott appeared at the entryway to the kitchen. "I made some chili for us."

"I can smell…that's fantastic."

After the microwave beeped, I pulled the carrots and peas out. I drained the bowl and then set about mashing them.

"So…" Scott winced. "What's up with your father? Why is he not supposed to be in Southern California?"

"I don't…" I took a breath. "I can't really talk about it." I felt like a hand was gripping my throat.

"And I'll respect that…but if he's going to show up here unannounced, maybe I need to know what's going on? I mean, I totally respect that it's your business—"

"You're right, it is my business." I slammed the bowl with the mashed vegetables down on the table. "I'll deal with my own fucking mess."

He held up his hands. "I didn't realize it was a mess." His green eyes softened. "You know you can talk to me, right? That I'm willing to listen."

Guilt gnawed at me. "I know. I just…"

Silence.

I turned in time to find two babies by my feet. One was about to grip my leg, while the other had her fingers shoved in her mouth. I watched in horror as she reached for a magnet on the fridge.

"No."

I nearly tripped over Zayden in my haste to get to Alicia. I thrust my finger into her mouth, but came up empty.

She started howling as Scott scooped up Zayden, who'd also begun to whimper.

"What happened?"

I pointed to the fridge. "How many magnets were there?"

Whatever color he had in his pale complexion completely vanished.

"You think—"

"How many?"

He rubbed his forehead. "I think they were a set of twelve. I mean, they were a gag gift from Mikayla last Valentine's Day."

I quickly counted the small unicorn magnets. "There are only eleven."

"But…" He floundered while I scooped Alicia into my arms.

"Chances are, they didn't sell an uneven number." I held her close. "Do you remember one breaking or throwing one out?" Even as I asked, though, I knew the answer. "Okay, should we make her throw up?"

Scott winced. "I don't think so—she might choke." He yanked his phone from his back pocket. "Let me just check…"

Somehow he managed to hold Zayden and scroll through his phone.

I continued to grip Alicia, berating myself. Here I'd been so concerned about my father that I hadn't given any consideration to the twins. Hadn't noticed the banging had stopped. Hadn't properly babyproofed the house. How could I have missed the magnets? And why was there one so low on the fridge? Had it slipped? Were they poor quality? What if they had lead or arsenic or—

"If it's just one, we can monitor her. If there's any chance it's more than one, we need to take her in to the hospital. They might separate and then reattach through the intestines —it could cause a perforation."

"Jesus." I gripped her even tighter, and she whimpered. "Do we call an ambulance?"

Scott quirked an eyebrow. "No. We get the car seats. The bases are still in your SUV, right?"

God, he was right. We hadn't gotten around to moving them to his car yet.

This felt surreal.

He placed a hand on my arm. "Are you going to be okay to drive?"

"Of course."

I might've snapped that.

"Right. I'll grab a diaper bag. Hey, don't you have a counseling session tonight? I can take the kids on my own—"

"No." I might've snapped that as well. "My client is a lovely lady who's doing really well. Unless she's had a major relapse this week, she'll be okay for a day or two." I glanced at the clock on the microwave. "I can email her once we get to the hospital."

Scott turned off the burner and moved the chili to a cold spot.

As hungry as I'd been twenty minutes ago, my stomach was now all knots and the thought of food revolted.

"Should we bring something for Zayden? What if we're there for a while?" I had no idea how long this would take. Some nights the ER at the hospital was a nightmare—other nights it was completely empty. On a Monday, we'd be okay, right?

"You can make a bottle we can feed him." Scott placed a kiss to Zayden's head. "Everything's going to be okay."

And I wanted to believe him. We loaded the kids into the car seats. Neither squawked. Instead, both seemed subdued. Whether they were reading something from us adults or whether they'd just run out of energy after the music fest, I wasn't sure.

Scott wanted to hold Alicia in his arms, but I convinced him she was safest in the car seat in the back. Odds were, we wouldn't have an accident between his house and the hospital, but it wasn't worth the risk. And, of course, it was illegal.

Twenty minutes later, the four of us walked into Gaynor Beach General Hospital.

And into my biggest nightmare.

CHAPTER 14

SCOTT

THE AMIABLE LADY IN ADMITTING DIDN'T SEEM OVERLY concerned. Certainly not at the level I was enduring. Anthony alternated between calm and panicked—seemingly in tandem. His alarm would rise and he'd be cresting and it would start ebbing away just as mine would ramp up again. Seemed one of us was in a heightened state of panic at all times.

On the other hand, the twins appeared fine. Their eyes were wide as a young man ushered us from the waiting room into one of the curtained bed areas. Since I held Alicia, Anthony coaxed me to sit on the bed. In turn, he sat in a chair with Zayden.

"I keep thinking they're going to call Child Protective Services because I'm a bad parent." I pulled Alicia in tighter, and she pushed against my chest, so I relented.

A bit.

"As I'm the person they'd likely call, I can tell you they won't." Anthony smoothed Zayden's hair. "Kids swallow things. Kids get into mischief. Physicians report when they suspect abuse. Or neglect. Or an unsafe situation. Look, we can both say we did the best we could, and we thought the house was babyproofed."

"We need to go over it again."

He nodded. "Yeah. Maybe we should find a list on a website somewhere—I'm sure there have to be a dozen or six about what to look out for." He snapped his fingers. "I forgot to feed Crumpet."

I winced. "He's not really your responsibility."

"Yeah, but he's been given the short end of the stick, and his urinary diet is important. I notice he's given these two a wide berth."

The most handsome man I'd pretty much ever met entered the room. Tall. Like about six-and-a-half feet. Blond. Muscular. Sparkling eyes. And wearing scrubs. I shelved the attraction vibes and held out Alicia. "We think she swallowed a magnet."

He smiled. "I'm Jay." He turned to Anthony. "Nice to see you again."

Anthony nodded. "Yeah, you too."

"We called CPS?" He looked back and forth between the two of us.

"No." I met Anthony's gaze. "He's with me. Helping me. With the kids. You know…right?"

He nodded. "Yeah, I know." He touched Alicia on the nose. "So, sweetheart, what mischief have you gotten up to?"

She giggled and pushed back, then snagged his finger and tried to pull it into her mouth.

"Okay." He made an exaggerated motion of removing his hand. "Can't have your chompers getting to me."

"I, uh, don't think she has teeth yet. But she might. Oh, God, am I supposed to know? Is there something I'm supposed to be doing?"

Jay put a hand on my shoulder. "Breathe. Scott, right?"

I nodded.

"Dr. Bracken will be in shortly. He's likely to order an x-ray, and we'll go from there."

"Will that hurt her?"

Jay shook his head. "It's good you told us about the magnet—so we know not to order magnetic resonance imaging. But an old-fashioned x-ray won't hurt her at all." He acknowledged both of us. "Back in a few."

"I know Dr. Bracken." For the first time in what felt like forever, a calm swept over me. "He's great. And he's so good with his granddaughter, Marilee. But, of course, you know all this."

Anthony's jaw ticked. "Yes, Hugh and Oscar are good with their daughter Marilee. And Lacy's a good aunt and Miss Agnes is a good nanny. Marilee is well cared for."

"That's good, right? What you'd want for all kids—surrounded by people who love and adore them?"

"Of course." He scratched his scalp.

Dr. Bracken entered. The doctor was about my height with gray hair, a trimmed gray beard, and soft-blue eyes. He often brought Marilee into the library, and I frequently saw him around town. Overall, I thought he was a great guy.

Anthony visibly stiffened.

The two men stared at each other for a long moment.

"Mr. Rodrigues."

"Dr. Bracken."

Wow, the temperature in the room just dropped twenty degrees. I didn't have a clue what was going on—but it wasn't good.

Hugh pivoted to me. "And this is Alicia?" He ducked his head down to meet her gaze. He poked her little belly.

She giggled.

He straightened and met my gaze. "You're pretty sure she swallowed a magnet."

I pulled one from my pocket. "One of these. We counted

and there were only eleven. And we figured it wasn't likely the package only had eleven and I suppose maybe there was a baker's dozen and we saw her swallow—"

Hugh held up his hand. "I've got the picture. We're going to do an x-ray to confirm. If it's just one and it looks like it might pass, we'll likely let it go. If there are two, it's definitely surgery."

My throat tightened, and I said a little prayer, begging that it only be one.

"Is it safe to take a wait-and-see approach?"

Hugh turned to Anthony. "It is. Inducing vomiting at this time isn't advised, and I don't want to put her through surgery if it isn't necessary." He held up the magnet I'd given him. "This is pretty small and doesn't have jagged edges. We'll want to keep her on foods that'll keep her regular. If she experiences any constipation, then bring her in immediately."

"And, uh, how will we know if it's passed?"

The doctor looked at me for a long moment.

"Oh."

"Yes. You'll need to examine her stool until it comes out. If we go more than a few days and it hasn't appeared, bring her back. We can do a repeat x-ray and, if it's stuck, we can operate. I'm really hoping not to."

So was I. And sorting through poop wasn't the worst thing in the world...right?

Even the thought had my stomach dropping.

Hugh yanked his stethoscope from around his neck. He put the earpieces in, warmed the disc with his hand, and pressed it to Alicia's belly where he'd pulled up her shirt.

She giggled.

That was a good sign...right?

After a few moments, Hugh stood and put the stethoscope back around his neck. "All sounds good. Why don't you carry her with me to x-ray? We're quiet here. I can check the radiographs right away and you can be on your way."

I'd expected longer waits—for everything. The speed was easing my stress. I scooped Alicia into my arms. "Hey, baby girl, want to have some fun?"

She grabbed my T-shirt and shoved it in her mouth.

"Is she teething?"

I met Hugh's gaze. "I don't know."

"Well, I can give her a quick exam, if you'd like." He pointed to Zayden. "Both of them. Unless you already have a family doctor."

"They don't need—"

"That would be great—"

Anthony and I caught gazes. Mine turned into a glare. "As I'm sure Lacy told you, they're newly in my custody. I don't actually know when they last saw a doctor. They're up-to-date with their shots. That's all I know."

"Which would've been my next question." Hugh's gaze traveled between Anthony and myself.

Finally, Anthony relented, his expression guarded but with a forced smile. "Yeah, okay, that'd be great. But they don't have insurance yet."

Jesus—something I hadn't even considered. I made a mental note to contact Ms. Wallace and arrange to get these two on my insurance as quickly as possible.

Hugh shrugged. "Like I said, we're not busy tonight. I'm happy to take a look once we've done the x-rays. Free of charge." He bent over to meet Zayden's gaze. "I need to know these little ones are okay. Part of being a member of the community."

Anthony twitched, but didn't speak again.

Whatever.

An hour later, we had a list of food that'd help digestion, a clean bill of health for both babies, and an extracted promise from us that we'd come back at the first sign of trouble.

The drive home was pretty quiet. Alicia appeared subdued after all the stuff that'd happened at the hospital, and Zayden dozed during the quick trip. Nine o'clock had come and gone by the time we trooped into the house.

Anthony held Alicia tight while I hefted Zayden.

"Bottles and then bed?" I dropped the diaper bag by the front door, pulling out the unused bottle. We hadn't gotten around to it and, somehow, Zayden hadn't put up a fuss. He'd also been fascinated by the older man who smiled, made silly faces, and basically spoke baby. I was charmed by the good doctor as well.

"I can get them ready for bed if you prepare the bottles." Anthony didn't loosen his grip on Alicia, merely held the other arm open for Zayden. Once he had both secured, he headed for their bedroom.

I prepared the bottles and soon we sat in rocking chairs, each with a baby.

"You're going to be exhausted tomorrow." I cut a glance at my handsome…friend? Companion? Helper? Co-parent? None of those quite described our situation, yet all felt weirdly accurate. Anthony appeared more haggard. His hair was in disarray from having run his hands through it so often. His cheekbones seemed more prominent. He was a damn handsome man.

Now? You're noticing this now?

Well, in fairness, I'd noticed before. But having the man in my space continuously—my house *and* my bed—lent itself to new observations. Like the little smiles he bestowed on the babies. Or how he'd suppress a yawn when he thought someone was watching but let it take over him when he thought he wasn't being observed. How he looked like he was tapping out the rhythm to some unknown song at various times. If he were alone, would he hum? Or even sing? Suddenly, I wanted to know all these things.

"She's out." Anthony whispered the words. He executed a quick diaper change and had her in the crib.

Zayden was mostly asleep, so I did the same, and by the time his head hit the mattress, he was out as well.

We closed the door quietly and stood for a moment in the hall, just staring at each other. Even in the crappy light, I saw the anguish.

"Her swallowing the magnet wasn't your fault."

"I was distracted."

"Maybe, but I wasn't paying attention either." Hell, I couldn't even remember what our discussion had been about. In the end, clearly it wasn't something that needed to be picked up again.

"I told you the place was babyproofed."

"And I did a sweep and missed it. She only swallowed one. Chances are it'll pass. Like, in every conceivable way that it matters, we did our very best." *Make him see.* "What if you hadn't been here tonight? What if I'd had to handle that crisis on my own?"

"You did okay."

"Because you were here. And I get that you're not going to be here forever—"

"I want to be."

Stunned. I tried to make sense of his words, but meaning wouldn't come. He couldn't mean *forever* forever. Because, like, eventually I'd be able to manage on my own. Perhaps not for another few months, or, you know, five or ten years, but there'd come a day, when I'd have this parenting thing figured out. And I wasn't going to tie him to me—to us—just because he felt a sense of…obligation?

"You're tired. And you're worn out. You need some food, and you need as much rest as you can get." I ran a hand through my likely disheveled hair.

"Don't tell me what I fucking need." His voice was a near growl.

Right. Okay then.

"Well, I need food and as much rest as I can get. I don't think Lacy can help me tomorrow. And we'll likely have to get up with the babies in the night, so better to get a few hours."

I started forward.

He snagged my arm.

Our gazes met.

In that moment, something passed between the two of us. I couldn't identify it—wasn't sure I wanted to put words to it —but some kind of unspoken message was communicated. Or he attempted to say something with his eyes that he couldn't say aloud.

On impulse, I stepped into his personal space. I wrapped my arms around his torso, laid my head in the crook of his neck, and held on tight.

His hesitation was clear. At first, he didn't return my embrace. He was stiff and unyielding.

Have I made a mistake? Did I misinterpret that look?

I was about to pull back when he clasped me to him. His grip was firm as he encircled me. Crushing, in fact, but I didn't mind. How important was breathing when I had a sturdy embrace to tether me to the earth?

To him.

"We could've lost her." His voice caught. "One moment of inattention."

Part of me was disappointed that he sought and offered solace because of my daughter, but the rest of me didn't care because I was in his arms.

He pressed a kiss to my temple.

I turned my head.

Our gazes again collided.

He moved his hands from my back to cup my cheeks. Then, he coaxed me forward.

I obeyed.

Our lips met.

The kiss was light. Just a brush. Just a touch. Just the promise of something more without a firm commitment of delivery.

Then things changed.

He ran his tongue along the seam of my mouth.

After only a moment's hesitation, I opened for him.

He growled his obvious approval as he eased his tongue into my mouth.

The wild intimacy of the gesture startled me. I didn't kiss the guys I'd been with—it just hadn't been our thing. We'd fucked, of course, but kissing hadn't been our jam. But now, as Anthony sought the recesses of my mouth with his tongue, a strange languor overtook me. I pressed myself against him as my cock perked up and took notice. Funny, from the moment he'd delivered the babies, I'd figured my sex life was over for the next eighteen years. Or at least eighteen months. Now, though? All I wanted was to haul him into my bed and have my wicked way with him.

I curled my fingers into his hair, near the base of his scalp, and tugged.

He moaned and pressed up against me. His erection brushed my hip.

Yeah, okay, so this wasn't one-sided. I found that oddly reassuring—that I wasn't alone in my attraction. We'd both hidden it well. Aside from a few fleeting glances, I had no idea he felt this way. Heck, I hadn't even been sure *I* felt this way.

But I did now.

His hand strayed down to cup my ass. He pulled us closer and our cocks brushed. Even through fabric, that connection hit me low in the belly.

Anthony's stomach rumbled.

Speaking of bellies...

I grinned.

He groaned.

I pulled back without losing my grin. "See, I told you that you need sustenance."

"I'd rather have you."

The low growly tone he used had me wishing for the same thing. "Food, Anthony." I wanted to say *and then bed*, but that felt like a step too far. We were, after all, going to be sharing the bed platonically. I was too exhausted to contemplate anything else…but we'd be together.

With obvious reluctance, he pulled back. "We can heat up some chili."

"I'll do it. You go get into your pajamas. By the time you make it to the kitchen, everything'll be ready." I'd make some toast, and we'd be good to go.

He rubbed my nose with his before moving away.

I pressed one quick kiss to his cheek before letting him go.

His hesitation was slight, but it was noticeable. "Do you think we're making a mistake?"

I was surprised to hear him vocalizing that—he always seemed so self-contained.

"We haven't even figured out what *this* is, so I can't see how it's a mistake." I patted his ass. "Get changed. Food, bed, and we'll sort the rest out in the morning." Except we wouldn't—we'd have to deal with kids, and he'd be heading to work. Then we'd have to do it over and over and over. I felt like I was on a treadmill I couldn't get off of.

And this was just day four.

He moved toward the bedroom while I hustled to the kitchen.

Ten minutes later, I had everything organized.

He appeared in his T-shirt and sleep pants. He looked adorable. His hair was a bit tousled. His eyes were a little heavy-lidded.

I encouraged him to sit—which he did—and I indicated he should dive in. He didn't hesitate.

Our meals were consumed in silence. And, really, what was there to say? I suppose I could ask him how his day went. Or how his boss was taking the news he was staying here. Hell, if his boss even knew. Oh, wait. Someone from his office had told his father to find him here. So at least one person had an inkling.

Which circled me back to his father. Given his reaction when I first brought the man up, I wasn't going to touch that one again tonight. I still knew so little about Anthony. Did he have siblings? What about his mother? And why had his father's appearance rattled him so much?

"That was perfect." He scratched his beard.

"I can honestly say it's one of the easiest meals to prepare —and I'm glad I did. And there are tons of leftovers, so feel free to take a container for lunch."

On cue, he yawned.

Then, because I was a sympathetic yawner, I did as well.

We rose. I attempted to lift my bowl, but he swatted my hand away.

"You cooked—I clean. You can get ready for bed now. I'll be there shortly."

His words did all kinds of wonderful things to my insides because, of course, we were sharing. Memories of me cuddled next to him flashed into my mind, but they must've been dreams because I'd fallen asleep on my side of the bed and awoken alone. Surely if I'd curled against him, I would've roused.

Still, I wasn't going to dither. I checked on the twins quickly before heading to the bedroom. I stripped and tossed my clothes aside before heading to the bathroom. I did every-thing I needed to do and found him loitering outside the door when I came out.

"Need to brush my teeth."

Ah, those perfect white teeth. So perfect that I wondered if orthodontia had been in his past.

I scooted past him and headed into the bedroom. An ensuite would be nice because, frankly, sharing a bathroom with Anthony and the twins was likely to be a little much.

And how long do you think he's sticking around?

He said forever.

And you're taking him at his word? You're going to hold him to that?

Of course I wouldn't. He hadn't actually meant *forever* forever.

Right?

I got into bed, put my glasses on the nightstand, and turned off my lamp. I didn't have long to wait—or time to get nervous—before Anthony slid into the bed next to me. The queen-sized bed that suddenly felt much smaller.

He flipped off his light.

The bed hadn't felt so miniscule last night...but then I'd been so freaking exhausted I barely remembered anything.

Anthony cleared his throat. "You can move closer."

"Huh?"

"You're perched on the edge of the bed—you can move closer. I won't bite."

"Unless I want you to?"

"Huh?"

I winced. "Bad joke." Still, I wiggled back a few inches.

"A bit more would be okay."

"Gracious, dear Sir, I'd think you wanted me in your arms." I mimicked the best Southern Belle that I could pull off.

"Maybe...maybe I do. Maybe I liked having you in my arms last night."

Oh crap.

"You, uh, didn't realize?" Now he sounded uncertain.

Fuck it.

I scooted back until I hit a warm, solid body.

He slid his arm around my chest. Then, unexpectedly, he kissed my neck. "Try to get some sleep."

With a sexy-as-fuck man holding me? Wasn't likely.

And yet I went down hard and fast, only waking when I heard crying on the baby monitor. I gently eased out of Anthony's hold.

He stirred.

"I got this."

He mumbled.

Somehow, I managed to do bottles, diapers, and get them back to sleep in under an hour. That felt like a monumental accomplishment.

I crawled back under the covers.

Anthony reached for me.

Life was pretty fucking amazing.

Or so it seemed until the next day when I opened the front door to find another strange man on my front porch. He held out a business card.

I snagged it, scanned it, and my stomach sank. I opened the door and ushered him in.

As I closed the door, he opened his briefcase and took out a notepad with an expensive-looking pen. My first instinct was to mention Anthony, but I still wasn't clear what his boss did or didn't know about our arrangement. I'd been warned this visit was coming—so I should've been prepared.

I raced through a mental visual of the house. Had I left anything lying about or missed something important?

Nothing came to mind.

Alicia banged her spoon against her tray.

"We're just having snacks." I gestured toward the kitchen. "I need to get back. Uh, feel free to look around."

He arched an eyebrow.

I drew in a breath. "I know you have to do a home visit to

ensure my suitability. I get that. I have nothing to hide—you do whatever you need to do to ensure yourself that I'm a fit parent."

I'd almost said guardian, but caught myself in time. I was their father—and I wanted to be judged as such. I headed for the kitchen.

He followed.

Naturally, Alicia was smooshing avocado into Zayden's hair. I thought I'd separated them far enough but apparently had missed how long her reach was.

Or her brother had angled himself closer.

I snagged a cloth and tried to mitigate some of the damage. "Sweetheart, we don't put food in our brother's hair."

She scowled.

Mr. Winters cleared his throat.

My heart sank.

And yet, when I ushered him out of my house an hour later, I felt good.

He hadn't judged. He hadn't criticized. He'd observed. He'd asked questions. He'd offered suggestions.

After I settled the kids into the playpen, we did an entire tour of the house and I was able to show him—thanks to Anthony, Hugh, and Lacy—that the house was safe.

I didn't mention the magnet incident.

In turn, he took me through all the steps I'd need to follow to get permanent custody, and what his role was going to be going forward. I didn't dare ask why Anthony couldn't be my caseworker. Instead, I nodded, jotted down some notes, and tried to ask intelligent questions, all the while holding in the panic.

After he left, I placed a call to Wynn Cavannah, a local lawyer. I explained my situation, and he promised to secure a court date as soon as possible and set up a time for me to go see him in his office. Lacy'd be around on Friday, so I set up the meeting for then.

Finally, after all that, I climbed down from the edge of panic and was able to enjoy some play time with my babies.

We weren't out of the woods yet, but daylight was slowly appearing.

CHAPTER 15

ANTHONY

"We need to take the twins to see Mr. McIntosh today."

I glanced up blearily from my cereal to look into Scott's bright-green eyes.

"Huh?" I'd been up twice in the night with the twins and, after the second time, hadn't really fallen back asleep. Still, it'd been Friday night, and since he'd handled every night as well as the entire day with them all week, I figured I'd better take a turn so he could get a good night's sleep.

And he had.

Gotten a good night's sleep.

He was all bright-eyed and bushy-tailed while I was bleary-eyed and…

Nope, coming up with something was far too complicated for this morning.

"Mr. McIntosh is a children's performer. I know the twins will be too young to enjoy his show, but I promised to be there. At the library. So we need to arrive by eleven."

I'd planned a quiet day in, with maybe scooting out to get some shopping done. We were running low on supplies. Sure, we could order some, but I wanted to take a break. Or, perhaps, let Scott head out to take a break. He'd been with the little ones for the entire week. I only did evenings, and that was exhausting enough.

And, at some point, we needed to talk. I'd tried several times to engage him in discussions.

No dice.

He always had one excuse or another. Want to talk about the twins? No problem. About the two of us? Oh, that can wait. Or I'm too tired. Or—the one I dreaded that he'd only pulled out once—let's just play it by ear.

By ear? What did that even mean?

"Mr. McIntosh, you say? Well, let's go."

Going out was always such a nightmare. Two kids, the stroller, the diaper bag, organizing car seats...I was exhausted, and we hadn't left the driveway. "Are we set?"

Scott patted his pockets, then nodded. "I have my phone and wallet. We have the diaper bag, the double stroller, and the twins."

Admittedly, having the twins was important. Crumpy sat at the front window, and I couldn't tell if he was sad his human was leaving or if he was relieved the two chaotic demons were. He'd continued to give them a wide berth. I felt bad for the cat—he hadn't signed up for mayhem.

I chanced a glance at my ginger companion who, on cue, yawned. Yeah, he hadn't signed up for this either.

The drive to the library didn't take long, and soon we'd unloaded everything and were heading inside. The day was a bit cooler than usual, so we'd put the twins in little fleece coats. Those coats were already a tight fit. Good God. I knew kids grew quickly, but I couldn't fathom we'd have to go clothes shopping soon.

A younger woman greeted us at the front door with the widest smile I'd ever seen. She squealed when she saw the twins. After giving Scott a big hug, she crouched down to poke noses, tickle tummies, and make the two formerly cranky babies quite happy.

Scott cut me a glance with a grin on his face. He seemed more relaxed—but then this was his second home. I'd always known that. Seeing it in action just brought the reality home. I never smiled like that in my office. Was never greeted with enthusiasm. Never felt like I made someone's day just by showing up.

"Oh, sorry." Scott placed a hand on my upper arm. "Mikayla, this is Anthony. Anthony, this is the best assistant librarian ever."

That he hadn't defined our relationship didn't go unnoticed. I wasn't hurt or anything like that.

Or so you tell yourself.

And what was I, anyway? More than the social worker at this point. It'd been more than a week, and I'd moved more clothes into the front-hall closet. I'd set up a space in the spare room where I could conduct my video counseling appointments.

You're sleeping in his bed every night.

Yeah, that was very true. It also didn't change who I was to him. Who he was to me.

Or so you tell yourself.

"Anthony?"

I shook off my thought and refocused on Scott. "Yes?"

He gave me a quizzical look. "I was just saying we should stay near the back so we can duck out if either baby becomes unmanageable."

"True." I eyed the little ones who appeared fascinated with all the chaos of kids, parents, and what appeared to be one or two library staff. I liked kids, but I couldn't fathom wrangling this crowd on a regular basis.

Mikayla stepped to the front of the crowd. Amazingly, a hush fell over the group.

"We're so lucky to have Mr. McIntosh coming to read one of his books to us today. Can we give him a Gaynor Beach Public Library welcome with big cheers?" She waved her hand in the air.

The kids broke into raucous applause. One little boy looked utterly confused and ready to start crying, but his father knelt and whispered something. The boy's demeanor changed immediately, and he started clapping as well. The magic touch—some people had it, and some didn't. I'd calmed a few kids over the years, but was just as likely to intimidate because of my size. I chose social work, and child protective services in particular, because I wanted to help kids. With hindsight, I appreciated that I probably should've spent more time around them before making such a monumental decision. Just…I loved my siblings, and wanted to honor what I'd shared with them. They were gone, and I wanted my work to be the legacy of that relationship.

In retrospect, I could see that was too much pressure on me. And too heavy a burden to carry for my memories of them.

Suddenly the man I assumed to be Mr. McIntosh appeared. He was about my height, with brown hair and brown eyes. And a huge, wide smile. Objectively, I could say he was attractive. Not my type, but attractive nonetheless.

And what is your type?

Over the years, I tended to gravitate toward larger guys. Certainly not slender redheads who were almost my height.

And I didn't fit his ideal. Or I didn't think so…if the twink the other day was any indication of his preference. Young *boys* who wanted a *daddy*. I still internally snickered at the *Who's Your Daddy?* T-shirt. Man, the guy'd had no idea what was coming. Yet I couldn't find fault in how he'd adapted. Aside from one panic attack and one or two near-misses in the stress department, he did exceptionally. Plenty of hiccups and missteps for sure—like the magnet, which appeared in the poop two days after the *incident*—but otherwise smooth sailing.

Did that mean he didn't need me anymore? As Mr. McIntosh read his book, I grappled with the thought of our future.

McIntosh had a talent, no question about it. He mesmerized the crowd—young and old alike. He even held our two, whom we thought would be too young, captive.

This offered a moment's respite and, as I stood behind the stroller, I took a minute to just breathe. To let the chaos wash away. To remember why we were doing this.

Alicia and Zayden.

They'd become my talisman. My reason for being. And if I felt that way, after just a week, how must Scott feel? They were his blood. They were of him. They were entirely his responsibility.

Applause broke out as Mr. McIntosh waved, thanking everyone. Within moments, he was besieged by a number of eager children.

"Should we head out?" I directed the question at Scott, but kept my eyes riveted to the scene of ordered chaos.

"He doesn't sell books here." My companion met my gaze. "He only sells them at the bookstore. He doesn't want the kids whose parents can't afford it to ask. We keep plenty on hand here, and they'll all wind up being signed out for weeks."

Alicia, clearly not pleased with the show being over, started to fuss.

Within moments, Scott had her in his arms.

She grabbed for his glasses.

Zayden, clearly not pleased with being left out, also started to fuss.

Within moments, I had the little guy in my arms.

He grabbed for my hair.

Yeah, I needed to start tying it back. Or even get a haircut.

Except I had the distinct impression that Scott liked my hair. Once, when we'd exchanged what I thought was a casual kiss, he'd run his hands through it. Then he grinned and sauntered off.

Leaving me dazed and confused.

But that was par for the course these days.

Finally, after the last child and parent duo'd been sent on their way, Mr. McIntosh approached.

Oh, shit.

How had I not recognized him?

Because he looked so different. His clothes were definitely not that of an on-duty social worker. And he looked lighter. Brighter. Not like the stressed-out guy I met five years ago when I took over his job as social worker at the local high school. His eyes didn't carry the weight of the burden. His cheeks, although still gorgeous, had some color. *He* had some color.

He'd honed in on Scott, though.

His smile faltered as he spotted Alicia.

Had I not been watching carefully, I might've missed the micro expression.

Grief.

Profound grief.

At seeing the baby?

Then, just as quickly, the pain passed, and he put on what I could only call a genuine smile.

"Scott, so glad you made it." He pulled my companion into a sort of one-armed hug, clearly mindful of the baby.

"Well, I promised." Scott offered up a wide grin. "Sorry I wasn't here to greet you—"

The man waved him off. "Mikayla was brilliant—and I think the show went well." He pressed a hand to Scott's biceps while watching Alicia intently.

"It did. Oh." Scott angled his body toward me. "Mr. McIntosh, this is Anthony Rodrigues." He met my gaze and cocked his head.

"Nice to meet you again, Ethan."

Ethan Mack quickly looked around the room, then shot me a look. "I prefer Mr. McIntosh around the kids."

And I'd prefer you stop touching my guy.

Wait…what? If they wanted to be close, and even affectionate, who was I to stop them? I didn't have a claim on Scott.

Yet I moved to his other side and pressed myself against him. "This is Zayden." I indicated with my chin. "And his sister, Alicia." I pressed my hand to Scott's other arm. I wanted to claim ownership on both him and the twins but, damnit, I didn't have the right. That pissed me off more than anything.

Ethan turned his attention to the twins for a moment. He made exaggerated faces as he repeated their names.

Both were, to my frustration, charmed.

Then the man feathered his hand through Scott's hair. "They look so much like you—but I didn't realize you had kids."

Scott blew out a long breath. "It's complicated. Really complicated. But yeah, they're all mine."

Ours.

I wanted to shout the word but, again, I didn't have the right.

Ethan cut me a glance. Sizing me up? Was I competition? He didn't seem like Scott's type—but then I wouldn't have said I was either. And here was a single man who was amazing with children. Hell, the man wrote books for them and performed for free. How could I begin to compete with that?

Except…was he single? For the life of me, I couldn't figure it out. No ring meant nothing. And I hadn't heard anything.

But then our paths hadn't crossed. Heck, maybe he had a pile of kids at home.

And yet, based on the yearning look he gave the twins, I didn't think that was the case.

"We should get together—you, me, and the twins." Ethan brushed Scott's shoulder and—I swear to Christ—batted his eyelashes.

Jesus.

"Sure. Or I can babysit them while you go on your *date*." I wasn't sure I could inject any more sarcasm.

Scott, apparently oblivious to this point, seemed to snap out of his daze. He glared at me. Then he turned to Ethan. "We're pretty busy these days—getting the kids settled and all. But when I'm more organized, I'd love to see you. A lunch at Boardwalk Books and Bites, perhaps?" He shot me another glance, this one indecipherable. "Anthony has to work a lot, but I'm on leave from the library for a couple of days." He turned back to Ethan. "Perhaps between Christmas and New Year's? Not Boxing Day, obviously. The store will be jammed."

"As long as you don't mind being interrupted. I do a lot of readings there, so people always recognize me." He winked.

I wanted to gag. *Jesus Fucking Christ.*

A lovely young woman came up to Ethan. "Mr. McIntosh? It's time to be going." She gave us all an apologetic look before heading back over to the circulation desk where Mikayla stood.

Ethan offered a sheepish grin. "In demand." He gave Scott another awkward hug. "You have my number—I'd love to do lunch." He offered his hand to me.

Short of being a dickwad, I had no option but to shake. But that meant letting go of my grasp of Scott. So I gave a hard shake—squeezing more than necessary—and taking no small measure of satisfaction when the man winced. Then, as soon as I could, I put my arm around Scott and pulled him close.

He stiffened for a moment, then allowed me to pull him in.

I tried to hide my triumphant smile.

Ethan winked, then headed off.

Scott pulled away. "What the hell was that?" He spat the words.

Alicia stirred and gave me a wary look.

"He's not right for you."

"He's not interested in me." Scott's look was pure exasperation with his eyebrows raised.

I bristled. "He was flirting with you."

Now, he rolled his eyes. "To make you jealous. Which, apparently, worked well. What's with the caveman impersonation?" A small smile crept through. "Not saying I didn't like it…"

My anger dropped away. Annoyance replaced it, but the sentiment was far less potent. "You were flirting back."

"Seriously? You think *that* was flirting? Either you're way out of practice or are truly clueless."

I was a little uncomfortable with how close to the mark he was. I *was* out of practice. This wasn't my *thing*. I didn't do jealousy. Truthfully, I'd never been in a relationship long enough to get to that stage. I was always fine with just walking away if things got too serious. And, if I was brutally honest, I hadn't met a guy worth getting jealous over.

Is Scott the guy?

My brain told me no. We hadn't known each other very long. We'd barely kissed. We hadn't even had sex.

At which point my libido kicked in and demanded to know what was taking so fucking long?

A week. We'd had the twins a whole eight days. We'd already had emergency visits both to the vet—where, after major surgery, a new diet was in order, the cat'd received antibiotics, and was on a urine acidifier—and the hospital, after which we'd spent a significant amount of time sifting through shit to find the magnet. Scott'd had a home visit and had consulted with a lawyer. Surely that was enough, right? Those stressors were why we hadn't progressed further. Because…twins…

Right?

I no longer had a good answer for that.

CHAPTER 16

SCOTT

THE ENTIRE DRIVE HOME, I KEPT THINKING ABOUT THE FACT Anthony'd been jealous when Ethan had shown some physical affection toward me. Ethan and I were like that. Just hugs and the occasional brush of fingers. His touches never lingered.

I had the distinct impression I wasn't his type. And even if I were, we had a professional relationship we had to maintain. He visited us frequently—which was wonderful. I was certain his shows encouraged people to visit him at the bookstore when he did signings there. He must have one planned for Christmas—likely a big time of year for him.

We fed the babies, and they settled down for a nap. All the morning's adventures must've worn them out. Pleasantly, they hadn't been cranky.

Even Alicia hadn't fussed.

I flashed back to Ethan's reaction upon meeting her. Upon meeting both the twins, sure, but he'd had a particular reaction to my daughter. Was it her age? Did she bring back some kind of memory? Or, was I overthinking this, as I was wont to do? Of course he was taken aback—I'd appeared with two babies, who had my coloring, and informed him I was a father.

Likely, there'd be more stares as I navigated my way through the introduction of my children to society. I wasn't a prominent member of the community per se, but plenty of people knew me. I was the public face of the library—popping up whenever appropriate.

I dropped to the couch, half-expecting Anthony to join me. Instead, he loomed above me.

"I'm going grocery shopping. And…" He hesitated.

"And," I prompted.

"I'm wondering if I should bring more of my things. I mean, I'm not sure you need—"

All lethargy swept away, I pushed myself up to get as close to him as I could. "Don't think—not for one single second—that I don't need you." I gestured to the bedroom. "That they don't need you."

Our gazes clashed.

I read the uncertainty, and that had me sitting up and taking notice because that hesitation wasn't like him. At least to me, he pretty much always acted liked he knew what he was doing. Whether that was just bravado, or whether he had lots of faith in himself, I wasn't sure.

"You'd like me to stay."

"Yes."

"For how long?"

My gut reaction was to say forever, but that made zero sense. That was just the panic at the thought of being a single father. That was just the fright of having to deal on my own with children who might eat magnets. That was just the terror of facing life alone. Last week, I would've said I was happy being single with my hookups and boys. This week, everything had changed.

"How long?" His repetition was quiet.

"I don't know." My answer was honest. I reached out to caress his cheek. Such sharp prominent cheekbones. Such lovely rich, soft skin. Such amazing eyes whose pupils widened at my touch.

Slowly, he nodded. Then, unexpectedly, he took my hand and pressed a light kiss to my knuckles. He dropped my hand, and within moments he was gone.

What he left behind was chaos in my mind.

And also a house that needed some cleaning. I couldn't vacuum, but most of the floor except the living room was laminate. I did a thorough cleaning of Crumpet's litter box— and made sure he was peeing properly—which he seemed to appreciate. I scoured the fridge for expired foods and things that were questionable. I loathed throwing food out, but I couldn't take the risk of anyone getting food poisoning. While I did all that, I settled on cooking burgers on the barbecue. I'd do mashed potatoes as well as corn and peas. The twins, for all their attitudes, weren't picky eaters.

The book I'd snagged from the library on Monday suggested slowly introducing new foods. I'd do whatever it took. My kids weren't going to be the ones who'd only eat canned pasta.

Or so you tell yourself.

I wanted to raise good kids. I'd met plenty of spoiled brats at the library. Although, in fairness, some were merely reacting to the overstimulation of story time. Things could get pretty chaotic with twenty or so kids. And other kids who threw fits were often special needs kids. I was as patient as possible, but sometimes screaming children got on my nerves. Hopefully my own would be the exception.

By the time I was finished organizing things, I was exhausted, and the kids were up from their naps. After I changed their diapers, we settled down for a snack. Slowly, we were adjusting to the schedule Eliza'd provided.

Eliza.

I hadn't thought of her in several hours—possibly a new record. Slowly, her problems, which admittedly had become my problems, were receding. I wished her well, but I didn't have the same animosity. Or anger. Truthfully, I felt only pity.

Or so you tell yourself.

Maybe I was deluding myself. I didn't want to cling to the anger—I'd often found that a wasted emotion. But the enormity of what Eliza'd done couldn't be denied. This was fucking huge. Life-altering.

And she hadn't even given me a heads-up or an adequate explanation. Maybe I didn't feel only pity after all. Not yet.

Anthony's return heralded some excitement from the twins.

Are they becoming attached to him?

I didn't know. And, frankly, I didn't have the bandwidth to care. I moved to help him bring in the groceries, but he waved me off. When I spotted a rotisserie chicken, already cooked, I was glad I hadn't put the burgers out to thaw—we could do those another day. I put away the groceries while I heard him putting things into the hall closet. I could certainly offer him space in mine. I didn't have much that I hung there —enough khaki and dress pants to get me through a workweek.

"Hey, if you come and watch the kids, I can reorganize my drawers so you can have one."

He poked his head into the kitchen.

"So you have somewhere to put your underwear and socks and stuff."

"That would be…nice."

He offered me what I'd call a shy smile. He snagged the washcloth, wet it, and headed towards the babies. He made some weird noise that got them riled up and I slipped away unnoticed.

I needed precious little time to create a drawer for him. I didn't have a ton of stuff. And I did rifle through my drawers to find a couple of pairs of underwear that needed to be tossed. I loathed throwing things away, but those holes were indecent, and now that I might be spotted in them—

You're dreaming.

Am I?

Hasn't he seen me in underwear a couple of times?

My subconscious didn't provide a snappy comeback to that. We stuck to pajamas, which was fine in the winter. But come summer, unless I jacked up the a/c, which I hated doing, we were going to be sweating our asses off. Of course I'd do whatever it took to keep the babies comfortable.

They'll be toddlers by then.

Holy Lord—another thing I didn't want to think of. My kids. Growing up.

I eyed the bed. We needed clean sheets. I snagged a set from the linen closet and set about remaking the bed. Then I threw in a load of laundry. Which reminded me I needed to do one for the kids. And hadn't I noticed Alicia growing out of some of her clothes?

The dollar signs flitted through my brain. That was definitely one thing Eliza hadn't considered—librarians did okay, but we weren't rich. Living in SoCal was bloody expensive. Even with the great interest rate I had on the house mortgage, I was still making sizable payments every month.

"I could've helped you with that."

Spinning, I pressed a hand to my chest.

Anthony cocked an eyebrow.

God, even doing that made him look sexy. His eyebrows were neat.

Does he trim them?

Does he trim other parts?

Oh, my God, so not going there.

"Where are the kids?"

"Happily playing a new puzzle game. I snuck over to the toy store and picked up a few more things."

He held up his hand as I took a breath to protest.

"They don't have a lot of toys, as you pointed out. And the pots-and-pans game is fun, but it gives us both a headache. Much as we're loath to admit it, I think we're going to have to put them in front of the television on occasion."

Loath was the right word. I didn't want the kids growing up addicted to the screen, be it television, tablet, or phone. Reality meant, however, that some screen time was inevitable.

A squawk drew our attention.

I followed Anthony into the living room to find the twins in a pitched battle for a piece of the puzzle. A piece, I was pleased to see, that was too big for them to put in their mouths. Not that I wasn't sure my companion wouldn't have thought of that.

Anthony stepped in to play peacemaker.

Several more bags, bearing the toy store's logo, sat off to the side.

Crumpet was sniffing them. Thank God, he wasn't a territory marker. No spraying. Immense relief, because he'd been older when I'd gotten him neutered. And just the thought of that surgery got me thinking about my balls and how protective I was of them.

I moved to scoop him up. "Hey, buddy, how are you?"

He glared his ugly cat scowl.

After kissing him on the nose, I gently let him down.

He gave me one long look.

Oh, shit. Food.

I moved to the kitchen and selected a small portion of wet food for him. I put out a small bowl of kibble.

Naturally, he devoured the wet food first. Then he looked up at me, unblinkingly.

"You're not getting any more. Eat the special, expensive, designed-for-cats-with-your-illness dry food or I'm taking it away. I can't leave it lying around. I'm quite certain the twins will eat it."

Still, he stared at me. Oh, right, I was supposed to wet it. I prepared the concoction, amused that my cat seemed to remember the instructions I'd forgotten.

Crumpy, a grazer, hadn't taken well to not having his food around whenever he wanted it. His covered litter box was in the laundry room, and I'd emptied the container earlier today. I'd probably need to get a baby gate that he could crawl through but which would prevent the twins from venturing that way. The vision of them eating, let alone touching, cat poop, sent me into apoplectic fits. So much to worry about.

Once Crumpy was finished with the mush, I grabbed the bowl. "Are we about ready for dinner?" I poked my head into the living room. My breath caught.

Anthony sat on the floor with Zayden cradled in his lap and Alicia sitting nearby with a puzzle piece in her hand. Just a father and his two children. Except he wasn't their dad. And that struck me as all kinds of wrong. He loved these kids already—of that I had no doubt. He could've walked away at any point, but he hadn't. He'd stayed.

But had he stayed for them, for me, or for some combination of the two? And was his remaining here contingent on his perception that I needed help? If I became too self-sufficient, might he see that as a cue to leave?

Do I want him to leave?

I didn't have a ready answer for that.

"Dinner sounds amazing." He indicated Zayden.

I waved him off. "I can prepare it. Chicken and vegetables? Oh, and I can quickly whip up some mini roasted potatoes."

"Sounds perfect." He pressed a kiss to the crown of Zayden's head.

The baby sat curled, playing with his toes. Apparently, the digits were fascinating.

The potatoes took the longest amount of time, but I was able to put everything together as well as do some pantry organizing. I wasn't a doomsday person, but I believed in being prepared. In my mind, we didn't have enough baby food in stock as well as some other essentials. It'd been one thing when I lived alone, but things looked different now.

I set the potatoes on a cooling rack and headed back into the living room.

Alicia and Zayden were back to playing amicably while Anthony scrolled on his phone.

"Anything interesting?" I pointed to the device.

He waved me off. "Just checking my calendar for the next week. Do you realize tomorrow is the solstice and Christmas is four days after that?"

Sure...sort of... The date had been in my mind somewhere, but it hadn't really registered.

Before I could answer coherently, he continued. "I'm off as of the twenty-fifth." He eyed my home. "Do you think we should, you know, decorate?"

A tactful way of pointing out that my home was not just spartan, but that I didn't have any Christmas decorations. "You were the one who said we didn't need to decorate. That the kids wouldn't even notice." I might've sounded a bit defensive on that one. The truth was that no one came to the house except my hookups. And I was pretty sure they weren't coming to trim my tree. Any entertaining I did was at various restaurants. I'd never considered bringing my staff back here—the place was simply too small. Still, I eyed the twins. "You said they're not going to remember their first Christmas."

"They won't." His agreement came easily. "But you were also right. They'll look back at photographs of this time and maybe wonder why we didn't put up a tree or hang some lights or something."

I didn't want to admit he was right—but he was. How had

this become a disagreement when we were essentially, now, on the same side?

"Maybe you can watch them tomorrow while I run to the store? I don't want to go overboard because I'll have to find somewhere to store the stuff once the season's over." I'd been trying to declutter and eventually get rid of Ms Ducking's things over the past few years—bringing home more stuff wasn't going to accomplish that goal.

"If you're asking if I mind watching the kids, the answer is *no*. Just be aware I'm on call and might have to leave in a hurry."

"I'll keep my phone close. Call if you need me to come home. Now, food's ready."

"Perfect." He scooped up Alicia.

I snagged Zayden and pulled him close against me. The sense of rightness permeated yet again. As I put him in his high chair, I marveled how far we'd come. Sure, there'd been tantrums, rough nights, and moments of sheer terror—but there'd also been quiet moments of joy. Silent times when I could just sit and watch them. Marvel at them. Be stunned they were actually in my care.

Be astonished I was their father. And that their mother had decided I'd be the best one to raise them. I'd do everything in my power to prove she made the right choice.

Dinner was a jovial affair. Somehow Alicia managed to get smooshed peas in her hair and Zayden played with his carrots and refused to eat them, but we managed okay.

Bath time was fun and, shockingly, both babies went down after just two bedtime stories.

As we snuck out of the twins' room, Anthony and I exchanged a look. Hope? Relief? Amusement?

Some combination of all three?

I wasn't sure.

"We should talk."

Anthony's words hit me. Panic skittered up and down my spine. Boldness overtook me. "I'd rather go to bed."

"Take advantage of them sleeping so we can get a good night's rest?"

"And other things." I gave him my best come-hither look and headed into the bathroom. We'd cleaned up after dinner, so nothing remained but going to bed. And talking was a great idea, but I knew there were things I'd rather be doing.

I tossed my jeans and T-shirt into the hamper—both had baby food on them. Likely I'd need to do another load tomorrow.

Good thing I'd stocked up on detergent when it was on sale last month. Awesome deal. I'd need to find many more of those. Plus I needed more detergent for the twins. Another thing to add to the grocery list. I slipped into my T-shirt and sleep pants for propriety's sake. But I had plans to shed them.

I exited the bathroom, and Anthony was on the other side of the door. He stood in his sleep pants and nothing else. As I raked my gaze from head to toe, I noted he even had his socks off. I cleared my throat. "Ready for bed?"

He cocked his head. "We can talk in bed as easily as in the living room. We *are* going to talk, right?"

My hand shook as I scratched my light stubble. Was he agreeing we do more than talk? For the first time in eight days, I didn't feel exhausted. I felt invigorated. "What do you think?"

"Sure, we can talk in bed. An early night."

He met my gaze and those dark-brown eyes mesmerized. What did he mean by an *early night?* I wanted to ask, but I didn't dare. Instead, I offered the smile that often got me action. "Yeah, bed. I'll meet you there." I almost pressed a kiss to his cheek, but chickened out at the last moment. Instead, I ducked into the bedroom.

Only once I heard the bathroom door close, did I take a breath.

First, I opened my nightstand drawer to locate lube and condoms. I had a decent stash. Out or just easily accessible? After a moment's debate, I put the supplies near the front of the drawer, but closed it most of the way. I whipped my T-shirt off and tossed it next to the bed—easy to reach, but a clear sign I was okay with more.

Sleep pants on or off?

Oh dear God, I'm way overthinking this.

Opting to leave them on, I scooted into bed. But I lowered the sheet so my chest was visible. I didn't have a lot of hair. That'd been a source of consternation when I was younger. One of my older brothers had a pelt, and he loved going around without a shirt on. Personally, I worried he might get a sunburn. My second thought was to wonder why he had plenty of hair and I didn't. That obsession stayed with me until I started meeting men in the dating context. I preferred guys with hairless chests. I preferred boys. Not in a disturbing way—everyone was always legal—but I preferred guys on the younger side. Guys who I could dominate. Guys who wanted someone to tell them what to do. Always consensually though.

Always.

Anthony was the opposite of all those guys. His tendency was to take charge. To make sure things ran smoothly. To work hard to ensure harmony and balance. He brought calm to chaos.

Living without him was unfathomable.

But was the desire to keep him with me merely panic at the idea of parenting the twins by myself, or was I feeling something toward him that I hadn't expected. Attraction or something even deeper?

My breath caught.

I wasn't falling for him.

Right?

He was so the opposite of everything I wanted in a partner.

Preferences change.

I scoffed. Not that much.

Yet when he appeared at the door to our bedroom—and I was coming to see this as *our* bedroom—my heart did a little flutter.

I'm a goner.

CHAPTER 17

ANTHONY

Talk? I'd thought we were going to talk?

Raking my gaze over all that pale, delicate skin with a smattering of red chest hair—arrowing down—all rational thought fled. Well, I took a moment to marvel at the dash of freckles on his upper chest. Then my gaze moved down, and I wondered what he'd look like without his sleep pants on.

So not the time.

We had a million and one things to discuss. We had futures to map out. We had to determine what, if any, my role was to be in this family. We hadn't had a complete debrief after his meeting with the lawyer yesterday, and we were still waiting to hear about an expedited court date. Mr. Winters's report had said Scott was an acceptable guardian for the time being and that further visits would be required to ensure the safety of the children was maintained.

So yeah, plenty to talk about.

Yet, as my cock stood up and took notice, none of that mattered. All thoughts of *what if* and *could we* melted into the background.

I palmed my cock.

He shoved the sheet aside and then shoved down his sleep pants.

His cock, thick and heavy, lay against his belly. Obviously he hadn't been thinking of co-parenting and legal quandaries while I'd been obsessing about them.

So not the time.

Okay, sex now, discussion later.

That worked for me.

I removed my sleep pants and joined him on the bed, sliding into the side I'd occupied for the past week.

This felt as natural as breathing.

Yet I still hesitated.

"Uh." I cleared my throat. "We've barely kissed—"

My next comment about penetrative sex was cut off when he launched himself into my arms. He maneuvered himself over me and slowly lowered so our bodies aligned. So our skin touched. So our cocks brushed.

Holy Lord.

He dove in for a kiss. Not just a peck. No, a tongues-tangling, teeth-clattering, soul-searing kiss.

I snagged the back of his head and dragged him closer. I wanted him—any way I could get him.

As he continued his assault on my senses, I became acutely aware of certain things. How his skin was so smooth. How when our cocks brushed, little shots of electricity arced through me. How if we didn't consummate this thing tonight, I'd die.

So much for worrying about whether it was too soon for penetrative sex.

I scraped my fingers against his light stubble, and he moaned. Finally, he pulled back. He met my gaze with lust-filled green eyes. "You're going to fuck me."

"I'm…" I tried to make sense of his words.

He rolled off me and dove for his nightstand drawer.

Within moments, he was back with a condom and lube. "You're going to lie there and you're going to fuck me."

I disliked using the term topping from the bottom—but sometimes you just had to call a spade a spade. I swallowed. Hard. "Don't you, you know, prefer to top?"

"You'd think." He straddled my thighs and grasped my cock.

I saw stars.

"I love my boys." He winced.

Reassure him. "I know what you mean."

"Right." He rolled the condom down my length. "And I'm all about being the dominant one—both inside and outside the bedroom."

Which I'd figured out, although I hadn't found sippy cups or actual toys, so his boys weren't, as far as I could tell, littles.

"But I also loved being fucked. And, amazingly, there are boys who like to do that."

I shouldn't have been amazed, but I kind of was. The rainbow community was so diverse, seeing variety shouldn't have surprised—but it did.

Before I could react, Scott coated his fingers with lube and started to work them inside himself. His cock bobbed as he thrust first one, then two inside. He worked himself and then, for a moment, stilled.

Our gazes met.

He mouthed *prostate*.

Ah, so that was why he loved being fucked.

Good to know.

Part of me wanted to slather lube on my cock, and part of me was fascinated with watching him. Not just the fingering part, but the whole thing. How he'd taken charge entirely. I'd never played passive participant before, and I was intrigued by my feelings. I would've assumed I didn't like being bossed around—but this was pretty fucking hot.

When he coated my cock with lube, I jerked involuntarily.

Apparently my appendage really liked the attention. Then he was there, easing himself onto me.

Impaling himself.

And for all my sexual hookups, I'd never done it like this either. With someone above me. Someone else controlling the movements. Someone else calling the shots.

He closed his eyes as he bottomed out. Then he pulled his lower lip through his teeth.

I grasped his thighs.

He batted my hands away.

I grabbed the sheets instead.

The orchestration of movement that followed was exquisite. He raised and then lowered himself—controlling every aspect of the joining. He scraped his fingernails against my abs.

I bucked up.

He moaned.

This, this, this.

Staving off the orgasm took willpower. With all the stimulation, my cock begged for release.

Hold out.

Aside from my first time, I'd never come before a partner. I took pride in making sure they achieved their pleasure before I ever considered taking mine. And I usually had the willpower to hold out until my partner climaxed. This time, though? He was testing my patience. The feeling of sinking deep within him—of being so intimately connected—was doing things to my mind.

"Jerk me off."

Ah, something he needed me to do. Of course he was responsible for maintaining balance, so needing a hand was perfectly logical.

I stroked him several times—just the lightest of touches.

He snagged my hand and encouraged me to encircle his cock.

Ah, such a bossy one.

I loved it.

I smeared a bit of precum along his length, then I stroked him—matching the rhythm he set.

His face was pinched as he concentrated—a little *v* forming between his eyebrows.

Then, without warning, he erupted. Cum spilled over my hand and shot onto my stomach.

I grasped his thigh with my left hand, using it for balance, as I thrust up into him a couple of times. Then I went over the edge myself.

Quite suddenly, he fell forward and into my arms. My cock came out with a bit of a pop and even before I could react, he was placing his head on my chest and wrapping his arms around me.

I hesitated for only a moment before enfolding him in my arms. A feeling of rightness settled in my chest as I brought him as close to me as I could.

He was a man I'd never seen coming, but I also couldn't envision letting go.

And that thought terrified me more than anything else in this whole clusterfuck.

Time passed, and I wondered if he might've drifted off when he finally raised his head. His eyes were clear as he blinked at me. "I need a shower. You need a shower. But we're doing this separately or I'll just want you to fuck me again. That was amazing."

I chose to believe him. Partners often told me that I was a competent lover—and I never tired of hearing that—but having Scott say it gave an extra layer of warmth that seeped into me.

He rolled off and padded out of the room and toward the bathroom.

I eyed the baby monitor, but the twins didn't make a peep. Then I did a quick survey of the bed. Most of the mess was on me, and we didn't have any noticeable wet spots. Good, one less thing to clean up. I removed the condom, knotted it, and dropped it into the trash can. Then I traced my finger lazily through the cum on my stomach. On a whim, I licked my finger. Generally, I was squeamish about stuff like that, but this felt right—just another way to connect to Scott.

"Hey."

A gentle hand on my shoulder nudged me.

I blinked.

And looked up into soft green eyes.

"You drifted off."

When I tried to rise, he put a hand on my shoulder to encourage me to stay in place. He couldn't hold me back if I wanted to get up, but I didn't want to get up. My limbs felt heavy and my mind was already fighting to return to sleep.

He applied a warm, wet washcloth to my belly, chest, and cock. The heat seeped into my skin. Into my muscles. Into my soul. No one had ever cared for me like this. Usually I was up and out the door before anything like this could happen.

Finally, he washed my hands, and when he was finished, he feathered a hand through my hair and kissed my forehead. "Rest, okay?"

"We were going to talk." The words seemed garbled as they came from my mouth.

Yet he smiled and cupped my cheek. "Tomorrow. We have all the time in the world."

Did we? As I slipped back into sleep, I doubted that statement. We didn't have all the time in the world. This conversation needed to take place now.

Five hours later, as we changed diapers and fed bottles to cranky babies, I despaired we'd ever have the conversation. And when we crawled back into bed, he curled against me and I held him like a lifeline.

Morning came with a brightness and lightness I hadn't

expected. Good sex always put me in the right frame of mind, but being awakened to a blow job was pretty fucking sweet.

I eyed the monitor for a moment, checked the time to check if the twins would be up shortly, then gave myself to the intense pleasure he was eliciting.

He tongued my slit as he swirled his tongue around the head of my cock. His warm, wet mouth enveloped me as he drew me farther. Then, as if that wasn't stimulation enough, he grasped my balls and rolled them gently in his hands.

This was a level of intimacy I wasn't accustomed to. Yet I found it to be something I could very much get used to.

Then, unexpectedly, he rubbed a lubed finger around my pucker.

Okay, that I hadn't seen coming. I didn't do this. I did the fingering, not the other way around. On the rare occasions I bottomed, I always prepped myself.

Yet, as he stuck that finger slowly into me, I tried to relax.

Probably helped that he continued to suck me.

He probed. He added a second finger. He scissored.

I fought the urge to ask him to stop. He would, in a heartbeat, but suddenly I wanted to know. Know what it was like to have someone touch me so intimately.

Then he crooked his fingers, found my prostate, and pressed gently.

My world came into sharp focus. As pleasure washed over me, I continued to give in to the sensations he was bombarding me with.

When he swallowed me down, I was a goner. "I'm coming."

He crooked his fingers again.

I flew. Right off the cliff face and down toward the ocean. I feared crashing, but he held me tight. And as I climaxed into him, he continued to suck.

Heat suffused my body as—

A screech I'd come to recognize as Alicia's resounded

through the monitor and filled our room with the discordant sound.

Scott withdrew his finger from my ass, and my cock fell from his mouth with an audible *pop*.

"I'll go." I was already pushing myself up.

"You just had an orgasm."

"And you need to get cleaned up." This time I succeeded in rising. "Once you're clean, you can join me because you know—"

The second wail came through the speaker. I adored Zayden, but when Alicia riled him up, he could be a holy terror as well. Both were capable of going from completely asleep to completely awake and cranky in a heartbeat. I'd witnessed Scott take long moments to even begin to crawl into consciousness. So obviously they didn't inherit his gentle method of rousing.

Or maybe they'd outgrow this *must be at a ten to get attention* phase. Hopefully they'd trust us to meet their needs without blowing a gasket every time.

I managed to pull on sleep pants before I padded over to their room.

Since Alicia's face was redder, I scooped her up first. I jiggled her as I ran my hand over Zayden's forehead.

Hot.

Oh, Jesus. How could they have caught something?

Right.

I winced.

Being out in a roomful of toddlers and children wouldn't help us. No, kids were germ factories—as I had known—and ours weren't likely to be immune.

Scott sauntered in and scooped up Zayden who, unlike his sister, immediately calmed.

"I think they might be sick."

Watching Scott's instinctual reaction to push the baby away would've been comical if it hadn't also been practical.

Also, likely too late.

He pressed the back of his hand to Zayden's forehead and winced. Then he repeated the action with Alicia. He cocked his head and frowned.

"She doesn't have one?"

"Nope. Perfectly cool."

"Maybe they're going to be staggered."

"And that only he was exposed? Highly unlikely, but I suppose…"

Gently, he inserted his index finger into his baby's mouth and swirled it around. Then he grinned. "A tooth."

"Huh?"

"The book says teething can cause a temperature. He doesn't appear to have nasal or chest congestion—he's not sneezing or coughing. I mean, there might be something else going on…or he might just be teething."

Alicia was finally bringing her cries down to a whimper.

Scott gently stuck his other finger in her mouth. "None yet, but it'll happen. Soon, according to the book."

I really needed to find time to read this book. Just the thought made me weary. Maybe they made an audiobook version I could listen to in the SUV? I'd have to look into that.

"Diapers then breakfast?" Personally, I was starving.

Scott nodded as he headed to the changing table.

Fifteen minutes later, I was cooking scrambled eggs while Scott managed a bit of oatmeal. He touched Zayden's forehead again. "I think it's a little better. I have a couple of teething rings in the freezer. Hopefully he'll be willing to chomp on that. But if he develops any worsening symptoms, I might text Dr. Bracken."

I stiffened at Hugh's name. The wrong response, I was sure. The doctor'd been unstintingly kind and helpful earlier in the week. I should've been grateful—not resentful that we'd needed his help at all. "We have a pediatrician in town. Dr. Coral Llewellyn. I'm certain she'd be willing to take on the twins as patients. I've consulted with her on a number of cases over the years."

Scott winced.

"What?"

"Only that you needed to consult a doctor."

I continued to cook the eggs. "Not all kids are raised in a loving and violence-free home." Not to mention the cases of sexual abuse. Fewer than I might've encountered in big cities with larger populations, but still more than I wanted to see.

That part of my job I tried to compartmentalize—to leave at work when I finished for the day.

But I didn't always succeed.

Scott cleared his throat. "Yeah, I'll call Dr. Llewellyn's office tomorrow and see if I can get an appointment after Christmas. Jesus, Christmas."

"I think it's Jesus Christ." Obviously he was able to leave behind some of his fundamentalist upbringing that he'd mentioned.

My family'd been religious as well. Every Sunday my mother'd trooped her three kids off to mass.

After her funeral, I never stepped into a church again.

No, that wasn't true. A young mother had taken refuge in one of the interdenominational churches here in Gaynor Beach. With her two daughters, she'd waited for the cops. When she refused to take the children to a hospital or a police station, I'd been called in. I'd helped find her a shelter in San Francisco—up near where her parents lived. They lived in a studio apartment and would've taken in the woman, but she wanted some modicum of independence. After having lived four years in a terrifyingly abusive marriage, she wanted to know she could stand on her own.

She'd sent me a Christmas card last month. The girls were in primary school and she was working as a receptionist at a dentist's office. They managed in a small apartment, but she had the independence she craved. The girls were happy and doing well.

My only frustration was her unwillingness to press charges. The husband had left Gaynor Beach, and I could only imagine what he was up to today. A good news/bad news story. Because in no way did I believe he wasn't abusing the next woman. And maybe he'd even had more kids he could hurt.

"Hey, you're going to burn the eggs."

I moved the pan off the burner and shut it off. I continued to stir the eggs so they wouldn't stick to the bottom of the pan.

Ugh. They'd be rubbery, but they were likely still edible.

Scott wrapped his arms around me, the powerful presence of his chest against my back.

I grasped his hands which were clasped tightly against my pecs. "I'm okay."

"Clearly." He laid his head against my shoulder blade. "You know you can talk about it, right? That communication goes both ways."

I turned in his arms. "I really am okay. But we need to eat or it'll get cold."

He held my gaze for a long beat before nodding. "While you feed that to the kids, why don't I cook up some sausages?"

"Sounds divine."

"Good thing you're not a vegetarian."

"Yeah, well, I should be…" And maybe some day I'd find a good source of protein beyond meat and aside from eggs. I eyed the twins. I was well-versed in overpopulation and the negative effects of factory farms. But, for now, I needed to get these little ones fed.

Scott blew on some egg to cool it while the twins watched in fascination. "I still think we should have a couple of things that are Christmassy. At least when they look at pictures, I want them to feel like we put in the effort."

I sighed. "Personally, I don't want to drag the kids out again."

"You're afraid they'll catch something."

"Well, something is going around."

"Something's always going around, and they won't have robust immune systems if they never get sick."

Personally, I thought that theory was nuts. Then I remembered my mother used to tell me how I ate dirt as a child and I grew up to be a big, strong, healthy boy.

The sound of the doorbell ringing pulled me from that instant of memory. Another dark place I didn't need to go.

Scott moved the pan of sausages to the back burner that was off. "I'll go."

I didn't even have a moment to argue. And really, what was the point? Scott was perfectly capable of answering his own door. Although the last time he'd done that had been me—

My breath caught. Because at the exact moment I remembered Scott'd had a guest earlier in the week, my father's voice carried into the house as he called my name.

How could I have forgotten?

CHAPTER 18

SCOTT

Somehow, in all the chaos of the hospital visit—and everything that'd happened since—I'd managed to completely forget about Anthony's father. Now, facing Mr. Rodrigues, I recollected Anthony's upset.

And things were going so well.

I still knew he wanted to talk, but I figured I could push that back again. The longer he stayed and things went well, the harder it'd be for him to extricate himself.

Right?

The man before me pointed a shaking finger. "I want to see my son."

I seriously considered lying. Something told me this guy didn't know what vehicle his son drove. And we hadn't left the house since yesterday, so he'd have no proof I even had Anthony in my house.

Yet, when a cold hand touched my shoulder, I knew the confrontation was about to happen.

I shifted, but didn't entirely step aside.

"What do you want, Carlos?"

The venom in my lover's voice caught me off-guard. Even

when he was at his angriest—which I admitted I hadn't seen often—he wasn't this frigid. Like Arctic cold.

"I want to talk to you."

"Well, I don't want to talk to you." Anthony grasped the door and tried to close it.

Stupidly, I reached out a hand.

He stopped his forward motion.

Our gazes clashed.

"You'll never know what he wants if you don't hear him out."

"I don't care what he wants." Those dark-brown eyes were granite-hard. "I don't want anything to do with him." He shot his father a venomous glare. "And he knows why."

Well, I didn't know why and, frankly, I was curious. I knew so little about Anthony—and I suspected this encounter could offer me insights I might never get. And I knew it wasn't any of my business. But I couldn't help myself. "Give him five minutes?"

"He doesn't deserve five seconds." Said through gritted teeth.

"You'll have to live with not knowing."

Something in Anthony's expression shifted. An eyebrow twitched. His jaw unclenched. "Fine." He pivoted to his father. "You have one minute."

"Can I come in?"

"Yes."

"No."

Anthony and I glanced at each other.

I was more hesitant than I was letting on—I wasn't sure what Carlos was capable of—but he appeared even frailer than before. I figured Anthony would ensure things didn't get out of hand. "I don't want my neighbors to observe this inter-action, and you shouldn't want that either. Let the man come in. One minute, as you said."

"The man is a murderer. I don't want him anywhere around our children."

Which was a reminder that I'd left them in the kitchen. Not such a bright idea.

"Go." His voice softened. "I'll let the man in—for one minute and by the front door—then he'll go. Or I'll kick his ass out myself."

I had no doubt of Anthony's ability to do exactly that. The older man was almost the same height, but didn't have the bulk. In fact, upon closer inspection, he appeared like a breath of wind could knock him over. Still, I couldn't leave the kids any longer. "Maybe listen to what he has to say? It might bring you peace." I said the words as quietly as possible.

Anthony met my gaze and, after a long moment, nodded.

Feeling somewhat relieved—and not really knowing why —I headed back to the kitchen.

Only to find Alicia reaching over to smoosh eggs into Zayden's hair.

And him grinning.

I sighed. We certainly never taught her that putting food in anyone's hair was a good idea. And I doubted Eliza had either. So where did these tendencies come from? We always seemed a step behind this child.

My daughter.

Our daughter?

Yeah, that felt right. She wasn't just my responsibility. I had help. Really good, reliable help. Anthony had my back. He'd make sure I didn't face this alone.

I wiggled my ass. And if last night was a preview of nights to come, we'd do okay in that department as well.

Anthony still wants to talk.

Why did that feel ominous? Maybe he wanted to talk about making our relationship more permanent. Maybe he wanted to suggest he move in full-time.

Maybe he's trying to find a way to extricate himself from me.

Nope, I didn't believe that. If he wanted out, he'd have found a way to do just that. He was a strong-willed individual. He didn't do anything he didn't want to. Although he was talking to his father at my urging. And, well, at work. But as long as he was an employee with a boss, he wouldn't have autonomy.

Which was why I liked being the boss.

"All right, young miss, we're going to clean you both up. Then I think we can play in your room—"

Anthony's voice came loudly. "I don't give a shit what you're trying to say. You've had your minute. Get the fuck out of our house."

The *our* gave me hope. The words tore at my heart.

I wet the washcloth and set about cleaning Zayden's hair. Since eggs appeared to be the only damage, I estimated we could get away without baths. Tonight, though, we'd have to make sure to do a thorough scrubbing.

"I don't give a fuck that you're dying. You're already dead to me. And hell, I'm not sure I even believe you."

Alicia's eyes widened at Anthony's raised voice.

The door slammed. The following silence resounded.

"Uh, Anthony, I could really use your help." I hoped this might distract him and pull him back into a happy place. On the other hand, what the fuck did I know about anything?

Anthony strode in.

"I was wondering if you could wash Alicia while I get Zayden set up in the bedroom."

For a moment, I thought he'd refuse. His face was set in stone, a look of anger radiating. Yet when he looked at the twins, he softened. "How did you get egg in your hair, my little angel?"

Alicia reached out her hand to him.

I gave him the washcloth as a protective shield. Fortunately his arms had a long reach, and he'd be able to evade her while he scrubbed the egg out of her hair. "Did you consider a bath?"

"Tonight for sure."

"Right, because God only knows what they'll get up to today."

We hadn't had a repeat of the shit incident from last week, but that didn't mean they couldn't get into plenty of other mischief.

"Son, you need to listen to me."

Carlos appeared at the kitchen window.

Jesus, had I not locked the back gate?

"No, I really don't." Anthony plastered on a smile, but I couldn't have missed his tone of voice.

"I *am* dying. It's why they released me early. I need a liver transplant—"

"You're not getting part of mine."

"I wasn't asking." The man wiped his brow. "I just wanted to let you know. Because of my criminal history, I'm not likely to make the transplant list—and my health is deteriorating."

"Whose fault is that?"

"Anthony." I hissed his name, hoping to knock some sense into him. Yes, his anger toward his father might be righteous —but the man was also dying. And now that I looked closely, I could see the yellow tinge to his tanned skin even through the window. His eyes didn't look right either.

"I have prayed to God for forgiveness for what I did."

"I hope he didn't give it." Anthony gently washed Alicia's hand, and she gave him a coy smile. This child was going to be hell on wheels.

"Maybe you could find it in your heart—"

"What about Mama's heart? Or Laura? Or Mickey? Didn't they deserve to live? And yet you took that away from them. Because of your selfishness."

Carlos hung his head. "I was an addict, Tony."

"Don't call me that. Don't ever call me that. That boy died

the night you crashed the car into a tractor trailer with my entire family on board. I still don't understand why you got to live, and they all had to die."

"For me to suffer as well." Carlos ran his hand through his hair. "Do you not think I wish I'd died as well? That it'd just been me and not them? Do you think I don't weep inside every night and every day?"

"No, frankly, I don't. You were always selfish and self-absorbed. Always blaming everyone else for your failings. You never took responsibility for anything." Anthony's eyes blazed with fury. "So you can just fuck right off. Go back to wherever you came from."

Something in Carlos's eyes died.

I watched it happen. The man's shoulders slumped, and he appeared to cave in on himself. Certainly this wasn't the man who fifteen minutes ago had stood at my door and demanded admittance.

"What do you want, Carlos?"

"You used to call me Papi"

"That was before you became a drug addict and tossed away all our money on your illegal pills. Mama worked two jobs to support the family—"

"I was injured." The man held out his hands. "And the doctors wouldn't treat me."

"So you decided to self-medicate." No missing the derision. Still Anthony turned to me. "He was so drugged the night of the crash that they suspected he passed out while behind the wheel. He wouldn't let Mama learn how to drive—"

"Your mother didn't want to learn." A weak protest at best.

Anthony straightened. "That's not what Laura said. Mama confided in her that you liked controlling her. Controlling all of us. You wanted me with you that night. But the school counselor insisted I attend career night. I wanted to be a doctor. Do you remember that? Did you even care?"

Carlos hung his head. "Of course I remember."

"Well, after they died, my grades slipped. I couldn't get into a science program so I couldn't get into med school. I got into a general arts program and started taking social work and psychology classes."

"And I'm so proud of you."

Anthony shot his father a glare. "A little too late for that." He let out a long exhalation. "Just go, all right? No one wants you here." He scooped Alicia into his arms and stalked into the hall and then into the twins' room.

The old man looked at me with Zayden. Actually, not that old. But downtrodden, to be sure.

"Maybe you'd better go." Obviously arguing any merits of giving his father a chance would be completely lost on Anthony. I knew his stubborn nature—had come up against it a time or two. When his mind was made up, changing it was near impossible. So I wasn't going to.

Carlos pulled a scrap of paper from his pocket and put it on our patio table. "In case he changes his mind. I'm staying in a local hotel."

I pulled Zayden into my arms. "Can you afford that?"

He shifted. "I've picked up a couple of odd jobs to help." He met my gaze. "I really don't have much time."

Until the money ran out or until his liver failed completely? Had it been the pills or was it something genetic? Part of me wanted to know, and part of me dreaded the answer.

Without another word, he left. He slunk away and I winced. After I heard the gate shut, I opened the sliding glass door. I pocketed the note and rounded the corner so I could lock the latch in place. I went back into the kitchen, feeling somewhat reassured.

Although maybe I didn't have the right to be. I shouldn't

have pushed Anthony to deal with his father. If the shoe had been on the other foot, and my father had shown up dying, would I have afforded him the same privilege? And he hadn't killed most of my family. It'd been an accident, but that didn't excuse what the man'd done or the result of his actions. Anthony had a right to be angry, and I should've been more supportive.

Moments later, he appeared. "I think we should take them out to play in the backyard—the fresh air will do them good."

And that plan had the added bonus that we wouldn't be able to hear the doorbell if some wayward straggler showed up again. I couldn't imagine who else might show up on a Sunday morning, but I didn't dare tempt fate.

"Okay, we agreed to buy a few Christmas things. I'm quite sure we can make it a family outing."

Anthony eyed the twins. "Uh, no. You choose whether you go or I go, but we're not piling the kids into the car seats and then into the stroller and braving the Christmas rush."

Crap. I kept forgetting we were four days away from Christmas. "Uh, do you want turkey?"

"My mama used to make tamales." Then, as if realizing how much personal information he'd just imparted to me, he pressed his lips shut. After a moment, he continued. "Turkey's fine."

"Well, I'm not a fan of turkey—never have been. Too many memories of the farm. Usually I do a burger or some other quick meal from a fast-food restaurant. But I like the idea of starting a tradition. Or continuing one of your mother's." *Not that I have any guarantee he'll be around next year.* Still, I had to try. "Do you want me to try cooking them…?" I wasn't a terrible cook, but I wasn't the best either.

"Mama taught me." He brushed a kiss to the crown of Alicia's head. "She believed in equality—she insisted her boys know how to cook and that her daughter know how to fix things around the house. For all the good it did."

"Will you tell me about them?"

His eyes were bleak. "Not today. Today…" He glanced toward the door. "I'm too raw."

As honest a statement as he'd ever made to me.

"Then yes, let's just go play outside." I couldn't think of anything dangerous in my backyard. My garden was mostly done for the year, and all the fruit had fallen or been picked from the trees. I had a bird of paradise plant that was particularly prickly, but I'd keep the kids well away from that.

We were still early enough in the day that I didn't worry about sunscreen or hats. We also had plenty of shade.

While Alicia insisted on exploring the backyard while crawling backward, Zayden was dedicated to pulling himself up. He grasped onto a patio chair and wouldn't give up. I sat behind him while Anthony followed Alicia who covered significant ground. That she hadn't figured out how to move in a forward direction was of no impediment for her. She did enjoy some of the flowers, and Anthony carefully guided her through how to touch them without shoving each into her mouth.

"We should get a sandbox." I glanced around. "Or a play set or something."

"There's a playground a block from here."

Anthony wiped his brow with his forearm and I was treated to a nice bulging of the muscles beneath his T-shirt. "True. I never think of that. I should get in the habit of going. Maybe I'll meet some other parents." I almost suggested I might meet other single parents, but I realized that sounded wrong. I wasn't a single parent. Anthony stood six feet away from me, watching my daughter with hawk-like intensity.

Not lost on me was the fact he never checked his phone. He had it near him—likely in case he was called into work—but his attention never wavered. Had I ever seen him check it, aside from noting the time? I didn't think so. And I'd never been an obsessive phone watcher either. I was set up to receive notifications, but only texts and calls actually made noise.

I'd decided early on that everything else could wait until I was ready. Mikayla handled the social media for the library, and that was my only genuine concern. I checked it regularly, but my employee was reliable. Perhaps a little cheeky at times —but always well within the bounds of propriety.

"They're going to need baths before lunch."

Anthony's dry observation wasn't wrong. Both twins were covered in dust and dirt. We hadn't had rain for a while, so it could've been much worse, but we still faced two messy kids.

"After lunch, which of us is doing the shopping?"

"Would you mind? I have some paperwork from my other job that I need to tend to. I was hoping to do that while they sleep."

"Sure. You'll have to prepare a list for me—I have no idea what goes in tamales."

"I can do that." A wistful expression crossed his face, and he opened his mouth to speak.

As much as I wanted to push, he'd told me he needed space. If anyone understood family dynamics, it was me.

Anthony eyed the sky. "We might want to move them inside. The sun's getting high in the sky." He yanked out his phone and checked the time. "Or we slather them in sunscreen."

"I think we've had enough adventures for one day." I rose, then pulled Zayden into my arms.

He pounded me with his little fists.

"You can keep trying to stand up once we're in the house. You can do it while in the crib, so I have faith you'll figure out how to do it elsewhere." I eyed his clothes. "Well, after you've had a bath and are in fresh clothes, that is."

"I'll put in a load of laundry."

I offered a grateful smile to Anthony. "Don't forget to use the baby detergent. A mother came in one day and was adamant about using baby soap. Apparently, she hadn't realized soap choice made a difference, and her baby had a reaction to the harsh detergent she used for her husband's uniform. He's a mechanic, so she needed something strong that fought grease. At the time I thought she was giving me way too much information. Now, I'm glad she did." I wracked my brains for all the other times parents had taken the time to impart knowledge to me. Most of it, I'd shoved to the recesses of my mind. Sure, I was going to be a parent. Likely. Eventually. Certainly not mere weeks after the advice had been offered.

We carried our respective babies into the house and headed for the bathroom. By now, we had the routine down pat, and within a short period of time, we had two clean kids.

How was I supposed to do this on my own? When Anthony was at work and I took the twins to the park or even just played with them outside? I supposed a wipe down would be good enough. Still, I needed to find a book specifically about raising twins. I tried to be careful that each child had equal time with both adults. I didn't want one to feel left out. But kids, like adults, had preferences. And, generally, Alicia fussed less when Anthony held her. For which I was eternally grateful—but I also worried.

We settled the twins in the living room, and I sat with them on the floor while Anthony pulled out his laptop and sat at the dining room table. He'd said he wanted to work this afternoon while I was shopping. Perhaps he was getting an early start? Or maybe he had more work than he was letting on. That thought sobered. He'd mentioned a second job. And he already put in serious hours at Child Protective Services. He'd need downtime. Time when I wasn't counting on him to do things for me. That meant me trying to be more independent.

God, how did people navigate these treacherous waters? I wanted him to know we needed him, but I didn't want him to feel obliged to help. I needed to take my cues from him. And if I was good at that sort of thing, then I wouldn't be so panicked now. In truth, my relationships didn't exist at this depth. I kept things superficial—the easiest way to protect my heart.

I'd thought I had a strong bond with Eliza, but after Mark started giving her a hard time about hanging out with me, she backed away from me. She chose him.

I eyed the babies. And she'd chosen Mark over her own flesh and blood. I didn't suppose I'd ever understand. If it came down to Anthony or the twins? Wasn't even a close competition. I was coming to care deeply for Anthony. Hell, if I could admit it to myself, I was halfway in love with the man. But I'd choose Zayden and Alicia every time. Over him. Over anyone. And I knew, deep in my heart, nothing would ever change that.

"Lunchtime." Anthony shut his laptop. "Why don't I whip us up some grilled cheese? You can feed the darlings. Tomato soup sound good?" He came around the table and scooped Zayden into his arms and swung him around.

The baby squealed in delight.

His words pulled me from my introspection.

He caught my gaze.

I offered up a smile. Then I swung Alicia into my arms and held her above my head as well.

She giggled.

Yeah, everything was going to be okay.

CHAPTER 19

ANTHONY

I'D SNAGGED THE PIECE OF PAPER MY FATHER LEFT BEHIND IN THE wake of his monumental visit that Scott had laid quietly on the counter. I'd shoved it into my pocket—resolving to shred it as soon as I could. Yet all the while knowing I wasn't likely to. Scott's shock at my vehemence had given me pause but, in the end, I knew I'd done the right thing by sending the bastard on his way.

If he'd been a good man—a good father and husband—before the crash, then maybe I would've been understanding. And I'd studied the effects of addiction. Had tried to be empathetic when working with addicts.

To my everlasting shame, I'd failed.

Patricia Peterson.

Oscar Collins and Dr. Hugh Bracken maintained that if I hadn't ridden her so hard, she never would've started using again. And if she hadn't started using again, she wouldn't have overdosed. In their minds, I was responsible for the woman's death. For the orphaning of her beloved daughter. A daughter who now had two loving parents. The men were fierce in both their love for each other and their absolute caring for little Marilee. So, despite everything, things had somewhat worked out. Except Marilee's mother was dead, and nothing would ever change that. She'd grow up knowing she wasn't the same as the other kids. Likely, if I knew Hugh and Oscar, they'd tell her—when she was older—what happened.

Would she blame me too?

My father.

He'd sworn a million times he'd stop using the pills. Yet he never had. But he'd fooled my mother. She never would've gotten in that car with him—never would have risked her children. A huge part of me lamented her loss. An equal part of me was glad she died, because if she'd lived and one or both of my siblings had died, it would've destroyed her. As it was, I faced pain every day from having lost the three most-important people in my life.

I pulled into the driveway at home.

Home.

Well, Scott's home.

We still hadn't managed to have *the* conversation.

He knew.

Every time I tried to broach the subject, he'd come up with an excuse. Or, better yet, he'd initiate some kind of physical intimacy. Despite having two children under the age of one and me working a full-time job, we'd managed to have sex three more times, and he'd given me two more blow jobs.

And had ordered me to give him one.

Which I totally didn't mind.

But while my mouth was full of his cock and, I had three fingers up his ass, we weren't getting a lot of discussion going.

I'd never taken a submissive role—and I wasn't entirely taking one now—but I also wasn't really in charge of the physical aspects of our relationship.

In the bedroom, at least.

Out of it? I initiated little touches. Caresses. Kisses. Hugs.

Anything to show him how I felt. Because, damn it, I was falling for him. In less than two weeks, I was ready to admit defeat and ask if I could move in. Or, better yet, if we could combine forces and get a bigger house. My own was nice, but about the same size as this one. And there were fancier neighborhoods than this one, although I was becoming enamored of this location. Status was starting to mean a lot less to me. That being said, a second bathroom would be amazing. But my head screamed this was all too soon. That he'd go running for the hills if I made any kind of pronouncement. Or, worse yet, send me away. My heart would be torn to shreds—I was certain of it. And not just because of how I felt about him.

Alicia and Zayden?

My heart also belonged to them. In my mind, I used to think about kids in the abstract and ponder having them in the future. But that'd never solidified. Until this past week when I realized I'd do anything to protect these two. Hell, these three. The three humans just beyond the front door were my reason for being. My reason for living.

And wasn't that a mind fuck?

The front door opened, and Scott poked his head outside. He waved.

How long had I been sitting in the SUV? Obviously too long. I hopped out and grabbed both my messenger bag and my suitcase. I'd emptied it again yesterday and had run home on my lunch break to fill it again.

Scott's eyes lit when he spotted it. "I made some more room in our closet for your stuff."

Then he snagged Alicia who was desperately trying to crawl through his legs.

Forward.

"Hey." I moved quickly to swoop her up into my arms. "I'm so proud of you. Crawling the right way."

Scott snagged my abandoned suitcase. "There is no *wrong* way. There's a *better* way."

His admonition held no heat. But he'd made his point effectively—I needed to watch how I phrased things with the kids. Hell, with everyone. Words had consequences—which I, more than most, knew.

"Hey, kiddo."

Zayden, apparently having decided he didn't want to be left out, was crawling through the front door as well, but Scott snagged him.

These two were endlessly fascinated with doors.

Scott and I were definitely going to need a lock on ours before too long.

Well, admittedly the twins wouldn't be tall enough to reach the handle for some time.

And how long are you sticking around for?

I eyed Scott, trying to read something in his expression that might give me a clue as to what he was thinking.

All I saw was the affable guy who managed to smile through everything. Those two panic attacks from that first day felt miles away. Far in the past. I kept watching for signs of stress and anxiety, but I didn't see any that concerned me. Well, aside from standard parental stress about things. He worried he would make a mistake and fuck up the kids forever. He worried they might be too reliant on him and claimed he'd be happy when they went to day care and met other kids. Oh, and something about their college fund. I'd admit to letting that one wash over me.

I leaned in for a kiss.

He leaned toward me and our mouths brushed.

Alicia snagged my beard and tugged.

Zayden made a grab for Scott's glasses.

Yeah, pretty much as it always was.

And I wouldn't have changed it for anything.

Scott winked. "I have plans for us tonight."

My libido kicked up a notch. Completely inappropriate—

and terrible timing given the company we kept—but that was likely his intention. He liked to tease. He liked to torment.

Then he liked to make me come like a fucking freight train.

An electric SUV glided up and parked in front of the house.

I met Scott's gaze, and he shrugged

We turned to find Dr. Hugh Bracken stepping out of his vehicle.

When he spotted us, he held up a finger. Then he opened the back driver's side door, slid something out, and then slammed the door. He came around the vehicle and crossed the lawn to get to us. He had a tattered rucksack slung over his shoulder. The thing looked a little worse for wear.

Alicia clapped when she spotted him—likely thinking *here's a new human I can manipulate*. Ah, she was predictable.

Hugh grinned. He appeared to consider holding out his hand to shake then, realizing we both held squirming bundles, relaxed. "Hello little one." He held his hand out.

Slowly, I eased her toward him.

He touched her forehead. "I understand you passed the magnet."

Huh? Oh, right, someone at the hospital had called to follow up with us. And the twins were seeing Dr. Llewellyn in the new year.

"She did." Scott offered a grin. "You came all this way? Talk about a house call."

Clearly he was joking, but I didn't miss the vague unease.

Hugh offered a smile while looking over Zayden.

Nothing to see. Move along.

But I wouldn't say that. He'd obviously come for some purpose, and I was damn curious to know what it was.

He met my gaze, and the smile slipped. "Is there some place we can talk? Privately?"

I gazed at Scott. Was there anything I didn't want him to

hear? Well, more recriminations about somehow being responsible for Hugh's daughter's death would be one. And this might involve some kind of patient confidentiality. But I wasn't sure I'd be comfortable alone with the doctor. Something just didn't feel right—

"It's about your father."

I met compassionate blue eyes, and I knew. My chest constricted, but I managed to say, "He can hear it. We don't have secrets."

Hugh's gaze went between the two of us. Then he offered a brief smile. "May I come in? This story's going to take a few minutes."

"Really, that's not necessary. Obviously the man's dead. Or you're here to convince me to donate part of my liver, which I won't—"

He held up his hand.

I halted.

"Your father passed this afternoon. I...made it as comfortable as I could...but it wasn't a painless death."

"No less than he deserved." My tone bit, but I didn't give a shit. Was this guy here to give me grief? To heap on guilt? If so, he could just shove the fuck off and leave me to my peace.

"Dr. Bracken, why don't you step inside?" Scott nudged me, indicating the twins. "I can make you a coffee while you talk to Anthony."

"Don't you leave me alone," I muttered under my breath.

"I'm just coming off a long shift and want to sleep before midnight." Hugh offered a genial smile. "But I'll take a glass of water if you have it."

"Ice?"

Trust Scott to be nice. Of course we had water. And trust Hugh to be so accommodating. I was going to wind up looking like an asshole if I wasn't careful.

"Ice is perfect."

Another quick grin. Any trace of the man who'd chewed

me out and nearly gotten me fired just last year was completely gone. Had he forgiven me?

Have I forgiven myself?

As we entered the house, my resolve wavered. In hindsight, I could see how my treatment of Patricia, Hugh's daughter, had led to her stress. Based on my dealings with my father—who always relapsed—I'd decided Patricia was going to do the same, and that taking her daughter away from her was the only safe thing to do.

Once an addict, always an addict.

Except Oscar—Patricia's friend and Hugh's husband—had been clean for years. Had sworn he'd never use again. And, against my rational mind, I believed him.

Hugh followed Scott, while I brought up the rear with Alicia and my suitcase. I dropped it near the front hall closet and moved into the living room. I deposited Alicia on the floor and indicated Hugh could sit on a chair. While he did that, I headed to the kitchen.

Scott was valiantly trying to get ice into a glass while Zayden continued to grab for his glasses.

I scooped the baby into my arms. "We're going to have to have a conversation about what *no* means."

"Well, you can try." Scott eyed his son. "We're not doing well with that word today."

"Do I want to know?"

He ran water from the tap and filled three glasses. "No, you probably don't. But the damage wasn't permanent, so we'll survive." He offered up a smile, but I caught the hint of strain. Strain that hadn't been there before Hugh arrived. So, because of our guest or because of something else?

I kept telling myself I should feel something. My father was dead. And as we went back into the living room, I struggled to figure out what I was feeling. I placed Zayden on the floor with Alicia, and he immediately grabbed his yellow stuffed bear. She played with a puzzle piece. Not putting it in the puzzle, of course, but just gnawing on it. I made a note to ask Scott about whether she was teething as well.

Scott offered a glass to Hugh then sat on the couch and patted the spot next to him.

I sat.

He grabbed my hand.

I clung to him.

Hugh took a sip, put the glass on a coaster on a side table, and snagged the rucksack at his feet. He rose and brought it over to me. Then, as if seeing I wasn't going to take it, he placed it at my feet. He returned to his seat and took another sip of water. "I was the attending physician in the emergency room yesterday."

"Yeah, I figured."

"The ambulance brought your father in." He shifted. "He'd been staying at a local hotel. When he didn't pay his bill, security opened the door. They found him in bed and unable to move. They called an ambulance."

"Which hotel?" I'd have to go and settle the bill. More things to worry about.

Hugh named one I recognized. Then he continued.

"He presented with chills, fever, and other signs of an infection as well as some cognitive impairment. I was quickly able to ascertain an advanced case of cirrhosis and ran blood tests. They indicated spontaneous bacterial peritonitis. Despite his situation, I wanted to get his treatment started immediately. He refused."

My breath caught. "You said he showed signs of cognitive impairment. You could have overridden his refusal."

Hugh slowly tilted his head. "Yes, I could have. It would've been a battle. But, in his paperwork we found, in his possession, a DNR. Do not resuscitate. He was very clear with what he wanted—no medical intervention. None. That goes against every instinct a physician has—especially when there's treatment available. But I could see his point. He was dying. Even a liver transplant wouldn't have been possible, given the advanced nature of the illness."

A small measure of guilt lifted. Guilt I hadn't even known was there.

"Maybe, months ago, it might've been a possibility. But he was too far gone, and he knew it. He said he didn't want treatment, and I had to abide by his wishes." He met my gaze. "I did implore him to let me call you. I said that no matter the circumstances, you had a right to know. A right to decide whether or not you wanted to be there."

Part of me felt gratitude he'd thought of me at all and part of me railed at him for not making the phone call. It should've been my choice.

"He asked me not to. He said he'd caused enough grief to last you a lifetime and the last thing he wanted was for you to suffer more. I waged an internal battle on that score, but he was my patient and I had to respect his wishes." He indicated the bag. "He asked me to give that to you. And to tell you how truly sorry he was."

"Did he tell you what he did?"

Hugh nodded. "He came in last night. I…was supposed to be off in the morning but…I knew his time was short and I didn't want to leave him alone. We have a great staff, but assigning him someone might've been rough for them."

"So you did it yourself."

"I'll never assign to someone a task I wouldn't take on myself."

His sharp eyes flashed, and I had no doubt of his sincerity.

"He didn't have long. Soon after he arrived, he slipped into a coma, and after a long time, he drew his final breath."

Scott sniffed and his grip on my hand tightened.

I, on the other hand, felt weirdly disconnected. Like Hugh was relaying a story about just another patient. Not about my father. A man who'd loomed large in my life, even after he went to prison. A man who hadn't been particularly nice—even before the addiction. A man I both loved and hated.

A man who no longer walked the earth.

An empty void opened within me. I didn't know if I'd feel grief at a later point, but right now I was just numb.

"Thank you." Scott's words were barely above a whisper. "I appreciate that you didn't have to stay, but that you chose to."

Hugh's smile was tinged with sadness. "I rarely had time in my old job to spend with patients. When you're in a war zone or some kind of catastrophe, you treat and then you move on because there are ten more people who need your attention. When I first came to Gaynor Beach, I wasn't certain I'd adjust to the slower pace. I mean, we still get car crashes, heart attacks, strokes, and drownings. But it's rare for me to have more than a couple emergent cases at once—I can take the time to give proper care to my patients and not just rush through the triaged ones. A hospital ER is not where most people would choose to draw their last breath, but I try to make it as comfortable as possible." His attention pivoted to me. "His passing was peaceful. That's all any of us can ask."

A day ago, I would've wished a horrible and painful death upon the man who'd caused the death of the three people I loved most in the world. But somehow things had shifted. Now that he was really gone, I could take a measure of comfort that he went quietly.

I squeezed Scott's hand and met the doctor's gaze. "I would invite you to stay—"

He held out his hand. "Oscar's been cooking up a storm to give Miss Agnes a break, and his family's coming down from Los Angeles tomorrow—all seven of them. Organized chaos, is how I describe Collins family gatherings." He grinned. "And I love it. I was an only child—now I'm surrounded."

Like I'd been as a child. I glanced around at Scott and the babies, who still sat and played. Make that, like I was now.

We three rose, and I walked Hugh to the door while Scott crouched to check on the twins. When we got to the door, Hugh offered me his hand.

I shook it.

"The morgue is waiting for instructions. Your father said he wanted to be cremated. If you choose not to be involved, that's up to you."

"I'll…call them later today. I know a funeral home and… I'll make arrangements."

"I thought you would. I told them to expect your call."

My initial reaction was anger, but I tempered it. He had every right to believe the worst in me, yet, at every turn today, he'd given me the benefit of the doubt. Had fought for me. Had ensured a man he didn't know had a dignified end. "I hope you have a great Christmas. My best to you and your family."

He nodded. "And Lacy's looking forward to coming over to help more. Just make certain she doesn't run roughshod over you. And she has to attend school."

"I'll make sure. Has she been coming over?"

Hugh tilted his head. "Just about every day. For a few hours." Realization dawned and his eyes widened. "You didn't know."

I rolled my eyes. "I might've wondered how Scott managed to keep the kids wrangled and put delicious food on the table every night."

At the same time, we both said, "Lacy."

My guest offered one more smile and headed to his SUV.

I watched him get in and drive away.

A long time passed before I went back inside.

CHAPTER 20

SCOTT

THE RUCKSACK HUGH'D DELIVERED SAT UNTOUCHED—IT WAS THE elephant in the room and since Anthony ignored it, so did I. We ate the spaghetti I'd made. Well, that Lacy'd made. I'd caught Hugh telling Anthony my secret. Which shouldn't have been a secret, but I hadn't wanted him worrying about things.

Lacy, ditching school with Hugh's permission, gave me a couple of hours a day as well as child-rearing tips I couldn't get from books or blogs. This hadn't been on the schedule. And the twins adored her, so that said something.

Even Crumpet was less grumpy when she was around—going so far as to make several appearances when she arrived. I figured his deigning to share his presence was because the holy terrors who were obsessed with him were too busy with Lacy to notice him. Overall, my guy was doing okay.

In fact, when taken as a whole, we were doing okay. I was looking forward to getting the twins into day care. We'd met a few other kids in the park, but mine seemed to shy away from strangers and only played with each other. Made me wonder how much socializing Eliza'd done with them. Or maybe they stuck close to each other because of the trauma of being re-homed.

Jesus, like you'd re-home an animal.

My anger against Eliza was building with each passing day. I thought it'd ebb, but it hadn't. She had these two miraculous and amazing children, and she threw them over for the asshole husband Mark. Who did that? She could've come to me. I would've protected her and taken care of the babies.

Where was she, on this Christmas Eve? Regretting her choices, or celebrating? Thinking about her babies, or putting them right out of her mind so she didn't have to think about the monumental clusterfuck she'd dropped on my lap?

When Anthony first arrived with the babies, I'd had sympathy for my friend. Now, I had very little.

Three bedtime stories did the trick and soon the little ones were in la-la land.

"Thank God they don't understand the significance of tomorrow." I eyed their bedroom door as we headed back to the living room. "I doubt they'd have been willing to go to sleep."

Anthony shrugged. "Maybe next year?"

"Lacy said Marilee's still too young to grasp the whole concept. That being said, she picks up on other people's energy." I grinned. "Lacy showed me a picture of Oscar holding her while he wore a Santa's hat. So cute."

My companion offered a measured smile. "I suppose we should do something."

I grinned and headed to the front hall closet. Carefully, I yanked down the box I'd stowed. I almost lost my balance, but he was there to steady me.

"Watch out."

The admonishment washed over me and was gone as I watched his face when he saw what my box contained.

He met my gaze and frowned. "I thought we agreed we weren't going to go overboard."

"Well…yeah…" I eyed the mountain of presents. "Okay, except I was helping a woman out. They have four older boys, but she kept hoping for a girl. The doctors did an ultrasound with this latest pregnancy and discovered she was having a girl. So she went out and bought toys and clothes and all kinds of things." My heart lurched as I winced. "The next ultrasound found an abnormality. Like, life-ending." I swallowed hard. "They terminated the pregnancy—they didn't really have a choice—and the woman decided four boys was fine." I met Anthony's gaze. "She wanted all the baby toys and everything else out of the house. Immediately. This was part of her grieving process.

"She approached me. She'd heard about the twins through the grapevine and somehow deduced we didn't have a lot of stuff. She donated the infant clothes to a charity, but brought everything else here. I mean, everything her kids used practically from birth until age five. I have six boxes in the garage—one for each year. Now, we've only got boy's clothes, but I'm not big on gender stereotypes. But if Alicia wants pink and frilly, then we'll get her pink and frilly. Or if Zayden does. The point is…" I drew breath.

Anthony placed his finger against my lips. "The point is that you overcame your dislike of accepting help to do a good thing that helped someone and will benefit our children."

"Uh, yeah."

He leaned over to kiss me. "And I'm thrilled. I just…" He eyed the presents. "We haven't discussed finances. I don't know what yours are like."

"And I don't know what yours are like." I tried to read his expression. Normally, he vacillated between open and guarded. Tonight, since Hugh's visit, his walls had been up. Understandably, of course. Except I wanted to help him and I didn't know how.

"We really need to have a conversation."

Ugh. The words I'd dreaded all week.

227

Instead of answering him, I moved the box to the corner where I'd set up a fake tree on an immovable stand where little hands couldn't reach it. Not that they hadn't tried. Zayden was now able to pull himself up, and Alicia eyed him with a combination of envy and suspicion. I doubted she was far behind.

"If I put these out, how long do you figure before the kids tear into them?"

Anthony cocked his head. "Well, if they've never seen a wrapped gift, they might not initially know what do to. Once they've figured it out? I still think they're too small...but with Alicia, who the hell knows?"

His words brought a smile to my lips. "Yes, she's damn curious about everything." Still, I laid out the presents. In a moment of rational thought, I put Anthony's up and under the tree. I caught his curious glance, but he said nothing.

I'd planned a great seduction—after the kids were tucked in bed—but that didn't feel appropriate. I eyed the rucksack Hugh had brought, still untouched. Would talking about Anthony's father be preferable to talking about us, or was I better off doing neither? "*It's a Wonderful Life* is on the television. That's one of my favorite movies."

"I haven't seen it."

His words took a moment to register, as he still appeared distracted. "Oh, my God. It's such a great movie. We have to watch it." I snagged the remote, but stopped when he held up his hand.

"Not tonight."

Fair enough.

"Do you want to just go to bed? The kids'll be up in a few hours, and we should grab some sleep while we can."

He ran his hands through his hair. Tired eyes gazed at me. "Yeah, that sounds good."

Gingerly, I indicated the rucksack.

"Yeah." He snagged it. "The twins would likely get into

it." He moved to the front-hall closet, tucked it inside next to the abandoned suitcase, and closed the door. Then he held out his hand to me.

I took it and let him guide me to the bathroom door.

He pulled me in close and nuzzled my neck. "One day I want to live where we have two bathrooms. But for now, why don't you go first while I get the bedroom ready?"

He'd provided a lot for me to unpack in those two sentences. And as I headed into the bathroom, I contemplated them.

He wanted to live in a house with two bathrooms. Obviously so he and his partner could each get ready for bed without tripping over each other. Or maybe so the kids would have a separate one from the adults.

And did he want to live in that house with me? With the twins? If we combined our incomes, could we afford a bigger place? I was kind of attached to this place—I liked the coziness. Could we replicate that? Or, with truly pie-in-the-sky thinking…could we add a bathroom to this home? Extend one part of the house into the backyard and add a second bathroom and maybe a playroom for the twins?

Fanciful.

He'd implied he was tired of sharing a bathroom. I shouldn't be combining our lives just yet.

And, as I brushed my teeth, I remembered his comment about getting our bedroom *ready*. Well, I'd laid out fresh sheets and done a sweep, so the room was already clean. I even managed a load of laundry and put everything away before Lacy'd headed home.

The girl was a godsend. I'd bought her a copy of a fantasy series in hardcover as a gift. I wasn't sure if I should've chosen a gift card, but her enthusiasm was genuine.

She promised to read the books and get back to me.

I suspected she'd do just that.

I exited the bathroom to find Anthony waiting. He gave

me a hard kiss before swatting my ass and directing me to our bedroom.

The bed was turned down and a chocolate orange sat on my pillow.

I adored those and was absurdly touched by the little gesture. I put it on my nightstand, revealing the three condoms tucked underneath the orange.

I paused.

My lover'd had a big shock tonight. No matter his relationship with his father, losing the man had to hurt. And so much remained unresolved. That made me laugh because for more than a week I'd been trying to avoid talking. Now that I was ready, he was letting me know it wasn't on the agenda.

We need to get our shit straight.

Except…maybe not tonight.

I pulled back the covers and crawled into bed. Eyeing the small pile of condoms I'd moved to my nightstand, I contemplated. Generally, I wasn't a top. I might dominate in my relationships, but I preferred to be penetrated rather than doing the penetration.

Tonight, though, I felt different about it.

If Anthony wanted to have sex tonight, who was I to deny him?

Tomorrow, however, we were going to talk. I needed to know where we stood once and for all. I wasn't going to push either issue—but I was going to make it clear that talking was pretty critical to the success of this relationship going forward.

If I even have one…

Well, there was that notion.

No, goddammit, I wasn't going to think that way. He could've walked out at any point in the last twelve days.

He hadn't.

In fact, he could've used his father's death as an excuse to need space.

He'd left condoms where I could find them.

The shower turned off.

I snagged my cock and stroked it in just *that* way. If there was one thing I was proficient with, it was giving myself a hand job. With my other hand, I grazed my balls.

A drop of precum leaked.

When I heard the bathroom door open, I snagged the condom.

He always checked the twins before coming to bed and, with perfect timing, I tossed the wrapper over the side of the bed and was able to present him with my sheathed cock when he entered our bedroom.

His eyes widened.

Okay, clearly not what he'd expected.

But would he be game?

He let the towel drop, and he offered a tentative smile.

I held open my arms.

He slid into bed and allowed me to pull him into an embrace.

Affection flowed from me. Caring flowed around me. Love flowed through me. As much as I could tell myself a million times that it was too soon to make such a pronouncement—even if only to myself—I knew in my heart this was the truth.

I wasn't sure what to expect. Maybe making love after today was a bad idea. Or maybe I could take his mind off things. Or maybe we could find a way to solidify our bond— that I could tell him without words how much he meant to me. And given I worked with words all day, the fact I couldn't find them to share irritated me. Made me question my feelings. Except, after coming from a repressed household where words of love were never spoken, perhaps it was no surprise being able to express them was proving challenging. I'd tried out words of affection on Eliza—letting her know how much I appreciated her friendship. Mere months later, she'd picked Mark over me.

And now was so *not* the time.

Anthony clung to me, and I offered up what comfort I could. My erection was starting to wane. Should I just remove the condom and postpone?

Just as I had the thought, Anthony nuzzled my neck. Not a cuddle nuzzle. No, a nuzzle with the scraping of beard. A nuzzle with an inhalation—as if he wanted to imprint my scent upon him.

He adjusted so our bodies came flush, and he thrust his pelvis against mine.

Okay, so his impressive erection was really the only thing that mattered in that moment. Well, and my responding one.

He brought his mouth to mine, and the kiss was languid. Soft. Sweet.

"I want to make love tonight."

What had we been doing every night? Maybe he'd only seen that as fucking. And that realization might've hurt, except I was ready to make him mine. To claim him. I could count on one hand the number of times I'd topped, but tonight felt like it had to be one of those times.

I sucked on his earlobe. "Have you ever bottomed before?"

"Yeah, a couple of times." He met my gaze. "I don't like the lack of control."

"Then you call the shots." Simple. Straightforward. Easy to do. I'd gladly hand over the reins—if that'd make him comfortable.

He shook his head. "No, I don't mind being bossed around now and then."

Since I'd been a bossy bottom for most of my adult life, this worked for me.

Having some control—especially after having had none during my childhood—was important to me.

He drew his hand down my side to my hip. "I do want you in me."

I saw sincerity in his dark-brown eyes. "Okay, then. On your back?"

Slowly, he nodded. He rolled onto his back, but faltered with what to do with his legs.

I leaned over to snag the ever-present lube. Despite having two babies, we'd managed a fair amount of sex over the last few days. I said a silent thank you to my helper who came by every day. But I couldn't rely on her forever—at some point I was going to have to stand on my own two feet. Hopefully with this man by my side.

But that was up to him.

Crouching between his legs, I encouraged him to move them up and out of the way, exposing his hole.

Uncertainty flashed in his eyes.

I held myself still.

He nodded for me to continue.

I coated my fingers with lube.

His cock bobbed up toward his stomach.

My insides clenched and my own cock continued to throb.

I gently circled my fingers around his rim, only increasing the depth by a millimeter each time.

"Oh, for God's sake, just get it over with."

My amusement warred with just a touch of concern. Was he encouraging me because he really wanted this, or because he was so over this? I eased a finger in.

He sucked in his breath. Then he closed his eyes.

"Please open your eyes."

At my entreaty, he complied.

"I need to see you—how you're feeling and how this is affecting you." I still worried if we were doing the right thing. On the one hand, he'd had plenty of off-ramps. On the other hand, I *had* donned a condom before he came in—so my wishes were clear. I just hoped that hadn't superseded his.

"I'm okay." His eyes shone. "I want this."

Believing him, I eased a second finger inside.

He clenched around me.

I twisted and scissored. I thrust in and out. I did everything I could to acclimate him to the intrusion. Then I twisted my wrist and hit his prostate.

A tremor shot through him—the good kind, as far as I could tell.

His cock leaked a drop of precum.

I moved to lick it. I would've been happy to give him a blow job, but I didn't want to stop our rhythm. "Pull your knees up and out of the way."

He complied.

After taking one long last look, I positioned myself at his entrance. Slowly, I pushed in.

"Oh, for God's sake, just fuck me already."

No missing his exasperation. Still, I didn't feel like obeying. I took my time, gradually easing in and back. Never pulling all the way out, but coming pretty darn close.

He wrapped his legs around my waist and dug his heels into my hips.

I bottomed out.

Still our gazes held.

He nodded.

From there, things progressed as we engaged in a ritual that came as naturally to us as breathing. This feeling—this connection—carried all the way from the top of my head to the tips of my toes.

I pulled back and pressed forward.

He nodded again.

I flexed my pelvis to drive deeper.

He grabbed my hips to encourage me to go faster. To go deeper.

Talk about a bossy bottom.

Still, I could give him this—I could give him what he

wanted. I steadily increased my thrusts as I sped up the pace. As I drilled him into the mattress, his eyes rolled back and he shut them.

I didn't order him to open them this time. Instead, I let the feeling of his tight body around my cock spur me on. I hadn't realized how much I needed this—this connection. Hadn't figured on the depth of feeling that this joining would bring.

Ordering him to jack himself was on the tip of my tongue when his body stiffened.

A moment later, cum hit my belly and chest.

His eyes shot open and sought mine.

I grinned.

And then I redoubled my efforts chasing my own orgasm. A few more thrusts and my balls drew up.

Then lightning crashed through me. My cock spurted cum into the condom and I held myself still as the aftershocks of his climax continued to rock him.

"I think I love you." He uttered the words softly—and I could chalk them up to post-orgasmic bliss—but they mirrored my sentiments exactly.

Only I wouldn't have said *I think*. No, I would've just said *I love you*.

And should have. Except he'd already dozed off, his gentle breaths fanning against me. *Next time.*

CHAPTER 21

ANTHONY

Scott insisted on wiping me down with a hot washcloth, pulling me back into semi-consciousness. Then he did himself. A shower might've been nice, but I was clinging to consciousness with a ferocity that drew every last ounce of strength I had. It'd been a brutal couple of weeks. My emotions had been all over the place. That Scott hadn't returned my perhaps ill-conceived declaration of love wasn't lost on me. Maybe he hadn't heard. Or maybe it'd just been too damn soon. Maybe it was a good thing he hadn't commented because if he had said anything less than a return declaration, my feelings might've been hurt.

I was overthinking this.

And then today…

Scott making love to me hadn't changed the fact my father was dead—it hadn't even blunted the news—but it'd given me perspective. I'd grieve for the old man. In my own time and in my own way. I had a few memories from my child-hood of really good days—including one trip to Disneyland that I knew he'd saved almost two years for. Before his work accident. Before the pills. Before the spiral of addiction. And even though he might've had reasons for that addiction, I could never forgive him for taking Mama, Laura, and Mickey. Some things you just couldn't come back from. Maybe—with time and distance—I might come to understand.

One thing I could do—that I'd been actively working at more recently—was to be more empathetic to people with addiction issues. To find ways to get them help. To encourage them rather than assuming they'd relapse.

Scott feathered my hair after climbing into bed and cuddling against me. "You need to sleep. I'll get up with the kids tonight."

"We can both do it." Said on an enormous yawn. My eyes shut and, as my limbs felt heavy, I drifted off.

I'd have sworn Scott said he loved me, but I couldn't have been sure.

Come morning, I was revitalized.

During the night, we'd spooned—as we always did—and Scott was in my arms. I inhaled his scent as a feeling of rightness settled over me. My mind told me it was way too soon to be making long-term plans, while my heart knew I belonged to Scott and the babies.

Speaking of babies…

Little babbling sounds carried through the monitor.

I extricated myself, and even as I stood, Scott burrowed farther under the blanket. I grinned as I pulled on jeans and a T-shirt. On impulse, I yanked it back off and pulled on a Christmas sweater I'd spotted in Scott's drawer. The thing was tight across my chest, and I'd likely be sweating in no time, but I wanted to get a picture with the kids with me in the sweater. As I headed to their room, I tried to work out logistics. Maybe when they were both in their high chairs? Could we do a selfie, or would we need Scott?

Alicia stood, gripping the side of the crib. She opened her arms, beseeching me to pick her up. I did, noting that Zayden was playing with a plastic toy we'd secured to the end of the crib. He was opening a door and peering inside to see some farm animals. Then, before I could stop him, he slammed his hand against the bell.

A loud clang reverberated.

I'd meant to tape that thing down.

A loud groan came from our bedroom.

I turned to the monitor—which I'd forgotten to turn off. "Go back to sleep." Then I switched it off.

Alicia snagged a handful of my hair.

Zayden clanged the bell again.

My heart leapt at the happiness of the moment.

Half an hour later, that joy might've slipped—but just a touch. I'd narrowly missed having oatmeal on Scott's sweater, but Alicia had tossed a handful on the floor before I could stop her.

Interestingly, Crumpy was licking it delicately. I couldn't imagine the goop contained anything harmful, so I left him to it.

Scott breezed into the kitchen with damp hair and a huge grin on his face. He leaned over and planted a smacking kiss to my lips. "Merry Christmas." He tweaked my nipple under the sweater.

My cock stirred.

Damn man—he knew my nipples were sensitive. That knowledge gave him a lot of power in our relationship.

And I'd happily given it to him. I worried far less about who was in charge or the *right* way to do things lately. Instead, I focused on making him happy. Keeping the twins safe. The rest was just icing on the cake.

"How about pancakes?"

My saliva glands kicked into high gear. "Oh, my God, I love pancakes."

He ruffled my hair. "Then you shall have them."

I tried to straighten my hair.

Zayden giggled.

I ruffled my hair so it stood up straight and made an exaggerated smiley face.

Both babies giggled.

Scott cracked an egg into the bowl. "So I was thinking presents and then maybe a stroll down to the park? There might be other kids, or even a dog or two."

He'd told me about the encounter with Zelda the dog their first night. Apparently they'd run into her and her owners on several occasions since then. He'd mentioned several other dogs he considered friendly and only one little holy terror of a dog that he gave a wide berth to. I liked the idea of the twins learning how to deal with animals. Better to have the skills to identify which dogs were safe and which were a threat than to be afraid of all dogs.

"Sure." I eyed Alicia, covered in oatmeal. "She's probably had enough. I'll go wash her off and change her. Again."

Scott nudged me. "Let her have a piece of pancake soaked in syrup. A Christmas tradition."

"You did that in your family?"

Even as the words left my mouth, I regretted them. The stricken look on his face assured me that I'd fucked up.

He cleared his throat. "Oatmeal. We were allowed a sprinkle of cinnamon on Christmas morning. No presents, or anything like that. Just another day working on the farm. *Animals don't take a day off*, my dad used to say."

Jesus, that broke my heart. We hadn't had money for luxuries in my home, but we'd had pancakes or waffles in the morning, tamales for dinner, and a fair amount of love in between. And one large present as well as stockings. My mother saved for most of the year to buy that one big present.

"Hey, get rid of the frowny face—you're not allowed to feel sorry for me."

I'd moved from feeling badly about his childhood to the reflections of my own, but I wasn't going to tell him that. If only because I didn't want sympathy for my issues.

Yet he met my gaze. "You okay? After yesterday—"

I waved him off. "I'll deal with it tomorrow. I mean I need to arrange for the body to be cremated and…I don't know." I shrugged. My father would've wanted to be buried with my mother, but no way was I buying a casket and getting him shipped up to Napa. The cost would be prohibitive and, as I gazed upon the babies, I knew where the money'd be better spent. On them. On their future. A future I desperately hoped to be a part of. "I'll keep his ashes and maybe one day I'll take them up to Napa and scatter them somewhere sentimental." I couldn't think of a spot at the moment, but I had time.

"We could drive up there some weekend. Make a little trip out of it." Scott eyed the twins. "Maybe to celebrate their first birthday? You can introduce them to where you grew up. I mean, I get that they're too young to understand—"

"That's a great idea." And almost three months in the future—which meant he intended to keep me around for that long.

Progress.

We still need to talk.

He poured the batter onto the griddle, and soon the aroma wafted through the room.

"Syrup's in the fridge. I hardly use the stuff."

"Well, we should plan to change that. How about we do one morning a week with pancakes? I know you work alternate weekends, but surely we can find one weekday morning before I go to work."

He leaned in for another smooch. "I don't start until nine on Sundays." He eyed the twins. "And since they're always up early, I can make them while you sleep in."

I shook my head. "No way. I want this to be a family event —so I get up and watch. Support."

"A family…"

His eyes softened, and my heart clenched. Had I said the wrong thing? Was I pushing too hard? Moving too fast?

"I like that." He turned back to flip the pancakes.

My jaw unclenched.

Twenty minutes later, we had two satisfied adults who'd consumed amazing pancakes and now sipped their coffee, and two babies covered in syrup.

"Baths first." I eyed Alicia. Of course she had it in her hair. Hair that would eventually grow longer. Would she want it long or favor a shorter cut? What about Zayden? How old would he be when we first trimmed his hair? Plenty of boys wore theirs long these days—what would he want?

"That's quite a frown." Scott nudged me. "I can do baths while you clean up."

"Huh? Oh." I smiled. "No, I was contemplating hair length and when we'll need to get first haircuts."

He feathered his hand through Zayden's hair.

The baby batted his hand away.

"I think we're good for a bit of time yet. It's so fine." He feathered his own hair. He kept it shorter, but I spotted curls.

"You have curly hair?"

He snorted. "Bane of my existence. My parents kept it shorn when I was young—vanity is the work of the devil—but I grew it out when I got to university. I had no idea what I was in for."

I cocked my head.

"Well, several guys heckled and called me Annie."

I couldn't picture him with hair that long, but I got the reference.

"So I went back to short. Eliza convinced me that wavy would be okay, but the hair turns into ringlets when it's damp. In the end, I decided short was good."

He snagged a lock of my hair. "Have I told you how sexy I think you are with the long hair? I should've grabbed it while we were making love. Ah well, there's always tonight."

Another promise. "We need to talk."

Our gazes met.

"Yeah...I—"

The doorbell rang.

I cursed. I wanted to say *fuck it*, but this wasn't my house. Wasn't my place to make the comment. Wasn't my right to get involved. Instead, I offered, "I'll get it."

Slowly, Scott nodded.

I rose and headed out of the kitchen and toward the front door. Logically, Scott should be answering the door—this was his house. But if I were to become truly entrenched, I needed to do things. Plus, I figured this might have something to do with my father.

As I opened the door, I *wished* it had something to do with him.

It didn't.

Eliza Markham stood on the front stoop.

My heart sank. My stomach roiled. My brain screamed *panic*.

Yet I schooled myself to show no outward reaction. I slipped into the social-worker persona and dispassionately observed her. Her ebony-black hair was pulled into a messy topknot. Her pale-blue eyes were bloodshot. Her white skin was translucent. She appeared even skinnier than the last time I'd seen her, and her small stature of just over five feet felt even more diminished.

And she sported a black right eye.

Sympathy welled within me. And anger. I'd offered her an out—had offered her a lifeline. If she'd taken it, I would've made sure she was safe. I would've ensured nothing happened to her under my watch. Instead she'd headed to parts unknown with a monster. A man who'd reject children because they weren't his blood. A man who would tear his wife away from the life she knew. A man who apparently would beat her as well.

I cleared my throat. "Are there any other injuries?"

She shrugged.

Okay, so that was a *yes*.

"Does he know where you are? Has he followed you?" Were the babies in danger? Scott? Her?

"I...I don't think so. I hopped a bus to Dallas three days ago from Little Rock. Then I went to Phoenix where I stayed overnight. Finally, I went to San Diego. I hitched a ride here."

Jesus. All that traveling. And I wanted to think she had her wits about her, but she'd been knocked around pretty good. As a single woman, she was bound to have attracted attention.

She patted her hair. "And he doesn't know where Scott lives. Or I don't think he does. And I told him that if he came after me, I'd report him to the cops. He might be a strong guy when it comes to beating up women, but he's terrified of jail."

My mind flashed to the slight man—even if he was incredibly strong, he'd have a tough time in prison.

A small part of me wished he'd face that. Wife beaters and child abusers were right up there with drug dealers as the scum of the earth.

"Did he ever hurt the kids?"

Her eyes flashed.

Well, shit.

Hugh hadn't detected anything in his thorough examination of both children, so obviously whatever happened took place a while ago. Should I have the babies examined more extensively? X-rays? God, my stomach roiled and bile rose in my thought.

She held up her hand. "He was just...rough with them. A few bruises."

Jesus, fuck.

"Please tell me you're not defending him." I pitched my voice low.

She swallowed visibly. Finally, she shook her head.

"Hey, babe, who's..."

Scott's voice trailed off.

I held up a finger to Eliza and pivoted to find Scott behind me with Alicia in his arms. It didn't appear she'd seen her mother.

Jesus, fuck.

"Please—"

I pivoted back to Eliza who ducked off to the side. "I just want to talk to Scott. I'm not here for the kids. I'm not…" She pressed her fingers to her lips.

Again, I held up my finger. This time, I pulled the door flush but didn't shut it as I stepped back into the house.

Scott's cheeks flushed, and he was incandescent with rage. "What the fuck is she doing here?"

Alicia squirmed under his tightened grasp and he pulled her close, then pressed a kiss to her temple.

"She's not taking them. That is not happening."

I held up my hands. "She says she left him. She said she's not here for the kids."

"And you believe her?" He spat the words.

Zayden banged his spoon on his tray.

Go to the baby or soothe his father?

God, was there a correct answer to that quandary?

I drew in a breath. "Look, Scott, I think you need to talk to her."

He cocked his head in apparent abject confusion.

"She says she doesn't want the twins—that she just wants to talk to you."

"What could she possibly have to say that I'd want to hear?" He pressed another kiss to Alicia's head. "She abandoned her children. My children."

"And I suspect she might be remorseful. Look…" I reasoned this out in my mind. "She's walked away, and we have the paperwork. But that doesn't mean a court wouldn't be willing to hear her appeal. Wouldn't it be better to know what she was planning instead of being blindsided? Isn't it better to be forewarned?" I advanced toward him and touched his cheek. "I'll regret not calling you before I showed up, but I can't regret what we have built. I don't think she can destroy us—"

"She can't—"

"But knowledge is a powerful weapon."

He met my gaze, and the moment suspended in time.

This could end disastrously. Eliza might convince him to let her in. He might even decide to give her a chance and walk away from me.

I'm being ridiculous.

And yet, in this moment, things felt perilous. Like everything was riding on this one moment in time. Our future lay in the woman's hands who stood just beyond the door.

Scott leaned in to press a broken kiss to my lips.

I eased Alicia from his arms.

He blinked several times. "I love you."

Before I could answer, he was gone.

Zayden banged his spoon again.

Alicia had oatmeal in her hair.

Whatever happened between Eliza and Scott could wait—my two precious hellions needed baths.

I offered up a prayer to a God I didn't believe in and focused on the kids.

CHAPTER 22

SCOTT

A MUCH-DIMINISHED ELIZA GREETED ME AS I STEPPED OUT OF MY house. I thrust my sunglasses on my face—partly to protect me from the glaring morning sun, and partly to protect me from Eliza being able to read me.

Bullshit.

She knew me better than anyone. Even more than Scotia. I fervently hoped Alicia and Zayden developed a genuine friendship. I should've been closer to my twin than anyone in the world, but we'd never developed that rapprochement. Part was the separation of genders by our religion and part was the fact she likely knew I was different from the beginning. Had she known I was gay before I had? She'd always been smarter, so it wouldn't have surprised me.

"What do you want?" I hitched my hand on my hip.

"This is a nice neighborhood."

I nodded, a little dumbfounded.

"Looks like a good place to raise a family."

For a moment, I spared a glance around. Several houses had toys scattered. The lawns were neat. The hedges were trimmed. The cars were clean. A typical street in a small town.

And more of a home than I'd ever known in my life. Ms.

Ducking selling me this house was the best thing that'd ever happened to me before Anthony and the children. Right up with landing the job in the library and finding Gaynor Beach in the first place. I was home and had a family, and no one—especially not my former best friend—was going to take this away from me.

"Yes, it's a good place to raise a family." I didn't meet her gaze. "What do you want, Eliza?"

"To talk."

Her voice was meek and unrecognizable. She'd always been brash and bold. And beautiful. Her looks had been ethereal—like a goddess. With otherworldly pale eyes and stunning black hair, she'd attracted attention wherever she went. But she'd always acted like she didn't need the attention and adulation. I'd believed that. Until I saw how quickly her head had turned with Mark's devotion. Or supposed devotion. A few pretty words and she'd been willing to walk away from all her dreams so she could become his wife. Then she'd distanced herself from me and, after I moved to Gaynor Beach, I never heard from her.

I'd tried not to look back, but that abandonment had hurt.

I wanted to snap at her, but Anthony's words of warning echoed in my head. I pasted on a smile. "Why don't we walk? There's a park down the way with some benches. We can sit there." *If we even have that much to talk about.*

After a long moment, she nodded.

I pointed the way, and we fell into step together. I'd expected us to talk—assuming she'd go first—but we made the three-block journey in silence. Words, for me, wouldn't come. I was so blazing angry. Yet, when I glimpsed the bruise on her face, part of my empathy kicked in. And I didn't want to notice that she cradled her left ribs—but it was hard to miss.

"You should go to the police. You should lay charges."
Great way to let her come to you.

Normally, I was a patient man. People came to me with problems and sometimes it took time to hear them out. To give them a chance to verbalize their needs. Or to communicate them in other ways. Not everyone could be articulate. But I helped people. Part of choosing to be a librarian. A way to give back to whichever community welcomed me.

We continued our walk in silence. When we finally arrived at the park, Eliza headed straight for the closest bench.

She dropped onto it, wincing as she settled.

I stood before her and glared down.

After a moment, she looked up. She shielded her eyes as the sun was behind me. "Please sit."

Personally, I liked the power dynamic of me standing. I wasn't normally an asshole, but I was sure feeling like one today.

She patted the bench beside her, still squinting. Her eyes were starting to water.

I sat. "Where are your sunglasses?"

After a long moment, she sighed. "I left them behind. I left everything behind. Fresh start, you know?"

"Or he might've seen you planning to leave and stopped you?"

She looked away, off toward a cluster of bushes.

Across the way, a family entered the park. The two eldest children made a beeline for the swing set while the youngest waved her hands in the air while still strapped in the stroller. Her? I squinted.

Then I realized it didn't matter. We spent way too much time on gender as a construct. What mattered was the happiness of the child—and that child was happy. So were the other two.

Eliza sniffed.

Goddammit.

I didn't want to care. I wanted to get up and walk away. To never deal with this clusterfuck. To go on as I had for the past two weeks—with Anthony and the twins. I didn't want the outside world to interfere with what we'd built.

Basically, I didn't want to give a shit about Eliza and her problems.

But I did.

I reached out to offer my hand.

She grasped it with one of hers, interlacing our fingers. She held on tight.

Time passed as the family settled in to play. Only now did I realize I was watching two dads. Funny, that hadn't even struck me because this was so normal in Gaynor Beach. Two dads, two moms…just lots of love.

"I made a mistake."

Her words were quiet.

"I would say so."

Her fingers tightened around mine.

Be nice.

"The question, Eliza, is what are you going to do about it?"

She drew in a long breath and let it out slowly. "I have an elderly great-aunt on Cape Breton Island in Nova Scotia. She's asked me to come and take care of her. She doesn't want to leave her home, and she's dying. Apparently she only has a few months. But that'd give me time—time to sort out my shit. Time to figure out what I'm doing to do with my life."

She made it all sound so reasonable.

"Will you come back to SoCal when she dies?"

An adamant shake of the head. "I have dual citizenship in Canada. I…I want to make a fresh start. I'm tired of the way things are going down here and, I dunno, I want change."

"Things up there could go just as sideways."

"Maybe." She sighed. "The whole world could go to shit, but I'm not sure I'd care." She slapped her thigh with her free hand.

I didn't miss the wince.

Her arm immediately cradled her side again.

"Ribs?"

"I...don't know. I don't think anything's broken, and I figure if I had internal bleeding, I'd be dead by now."

She'd been studying to be a nurse before she married.

"Might you go back to school?"

"I was thinking about qualifying to be a care aid or something like that."

"Helping people." Not a fantastic job, but one that could be extremely rewarding, given the right circumstances. Still, something niggled. "What about the babies? Are you planning to come back? To try to take them away from us?" I considered using *me* but I wanted to be honest—I saw Anthony as part of the package deal.

At least I hope he is.

"No." She sniffed. "I made a huge mistake. Tracking down your sperm donation and using it. Trying to pass the babies off as Mark's. Walking away from them without fighting."

"I would've helped you—"

"And I wouldn't have taken it." Finally, she met my gaze. "He said he'd kill them and he'd kill me."

Panic ripped through me. I'd left them alone with Anthony—

"I had a lady in Phoenix help me. She took pictures of all my injuries and I swore out a statement. If anything happens to me, she's to go to the cops. I texted copies of everything to Mark and then I blocked him. Then, at the next stop, I tossed the phone and bought a new one. It's just a burner phone— it'll get me to Canada. I plan to take a bus up to Vancouver and then catch a train to Halifax. Mark doesn't know about my aunt. Hell, I don't even think I told him about being half-Canadian."

"But he might still come after the kids."

Her mouth twisted. "No, I don't think he would. He's not

going to wind up in jail—especially as a baby killer. And he's so over the whole thing. Will he let me go? I think so. He believed the fertility issues were mine—despite what the doctor said. And I just wanted to be a mother so much. But being a parent turned out to be so much harder than I thought. Especially because I was essentially a single parent—Mark refused to lift a finger. Oh shit." She pressed her fingers to her mouth.

I tilted my head.

"I've made you a single father. Unless…"

I waited.

And saw the moment she put two and two together.

"Are you and the social worker a couple? What's his name?"

"Anthony."

"And you're together?"

Is there a right answer to that question?

"He's been helping me. We've…become close."

She stared at me. "You like him. You really like him." She didn't smile, but her nose twitched—which it always did when she was amused.

"Don't think you had anything to do with this. Whatever this is."

"But you wouldn't have met—if not for me."

"Eliza." I put as much of a warning tone in my voice as I could. I did *not* want her thinking that abandoning the twins on my doorstep had solved my loneliness problem.

"Sorry." She appeared appropriately chastened. "It's just… God, I haven't even asked how you're doing—or how the twins are doing. This entire conversation has been about myself. Which is why I think I'd be a shitty mother—I'm so self-centered."

I wasn't going to argue the second point because it was a good one. I loved her, but she *was* self-centered. I hadn't minded when we were the only two in the picture. She had enough personality for the two of us. I was happy to retreat into the background.

Well, no more.

"I think *shitty mother* would be an exaggeration. But you're right, you have to learn to put other people before yourself sometimes. Not all the time—but a good portion of it." I shifted. "The twins are doing great. Honestly, better than I would've expected. And yes, they adore Anthony. And I have a young woman who comes in and helps. We're making it work. But that's no thanks to you." I cleared my throat. "A phone call, Eliza. You owed me that much. Or a letter."

"He'd have found out. We had to do things his way or…"

"Or…?"

"It wouldn't have been pretty."

My breath caught. "Did he abuse them?"

The silence went on far too long.

She pulled her hand away from me and stood. This time, she gazed down at me. "Just bruises, which I know was wrong, so don't start in on me. But you'll make sure nothing ever happens to them again. You'll keep them safe. Right?"

If I hadn't known her so well, I might've bristled at the surety in her tone. But she'd nailed it. I'd protect them with everything within me. I'd love them and make sure nothing bad ever happened. Well, life happened—and I could only do so much—but I'd do everything in my power to ensure they made it safely to adulthood and beyond.

"Yes, I'll do my best."

She let out a long breath. "That's all I can ask." She patted her hair. "I have to get going. I've arranged for a ride to LA. There I can catch a bus heading north."

"It'll be a shitty trip. Why not take the train?"

"Easier to get missed on the bus. And I can stay somewhere for a night or two or just push through or…" She patted her hair yet again. "You know, whatever I need to do."

"Do you have enough money?" I only had a few bills in my wallet, but we could drive to the bank and I could take some out from the ATM. Again, I didn't have much, but I'd give her—

She held up her hand.

"I've been squirreling away cash for a long time now. I thought I'd leave it with the social worker but…"

"You thought you might need it."

Slowly, she nodded. "And my great-aunt has offered to wire me some more once I get to Vancouver. Something about exchange rates? Anyway, her bank has a branch near the train station so I just need to show up there and apparently everything'll be taken care of." She offered a small smile. "My very rich great-aunt."

"Well, I'm glad you're set."

"I'll try to send more, if I ever have some."." She again pressed her fingers to her lips and blinked repeatedly. She rubbed her nose. "All I ever wanted was to be a mother. And a nurse." She waved that thought off. "But mostly a mother. I thought that would fill the emptiness in my soul."

Part of me wondered why my friendship hadn't been enough. The rest of me understood that parenthood—motherhood in particular—had different meanings for different people. She'd viewed her self-worth as her ability to birth a child.

What did I see mine as? I'd thought being a good librarian and citizen. Now, I realized those had been too narrow. I could now find worth in being a parent, a partner, and someone who cared about others—who watched out for them.

I reached for her.

She backed away. "My bag is in a locker. I have to get it, and I have to meet my ride in an hour."

"Can I give you a lift?"

She shook her head. "No, I'd rather walk."

"With those ribs?" Honestly, now she was just being stubborn.

"Yes."

Some things never change.

"All right, then. You know the way?"

She pointed in the direction that would take her back to downtown Gaynor Beach.

I nodded.

She gave a little wave, spun around, and walked away.

Watching her go, I couldn't help feeling like something monumental had just happened. Yes, she'd confirmed she wasn't going to try to take the twins—but her paperwork had basically said the same thing. Yes, she'd told me, in general, where she was going. Would she be in touch when she arrived on Cape Breton Island? I couldn't even begin to predict. I thought I'd known her really well—now I questioned if I'd ever known her at all.

I rose, stretched, and headed back toward my heart.

CHAPTER 23

ANTHONY

Are you walking to Seattle?

Seriously how far were they going? When would they be back?

Most importantly—what would be the state of play when they returned? Would Scott usher Eliza in and let her become reacquainted with the twins? Would he usher me out and send me on my way?

I'm being ridiculous.

Yeah…maybe. But that didn't stop my mind from going to the dark place. A place where I was no longer needed. Where I was no longer welcome.

He said he loves me.

That should've been enough. Because Scott wasn't flighty. He was grounded and had two feet firmly planted to the earth. He didn't say things he didn't mean—he didn't bullshit. He could be tactful—when the situation arose—but he never lied.

Or at least I was pretty sure he hadn't ever lied to me.

Alicia let out an almighty howl.

I glanced away from my place at the window to find her trying to tear her stuffed dinosaur in two.

"Hey, sweetheart, let's not do that." I tried to pry the toy gently from her hands.

She scrunched her face in *that* way, and I winced.

"How about we play pots?"

She eyed me.

I scooped her into my arms and carried her into the kitchen.

Zayden was playing with a plastic book that he kept trying to put in his mouth—it'd be time for snacks soon.

With careful maneuvering, I managed to get the pot drawer under the oven open while not dropping the baby.

I was quite proud of myself. I was just trying to find the least noisy option when the front door opened. After a brief hesitation, I grabbed the wok. I nabbed a couple of large spoons and headed back into the living room.

Scott sat beside Zayden and stroked his hair.

The baby kept brushing his hand away.

"Guess he's not in the mood."

Both looked up at me in surprise.

Scott eyed the wok and spoons and arched an eyebrow.

I shrugged.

He held out his hands for Alicia and I placed her in them. He held her for an extra moment and nestled his nose in her hair.

She squirmed.

"I think she wants the pot."

"Can't we, I don't know, do anything else?" I didn't miss the distinctive whine in Scott's voice. He glanced over at the couch where I'd piled all the Christmas presents—out of the reach of little grabby hands. Hadn't stopped Zayden from trying to pull himself up to reach them.

"We can do Christmas presents." I put the wok and spoons onto the table—much to Alicia's obvious intense annoyance.

Before I could intervene, Scott scooped up a present and handed it to her.

Easily diverted, she grabbed it and shook.

Ah, a child after my own heart.

Zayden looked at me expectantly.

I grabbed one for him and handed it to him. Then I joined the crew on the floor.

Neither child could tear wrapping, so Scott and I helped. Soon Alicia had a large plastic football and Zayden had an anatomically neutral rag-doll.

Both held up their gifts in glee.

Slowly, one by one, we opened all the presents Scott had so lovingly wrapped. Most were gently used boy toys or brand-new for a girl. And I hated that I saw them in that light. I *would* remember to use neutral language with them.

Alicia's favorite toy was the football, and Zayden fought with Crumpy for who would get the large box that the hockey set came in. Overall, we called a draw as boy and beast settled into an uneasy truce.

Then both combatants promptly fell asleep.

My little girl curled into my lap as I leaned against the couch. We should've fed them and changed them, but today was Christmas. A time to break rules.

Right?

Scott tapped two stuffed animals against each other. Surely now that the stuffie quantity in the house had quadrupled, there'd be less squabbling.

Nah, likely not. Alicia always wanted whatever Zayden had. Hopefully, one day, she'd outgrow that habit.

"Do you want to talk?" I pitched my voice low.

Scott met my gaze. He shrugged. "There's not much to say. She's headed to Canada, and I doubt I'll ever see her again."

The vise around my chest loosened just a little bit. "That simple?"

Another shrug. "She said she can't be a mom right now. Or maybe ever, if I understood her correctly. She's got a relative who can use her help, and that person will take care of the finances. She's also positive Mark isn't going to come after us or the kids."

His eye twitched.

Yeah, okay, so he wasn't sure about that himself. Was he putting on a brave face for me? He didn't have to, but I appreciated he might need to.

"Do you think we should alert authorities?"

He tapped the stuffies again. "I don't think so. She said she has things set up so the authorities will be notified if something happens to her." He offered a crooked smile. "And she said he's worried about going to jail as a baby killer."

"Yeah, that'd wind him up in a heap of trouble." And if anything happened to Scott or the babies, that asshole would be at the top of the suspect list. He hadn't struck me as stupid. I hadn't understood his role in everything as he'd quietly loaded all the baby gear into my SUV, but I'd be quite happy to never see the fucker again. And we weren't likely to unless he came looking for trouble. Even if he wound up in SoCal, this gay-friendly small town wasn't likely to be on the top of any list of places to settle.

"Okay, so no Eliza and no asshole soon-to-be-ex-husband."

Scott scratched his nose. "Damn, she'll have to serve him divorce papers."

"There are processes to do it where the recipient doesn't get to know where the other party is. Courts are usually empathetic to abused spouses—even if they haven't gone to the police." And she should have because now he was free to abuse again impunity. No one to stop him. That thought had my stomach churning and I made a mental note to update the file at work with this new information. I gazed over at

Zayden who lay curled around the cat in the box. I made a camera clicking motion.

After a moment, Scott nodded. He yanked his phone from his back pocket and first snapped a pic of Zayden and Crumpy, then one of Alicia in my lap.

I'd managed to get a few while everyone was opening presents. We'd shoved the wrapping paper off to one side and a pile of toys sat in the center of the room. We'd put some away so we could bring them out later and the kids could rediscover them.

"Are you happy?"

Scott's question caught me off-guard. Instinctively, my grip tightened on Alicia. Was this the kiss-off? Where he told me he no longer needed me? That Eliza was no longer a threat so he could do it on his own?

When I met his gaze, though, I didn't see any of those things. I saw questioning, for sure, but in a gentle way. In a Scott way. "I'm incredibly happy." I pressed a kiss to the top of Alicia's head. "Honestly, I didn't know what happy was until this." I indicated the room in a wide arc with my chin. "I had a good childhood—my mother did her very best—but we didn't have a lot of stability. My father worked seasonally and then after the accident..." I cleared my throat. "And then, just as I was about to fly from the nest, the world crashed down around me. I took solace in my college classes, but something was always missing.

"But here? Now?" I gazed into his deep-green eyes. "I hadn't let myself think about kids because of the pain I endured losing my brother and sister. And I hadn't met a suitable partner, so why go borrowing trouble?"

"Now?" Softly asked.

"You make me want things." I indicated the babies. "They make me want things. They give me hope for the future—that I can be more than just the social worker in town. That I can have a lasting impact on someone. Two someones. That I can make a difference."

Scott tsked. "You were making a difference before. I'd heard about you—word got around. That you were tough, but fair. That you were one of the good guys."

"But…" How could I explain this? "Each of those kids would've likely been served just as well by someone else."

He held up his hand, but I continued.

"I didn't have the same empathy that I think I do now. Some other stuff has happened over the last while. Things that made me take stock—to figure out if this was what I wanted in life."

His questioning look was unmissable.

"It is," I rushed to assure him. "But I think when Mr. Winters puts in his retirement papers, I'm not sure I want his job. His office? Sure. But not his job. He does some work out in the community, but most of what he does these days is administrative. And yes, that helps indirectly, but I want more. I want to be actively involved in the community. I want to be at the high school and be out meeting parents, foster parents, and guardians. I want to be the one making sure the kids are safe."

"The hero."

I shook my head vehemently. "Never that. I don't have to take credit—I'm happy to work behind the scenes. I just want the kids to have a real shot at a good life."

"The life your father made so difficult for you."

My eyes drifted shut against the shaft of pain. All of it felt overwhelming. Maybe once I put him to rest, some of the demons inside me would quiet as well.

"Where does that leave us?"

I snapped my eyes open at his question. "I…what do you mean?"

He offered a sheepish grin. "Well, I'd say we've found a way to be compatible."

"In bed, you mean."

A giggle burst forth from him, held in check by the two sleeping babies. "Uh, well I'm not sure I would've but it so bluntly." His expression sobered. "Especially because that wasn't what I was referring to. I meant it when I said I loved you. Whether you accept that as romantic love or fraternal love is up to you. But I wouldn't have survived the last two weeks without you. And sure, I might be able to make it on my own. But I don't want to. Because, crazy as this sounds, I want you in my life. As a partner."

"It's so soon."

"I know." He gazed down at Zayden. "So we slow things down. With Eliza truly gone, and Mark no longer lingering in the shadows, we can take our time to get to know each other properly—to make sure this is what we both want."

"Sounds reasonable." Except I already knew. In my heart, I knew I'd found the man I was meant to be with. I didn't believe in soulmates, but I believed in compatibility based on common goals, mutual respect, and a deep, abiding love. I didn't know how deep our love could go, but I was happy to hang around while we figured it out. I grinned. "As long as *slowing things down* doesn't mean we, uh, spend less time in the bedroom. When we're not too tired, of course."

He grinned. "Of course."

Alicia stirred.

"Guess we'll have to wait until tonight to seal the deal." I was a patient man.

To a point.

Scott feathered his hand through Zayden's hair, and the little one stirred as well.

Crumpy, obviously sensing the movement, stretched and then scooted out of the box. He stuck his nose in the air as he leapt onto the seat of the couch and then up to the top—his favorite perch. He loved the kids—or at least I hoped he did

—but he was also sensible and tended to stay away from grabby hands.

"We'll do diapers, then you can do lunch while I clear up the mess." I hated how much wrapping paper we'd used. Maybe next year we'd choose reusable cloth bags. Not as much fun, but a new tradition we could try.

Next year.

Okay, not something I'd thought about. "Tomorrow I'll call Lacy and see if she wants to babysit on New Year's Eve. We can do something special."

Scott smiled. "Like sleep?"

I tossed a throw pillow at his head.

He caught it deftly, but my movement jostled Alicia.

She gazed up at me sleepily and smiled.

Anything. I'd do anything to protect these children.

And Scott, I quickly added.

Because this was my family.

And no one was ever taking that away from me.

EPILOGUE
SCOTT

WE CHOSE THE FALL EQUINOX FOR OUR WEDDING. NEITHER OF US were pagan, of course. Neither were we religious. We just liked the symmetry—as well as choosing a date we both had a prayer of remembering.

I called it parenting fog.

Anthony just ruffled my hair and gave me an indulgent smile.

He never forgot anything, while I struggled sometimes. My anxiety remained at bay, though. I'd had two episodes in the past nine months—both triggered by troubles with the kids. Both resolved with some TLC from my husband and reassurances from Dr. Coral that the twins were fine. I worried too much. I knew I worried too much. And yet, sometimes, I couldn't help myself. I still worried that I'd do something or say something that would fuck them up for life.

I'd heard of the terrible twos.

Nothing could've prepared me for the reality.

No was, of course, their favorite word. And often they'd tag team me. Fortunately, Anthony was usually a good arbitrator, and we'd survive the recalcitrance. Every morning, when I dropped them off at day care, I said a little prayer of thanks for Corey and her crew.

Corey who held Alicia as she walked down our aisle.

And Lacy held Zayden as they went next.

Anthony and I came behind them, already holding hands. I wasn't going for the superstitious stuff, and we wanted to be equals in this relationship. Plus, neither of us had family to *give us away*. I was okay with that.

So was he.

We'd done a trek to Napa in March to spread his father's ashes. A birthday trip for the twins—who'd been mightily unimpressed with the whole car-ride thing.

A way for my husband to resolve his lingering guilt over not being with his father for the last moments. He'd opened the rucksack to find some dirty clothes and an envelope with family pictures. That hurt his heart. Afterward, he'd spoken to a counselor friend a couple of times and had even reached out to Dr. Hugh again. Just closing that circle.

Dr. Hugh and Oscar were amongst the small group of guests today. And I knew what a leap that was for all of them. Burying a hatchet, as the expression went. We weren't what I'd term good friends, but we were getting friendlier. Plus, we wanted Lacy to have her brother and brother-in-law with her today. Oscar even held a very placid Marilee.

Why couldn't my hellions be calm like her? Did a year really make that much difference?

Anthony and I held hands and gazed into each other's eyes as all our guests, and even our children fell away. This moment—this marriage—was about us. We'd done a couple of sessions of premarital counselling as well. We'd needed help in navigating our relationship outside of being parents. The twins had brought us together—and were certainly part of the glue that held us together—but we needed a strong partnership. A fortified relationship. We needed something beyond just parenthood to bind us together.

As I pledged my everlasting love to the man I adored more than life itself, I knew I'd made the right decision. We were going to make it.

We kissed, passionately—much to the amusement of the crowd.

"Da, Da, Da," Zayden chirped.

"Papa," Alicia added.

I snagged my son and Anthony snagged our daughter.

As a family, we walked back down the aisle.

A bit later, when the reception was in full flow, I eyed the three toddlers as they now sat on a blanket guarded by Lacy, Oscar, Hugh, and Corey. Did it matter if they remained hellions for the rest of their lives and drove me to an early grave with white hair? Nope, I'd still love them.

Anthony came up behind me and slipped his arms around my waist, pulling me back toward him. "They look happy."

"They are happy." I sighed. "So am I."

"Still worried about taking a honeymoon?"

Just a long weekend in San Francisco. Nothing elaborate—just some badly needed time away. Lacy was staying at our place—our new place—with Hugh and Oscar as backup if she needed help. We'd both sold our houses and settled on a new home just down the street from my old one. Four bedrooms, two bathrooms, and a bit of distance between the twin's rooms and ours. We'd given them each their own bedroom.

They were still too young to understand their mother's absence. Quite a few of their friends had two mommies or two daddies, but—at some point—they were going to become aware and wonder about the woman who'd given birth to them.

We'd cross that bridge when we came to it.

"I'm excited about the honeymoon. Sleeping all night. Lazing around all day."

"I thought you had a couple places you wanted to see."

"Meh. I just want you. And sleep." I twisted my neck so I could plant a kiss on his bearded jaw.

"They sleep through the night quite often."

"Yes, but I'm a fan of morning sex and they're morning people. I've heard teenagers aren't morning people, but I don't think I can wait that long."

He chuckled. "And knowing our luck, one will be a morning person and the other will be a night owl, and it'll be battles all the way."

"Just so long as we have a good lock on the door."

"That's a given." He tightened his grasp. "Mr. Winters texted me."

My heart sank. Our going away was always contingent on there not being an emergency with Anthony's work.

"There's a girl in the hospital. She's going to be there for some time while recovering."

My breath caught. "But…"

"He asked if we'd consider fostering her when she's released. She's six, so she's in school, but she's going to need a lot of patience and—"

I spun in his arms. "I hope you told him *yes*."

"I told him I'd talk it over with my new husband. There's another family who might be able to squeeze her in, but they're pretty full—"

"We have space. Did you tell him we have space?"

My husband chuckled. "My boss *has* seen our house."

I scratched my nose. "Oh, right. When he evaluated us for fitness to be emergency foster parents." The town had run low on candidates earlier in the year. With the economy being in rough shape, some families had struggled to stay together. Others had faced drug or abuse issues.

Or both.

"Does she need us now? Because I'm happy to cancel the trip." I glanced over. "Heck, we could gift it to Oscar and Hugh."

Anthony rolled his eyes. "We're not giving away our honeymoon. Three days isn't going to make that much of a difference. But as soon as we're back, I'll start visiting her. Eventually you can join me. Like I said, her injuries are serious." He indicated with his chin. "Hugh treated her when she came in. I've read the report—it's bad. We're talking a serious amount of trauma, and now she'll have the psychological issues as well."

"I don't care."

He pulled me into his arms. "Which is why I love you so much."

Taking advantage, I rubbed against him. "I thought *this* was why you loved me so much."

"Or both."

Carole, the officiant for our wedding, drew alongside us. "You both look very happy."

"We are. Thank you." Anthony extended his hand.

She shook first his, and then mine. Her smile was wide. "I love when kids are involved. Just makes the day extra special."

I eyed our two. Both had flaming-red hair. And both had their mother's pale-blue eyes. The best of both, I guessed. Eliza'd sent a package with gifts on the twin's first birthday. Her letter was brief. She was enjoying Canada's east coast and had settled in for the long haul.

In other words—she wasn't coming back. Part of me was relieved and part of me mourned. She'd carried and then nurtured these two incredible beings for almost two years. I couldn't imagine she didn't have regrets. Anthony'd been right to insist I speak to her. And I'd admitted as much. Communication was our strength.

When we'd gone before the judge to secure custody, I'd said I wasn't sure where Eliza was. Which, at the time, had been true. Somewhere between the US and Canada. Or somewhere in Canada. To the best of my knowledge, at the time, she hadn't reached her final destination.

The judge hadn't been thrilled—had felt she, as well as Mark, should be on the hook for child support. My wonderful lawyer, Wynn, had convinced the woman that Anthony and I had everything we needed. That the twins were cared for. That we didn't want any ties to either Eliza or Mark. Disgruntled, she'd agreed.

Six months later, we'd returned and she formalized my adoption of them. Next up was getting Anthony listed as their second parent. A way to seal us as a family forever.

Carole waved and headed out the door. Lunch was a distant memory, and we should be heading home. We hadn't gone for fussy or dancing or anything like that. Heck, we hadn't even served alcohol. No, this was a family event. Our opportunity to share our luck and good fortune with our friends.

Lacy rose from the floor and approached. "So, tomorrow morning?"

"Bright and early." I offered her a smile. "We really appreciate this."

I expected a flippant response—her favorite was to point out how much we paid her.

She had an eye on a car as she was soon turning sixteen. Hugh and Oscar made enough to provide for her, but she had an independent streak a mile wide. Still, instead of glib, she grabbed one of each of our hands. "I just really want you guys to make it, you know? Like Hugh and Oscar."

I did know. Because I felt the same way.

Marilee, the men's daughter, clapped her hands in obvious glee.

Alicia screeched.

Zayden looked around frantically, undoubtedly searching for someone to save him from his sister.

"I think that's our cue." I scurried over to scoop Alicia up before she lost her cool. She was likely overtired, and getting her home, fed, and in bed, was a priority.

Anthony soon had Zayden in his arms, although he patted Marilee on her head at the same time.

Hugh laughed.

Oscar beamed.

Marilee clapped her hands again.

Lacy snickered.

Yeah, pretty much par for the course in our world.

Hours later, after the twins were settled, Anthony pulled me into his arms. We hadn't made love, and I was completely fine with that. Truthfully, I was exhausted. I had tried not to stress about today but, for his sake, I'd wanted things to be perfect.

He nuzzled my neck. "Today was perfect."

"Reading my mind?"

"I think you muttered the words a few times as a mantra." He rasped his stubble against my shoulder. "We did it."

I clinked our rings together. "Yeah, we really did." There hadn't been any grand proposal. Just one ordinary Sunday morning pancake breakfast when he'd suggested we make things legal. Well, we'd already named each other beneficiaries and sorted out custody should something happen to one or, God forbid, both of us. But he proposed making things permanent. And I'd agreed.

That simple.

The next day we hired Liz Campbell-Waite, a local realtor. She'd found great people to buy our houses and then found us the perfect home. Within a few weeks, we were officially living together in a home of our own. Now, three months later, we were married.

The last change was for all of us. We were now the Rodrigues-Wexler family. And yeah, hyphenated names sucked. Anthony would've been happy with just Wexler. But I wanted to honor him and his heritage, so we'd gone with both names.

And I couldn't have been happier.

"Can life get any better?"

"Well, it's about to become crazier."

I tilted my head back.

"After Mr. Winters confirmed we'd get Laura, Hugh told me they should be ready to release her in three weeks. She's facing an uphill battle."

I touched his jaw. "She has the same name as your sister."

He blinked. "Yeah, and she's got the same heritage as well."

Not that it would've mattered one way or another, but she'd fit right in.

"Forever."

He held me tighter. "Yeah, forever."

NEXT IN THE GAYNOR BEACH SERIES

HIROSHI BY ZARIA KNIGHT

World-renowned architecture professor Hiroshi Furukawa has never been one to back down from a challenge.

But for the first time, he's facing a problem he can't solve —being forced into early retirement after being diagnosed with heart failure. Only in his early fifties and a workaholic for thirty years, Hiroshi can't accept having to change his lifestyle. But he knows he has to keep his promise to his late wife and stay healthy and happy for their only daughter, Sara.

Gaynor Beach wasn't his ideal place to settle down, but Hiroshi knows that if he's going to support his daughter and his twin grandsons, they'll have to move into his old family home. Yet, there's something missing in their new lives, and Hiroshi finds it when he runs into a former student, Jayden.

Now pursuing a career as a firefighter, Jayden seems like the perfect match for his wayward daughter—young, handsome, financially stable, family-oriented, and, most importantly, *single*. Hiroshi's determined to play matchmaker to ensure his family will have a secure future.

But there are two big issues with his plan: Jayden is gay, and he's in love with his former professor.

Can Jayden convince Hiroshi that he's the perfect man for

him and not his daughter? Or is Hiroshi too stuck in his ways?

———

Hiroshi is a gay single dad contemporary romance set in the shared world of Gaynor Beach, featuring an age-gap, inter-racial, forbidden love story with an older bottom ready for a fresh start, a younger top eager to guide him, bickering pets, and two adorable grandkids.

https://books2read.com/hiroshi

ALSO IN THE GAYNOR BEACH SERIES